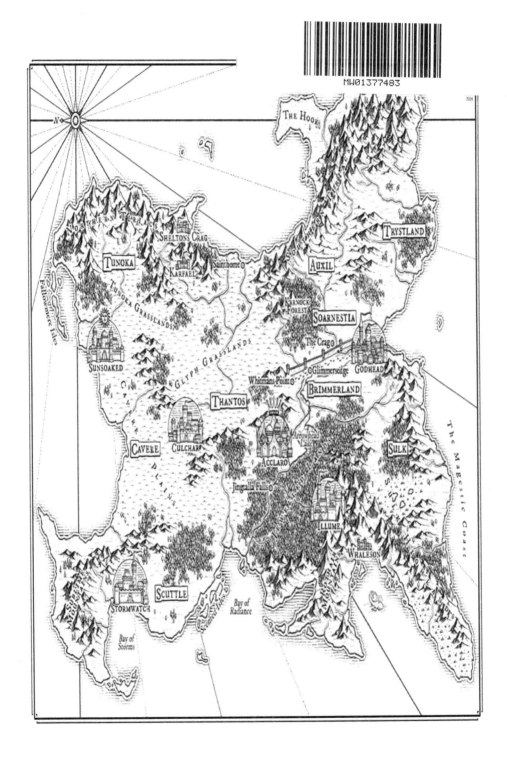

We're Golden

Troy Church

We're Golden by Troy Church
Published by T.A Church Perth Australia 6111
© 2023 Troy Church

All rights reserved. No portion of this book may be reproduced in any form without permission from the publisher except as permitted by Australian copyright law. For permission contact troychurch71@gmail.com

Cover by Justin Randall
Print ISBN: 978-0-6483115-6-0

Contents

CHAPTER 1	1
CHAPTER 2	9
CHAPTER 3	16
CHAPTER 4	22
CHAPTER 5	31
CHAPTER 6	35
CHAPTER 7	41
CHAPTER 8	46
CHAPTER 9	56
CHAPTER 10	63
CHAPTER 11	74
CHAPTER 12	82
CHAPTER 13	89
CHAPTER 14	94
CHAPTER 15	99
CHAPTER 16	106
CHAPTER 17	113
CHAPTER 18	121
CHAPTER 19	127
CHAPTER 20	137
CHAPTER 21	149
CHAPTER 22	154
CHAPTER 23	159
CHAPTER 24	169

Contents

CHAPTER 25	175
CHAPTER 26	183
CHAPTER 27	188
CHAPTER 28	195
CHAPTER 29	205
CHAPTER 30	211
CHAPTER 31	218
CHAPTER 32	226
CHAPTER 33	232
CHAPTER 34	240
CHAPTER 35	247
CHAPTER 36	254
CHAPTER 37	258
CHAPTER 38	264
CHAPTER 39	271
CHAPTER 40	282

Chapter 1

Lars leant all his weight back on the reins to deny the dappled grey stallion the chance of rising on its hind legs above him. He had no wish to be trampled beneath the hooves of this foul-tempered beast like the last stable hand. Jelo was making lamb stew with fresh bread. It would be much more enjoyable without broken bones. The stallion snorted and began sidling its body sideways towards him, seeking to knock him over. It nearly succeeded, with only his nimble movements coupled with prior knowledge of playing this game many times before keeping him safe. The stallion stamped hooves upon the flagstones, creating staccato notes, almost drowning out the approaching man's words.

'Kitty, enough!'

'About time,' Lars muttered beneath his breath as Lord Bertram sauntered from the growing shadows of the manor. The wind whipped Bertram's crimson cloak about his lithe form wrapped in damask finery, one hand holding the feather-endowed hat.

Kitty allowed the gloved hand to stroke his muzzle, leaning in to rest its head against its master's shoulder.

'I am eager to get going as well, girl.'

Pushing aside the fine sabre, a family treasure wielded by his very own father long ago, the young Lord mounted in one swift movement, his eyes falling upon Lars, who passed the reins then stepped back quickly, thankful to be free from the beast. A curt nod

Chapter 1

followed by a dismissive flick of a hand was the only thanks he received from the young Lord.

Whether commoner or noble, the youth lack the correct respect for their elders, Lars mused. Well, at least this lord treated the lowly servants of the manor kindly, unlike masters of the past whose scarred furrows still marked the skin of his back.

Glancing up at the lit room above them, Lars could make out a figure looking down, Lord Arlo Paxton, his intense gaze fixed, face void of emotion upon his only son.

With a kick of Bertram's boots, the stallion began trotting away from the manor. Lars expected the Lord Bertram to turn and acknowledge his father above like he should, but he didn't. Lars shook his head again. The youth of today.

Each step Kitty took away from the manor broke through the claustrophobic veneer of expectations Bertram could never attain. The eyes of his silent father wrapped a weight about him that need not be voiced, just felt, to deliver their lash. Looking back, meeting those hardened, flint eyes that had commanded obedience from thousands on the battlefield would be seen as weakness, acceptance that he desired to be more, to cast aside the title of boy, taking on that of a man in the eyes of his father.

He would not give his father that satisfaction.

The daily running of the manor left few precious moments for Bertram to devote to tallying exhaustive accounts. Brokering deals with arrogant, greedy merchants had bound him more tightly than the bars of a prison ever could. He feared he might go mad if he had to entertain one more ageing war veteran weighed down by medals pinned to their breasts.

Arlo would find him even at the slightest pause in Bertram's daily routine of running the manor and all the business that went with that. He would say if you have time to sit and drink mulled wine, then you have time to run this errand for me. Couldn't his father see how hard Bertram was trying to be a dutiful son?

The Cauldron, the only tavern of note, had become a beacon of freedom, allowing a reprieve from the stifling life that had him penned in, not unlike the livestock of the manor. As Kitty trotted down the familiar path beneath the warped, broad-leafed trees, Bertram closed his eyes, feeling his body relaxing. The dry, astringent taste of whiskey awaited, and the heaving crowd under the spell of bardic music was a looming promise.

The manor gates were closed now, their twisted iron framework barring the way to a night of indulgence. To Bertram's annoyance, the gates stayed shut as he approached. As Kitty pulled up beside the guardhouse, the bull-like figure of Martin came out, stroking his greying moustaches with one hand while the other held his worn, ivory pipe from which smoke languidly curled.

Bertram knew better than to demand the old warrior open the gates right that instant. More than a servant, less than family, yet still Martin walked to the beat of his own drum; a glare could silence the rudest person while the sharp bite of his tongue could reduce the most learned of men to a fool.

Martin peered up at Bertram. The old guard's moustache twitched, bushy eyebrows lending his visage a serious tone.

'I know you are not so pea-brained to have forgotten what night this is, Bertie. Couldn't you just stay in tonight? You know how Arlo gets.'

'That, Martin, is exactly why I wish to be far from here. She was my mother too? Or have you forgotten that? I just choose to remember her differently.'

'You are all he has now, lad. What harm can it do to spend the anniversary of her disappearance with him? Listen to his stories that you have heard countless times and allow his memories to guide him to sleep along with his wine. You are his only child. The old fool would never admit it since he's more stubborn than a bull, but we both know he needs you on this night more than ever.'

Chapter 1

'Why does it all have to be about him? I have given my father all I have. I may be his son, yet it hardly shows in the way he treats me. Withholding praise but quick to criticise maybe your idea of a good father, but it is far from mine.'

Martin's shoulders dropped as he leant forward, spitting out one of the seeds he always chewed, then regarded Bertram thoughtfully as he drew a deep inhalation of smoke from the pipe.

'It's for just one night, Bertram. Can't you go gallivanting around tomorrow night or any other night that doesn't have such significance for your father?'

'Martin, I'm just a tool he uses to do anything he now can't because of his accident. This little happy family life he has built here in the manor is nothing more than a lie that squeezes the life from me more every day. That's why I need to get away, do something normal like most young men do these days. Even my friends joke and ask who I am when we meet because they just don't see me anymore. I am always doing the good son thing, helping father. Well, not tonight! Now open the damn gate, Martin, or do I need to teach your old ass a lesson in blade work again?'

Martin started to reply, then laughed. He limped forward, swinging the gate open to let Bertram through, neatly avoiding the bite that Kitty attempted as he passed. The stallion hated everyone besides Bertram yet seemed to harbour a deeper hatred for Martin, much to Bertram's continued amusement.

'Get that damned beast away from me! If you plan to return before dawn, there will be Lucas at this post. He is new, young, and nervous, so just take it easy on him. I can't afford to lose any more of my men to your terrible moods.'

Bertram raised his middle finger, then thrust it at Martin with a grin. 'I will have a drink or two for you, Martin. Oh, and by the way, look after Arlo. You will do a better job than I,' he added with a wink, kicking Kitty into motion.

Bertram guided Kitty off the road, choosing instead to skirt the edge of the gully, enabling himself to cut the journey down considerably. The night was silent beneath the smiles of the two moons, Aspre and Tamul, their pale light enough to see by as Kitty meandered between the trees, her hooves only breaking the quiet when they occasionally cracked on fallen branches. No owls hooted; no insects buzzed. The forest life had fallen silent. This now was the case with nature, changed from the events of the past when nature had then accepted the races of the world, Bertram mused, his mind touching on the scholarly work he craved to finish writing. His paper explored the events leading up to the Severing, the famed coterie of the heart who now lived in the Elemental Heart built by the harlequin and finally, the changes the return of magic was having in the known world. The turning of the Mother against her children, the races of the world, was a major aspect Bertram wanted to explore.

As they emerged from beneath the trees into the field of fruit trees laden with plump peaches beside apple trees heavy with bounty, Bertram's gaze found its way like it always did to the field beyond the fruit where the wraith trees grew. Even from here, the ash-coloured trees gave off a silver radiance of fallen moonlight, creating a fey ambience that could prove alluring to unaware travellers. Sweet juice ran down Bertram's chin as he bit deeply into a plucked peach. Removing the stone, he fed the remaining half to Kitty, whose ears had flattened as they came close to the wraith trees. They continued parallel to the wraith down across the wooden bridge, the waters of the Gelded River trickling below.

The wraith plants had been the latest in Arlo's investments. The crop had gained popularity during the last twenty cycles of the Severing, being especially coveted for the access it gave the user to the astral world, which was usually reserved for travellers who had gained the focus and knowledge necessary for adventures in the amber realm. At the very corner of the wraith field, Bertram

Chapter 1

stopped Kitty, then dismounted, ignoring the goose pimples that sprung up across his skin. He removed a sack along with thick leather gloves, which he donned to prevent getting pierced by the sharp spines of the trees. One prick from such would assure him of a trip into madness itself.

With a small sack of wraith leaves tied to his saddle, Bertram started back down towards Fallon's March, trying to ignore his senses that screamed he was not alone. Twisting his upper body, Bertram looked behind him, seeing nothing. This was as it was now: if you ventured into nature, it was worse at night. The ever-growing town that sprawled out below had experienced their fair share of strange incidents since the return of magic. Farmers attacked while cutting trees for fencing; travellers disappeared at night, leaving only an empty campsite with a long-dead fire. More commonly, hunters who failed to pay the proper respects to the Mother after a kill or simply took more than they needed were being set upon by usually less bold species instead of the usual wolves that roamed the woodlands. The Mother expected a balance to be recognised, a price that was heavily exacted when ignored.

To Bertram, it seemed the Mother had cast the races out. Now no longer her children but trespassers watched warily. When magic had returned, the masses had expected great power to be suddenly available to them, only to find life continued not so different from before. Bertram had hungrily scribbled down the words of the one person he knew who had chosen the path of power. The problem was that Abe Grelson was on the wrong side of crazy.

'Like the mother hound tires of her pups biting her teats, climbing over her, nipping at tail or ears, so too has the great Mother become. Like the pests we are, she has shaken us from her coat. Use of her power by us nasty mortals soiled her blood, warped her bones, curled her nails, glazed her eyes, and broke her heart.'

Abe had motioned Bertram closer. 'Now Mother takes her due soon as we touch the power. Maybe you go mad, blind, grow old unnaturally fast or worse, that is the price we pay,' he said, giggling, then his eyes opened wide. 'Best thing is as the power takes from the user, it flows back into the Mother in the strangest ways, healing her, empowering her at our cost.' Abe grabbed Bertram by the shoulders, long nails digging painfully into skin. 'Do not reveal your birth date to anyone. There is power in knowing one's birth month now. That sacred date dictates what element you can tap and which element makes you weaker. It's all about the balance now. The Elemental Tower is a testament to that.'

Fallon's March lay tucked behind the Rothair Mountains south of Scuttle and the Scented Isles. The isolated location meant news took time to reach the town. The townsfolk who had not been conscripted to fight for Scuttle had seen the strange light illuminate the sky when the Elemental Heart had activated and magic returned to the world. It wasn't until Bertram and the other survivors of the battle at the Elemental Tower had returned that Fallon's March had learned how the world had changed. Many hailed their returning sons, brothers or fathers heroes. Bertram vehemently denied this title, claiming he was there simply to

record events as an apprentice chronicler. His father, for once, was proud of his son following in his footsteps in fighting for his country. He even held a dinner to honour the return of Bertram from the war. When Bertram had shattered any ideas of heroism during his speech by recounting his only part was as an apprentice to a historian chronicling the conflict, it had driven a wedge between him and his father.

As Bertram reached the edge of town, he spotted a lantern light bobbing toward him, its glow illuminating four armed men. A town patrol. The town had formed a militia following the brutal raid of an infernal war band prior to the siege of Acclaro City.

Chapter 1

Though the conflict had ended over a cycle ago, the townsfolk had voted to keep the patrols.

'Name yourself,' came the call.

'It's Bertram. I've come to drink the town dry, then deflower the maidens,' Bertram called out.

They met his words with laughter.

'You're out of luck, friend. This town has no maidens left,' came the reply as Bertram walked Kitty up to the four men led by Jarl Ergot, the carpenter.

'How's Arlo, young Bertram?'

'Fine as always, Jarl; he has his mind set on driving me mad, but he is well.'

'Must come up your way to visit him. It's been too long since we've seen him down here.'

'Arlo would enjoy the company, Jarl. You know you are always welcome at our home. Have a safe night! I will be at the Cauldron should you wish to slake your thirst with me.'

The patrol melted away into the darkness, leaving Bertram to trot alone again towards the Cauldron. From here, he could hear the loud music of the bards amongst the stomping of boots, whistles, and catcalls. The tavern was aptly named for the boiling over of intoxicant fuelled emotions, which often became deadly brawls. The townsfolk had done everything to close the establishment down. Many believed it gave their home town a bad name, but none could argue with the numbers of outsiders it attracted, allowing Fallon's March to prosper. It was the perfect tonic to forget the dull life at the manor with his father. Though a dangerous place after nightfall for the meek and unwary, Bertram had friends there; he supposed it was a good thing the townsfolk held the Paxton family in high regard after all.

Chapter 2

Bertram tied his horse out front of the establishment as a fight spilled out from the tavern. The two men came stumbling out of the doors. They fell in the dust, scrambling at one another with fists flying. The hulking figure of Sef followed close behind, bald head gleaming with sweat as he reached down to lift both men up, one in each hand. Muscles straining, Sef slammed them together, then threw them away from him onto the roadway.

A third man came into view from behind the giant with a heavy pitcher in hand.

'Sef, behind you,' warned Bertram.

Defying his large frame, Sef moved quickly in time to deflect the pitcher that was aimed at his head with a meaty arm.

'Thanks, Bertram,' he grunted as he planted a fist in the attacker's gut, who collapsed with a whoosh of air to lie, moaning, at his feet.

Bertram stepped over the fallen man into the tavern, the music washing over him. The crowd for the bar was four deep, which would mean Bertram's eagerness to wash away the dust that lodged in his parched throat would have to wait a time. He moved to join the queue. The tables lining the walls appeared full, while in the remaining standing space, heaving bodies cavorted to the bawdy lyrics of three musicians on a raised stage.

Bertram spotted the tall, curvaceous Rae as she stumbled between patrons, carrying a tray overhead. He pushed in front of her with a grin, her features knitting with annoyance, then softening as he planted a kiss before she could say a word. Her glare which could put most men in their place softened when she saw who it was.

'Bertram, it's been too long. I thought you loved me, but alas, here I am still slaving away, waiting, hoping to be made an honest woman.'

Barely tearing his gaze away from the deep cleavage before him, Bertram fixed Rae with his best smile.

'I love you, Rae. In fact, I must discuss something very important with you in the stables as soon as you are on break.'

'Oh, I hate it when you jest. A break, whatever is one of those?'

Bertram pushed the hair out of his eyes. 'I will make it worth your while.'

'You always do, dear,' she cooed, running a finger down his cheek before turning away to disappear among the customers.

As Bertram turned back towards the bar, he knocked into an old, red-nosed man who looked deep in his cups. The mug of ale he held clattered to the floor.

'That's gone and done it now, hasn't it, young man?' He glared up at Bertram through slitted eyes, his body weaving slightly. 'That was my last silver ketch of ale.'

A few patrons stopped to watch the exchange, turning away when Bertram put his arm around the man's shoulder.

'My apologies. I will buy you another to make up for it.'

'That would be the reasonable thing to do, young man. Lead on.'

As they waited at the bar waiting to be served, the old man regularly poked him in the ribs.

'Got my ale yet? Don't just stand there; make yourself heard. I haven't got all night!'

Finally, Dixie, a tall brunette who owned the Cauldron, sauntered over with a smile. She ran a hand through her short, spikey hair.

'Bertram Paxton, I would have thought this was too much out of your league to be mixing with the swine we have here. Now that you are an accomplished scholar and all.'

Bertram felt his cheeks reddening at the compliment.

'Hardly a scholar yet, Dixie, but working on it.'

'What can I get you, love?'

'A double of devil's breath for myself and a stein of golden ale for this old fellow behind me. I knocked his drink over,' replied Bertram, leaning forward to be heard over the din as the musicians began another tune.

When Dixie returned with the drinks, she waved away the three silver ketches. 'On the house, Bertram,' she said with a wink, 'and take care of that father of yours, okay?'

Bertram passed the ale to the old man, who slurped at it, and then Bertram tucked the four silver ketches into the man's other hand. 'For your trouble, sir,' he said, pushing away through the crowd.

Bertram made his way through the crowd enjoying the strong flavours of oak and hazelnut with a smooth blend of cherry aftertaste. He spotted Munn, who was the brother of the other giant, Sef, and husband of Dixie, waving at him from beside the musicians. He waded through the crowd towards him. Many folks whom he jostled as he passed asked after Arlo, shook his hand, or nodded respectfully when they saw it was Bertram.

Munn encompassed Bertram in one of his bear hugs.

'You should be out there showing us all those fancy noble dance moves, Lord Paxton,' bellowed Munn.

'More important things to tend to, I'm afraid,' said Bertram, his words trailing off at the sight of Rae wiggling her hips to the roars of appreciation at a nearby table.

Munn's elbow playfully caught Bertram in the chest, making him grimace. 'Seems to me you have a different style of dancing on the mind, Bertie?'

'Since when is it a crime to admire a woman? Unlike you, my tastes are for the fairer sex, not the hairy-ass brutes you frolic with, Munn.'

Munn caught Bertram by the shirt, pulling him close with a grin.

'You two are the town's worst kept secret, always flirting, sneaking off as if nobody notices. You could do worse than Rae, so why not make an honest woman of her?'

'There is no need to rush these things. I have much going on with running the manor and writing my manuscript. When the time is right, I will make my move.'

'All I'm saying is that Rae is an attractive woman who turns many a head. She will most likely take over the Cauldron when Dixie becomes weary of it. Married to a smart woman like Rae, along with the backing of a highly regarded family like yours brings endless possibilities.'

Munn shrugged his large shoulders as Bertram rolled his eyes. 'Don't get all uppity, Bertram, I'm just saying is all.'

Bertram looked back across the crowd where he had last seen Rae, and now she was walking towards him with a coquettish grin. She leaned in to whisper something, making Bertram jump as Rae pinched him hard on the ass. 'Meet me in the stables. You got me all hot and bothered. I will be there soon.' Then she scowled at Munn, who was laughing.

When Bertram turned back to Munn, he was nodding his head knowingly. 'Better go, Bertie, don't want to keep her waiting,' the big man said, pursing his lips for a kiss.

The cool night air washed over him as Bertram paused outside the front door to light his pipe from a lantern before pausing to watch Sef shake the rudeness out of a man.

'Next time you think to call my mother a whore, I won't be so easy on you,' Sef roared, setting the man down.

The man tried to flee but only careened into a wagon of empty barrels to lay on the ground moaning.

Sef shrugged his shoulders at the look from Bertram. 'What? I didn't put the wagon there.'

Sef strode over and took a long swallow from a wineskin. He mopped the perspiration from his brow. 'Leaving so soon, Bertram? You just got here.'

'Off to the stables for a time, then will be back to drink the night away.'

'Oh, some lucky lass is going to get some loving then. Might need to start charging by the chime for using it soon, Bertram,' laughed Sef as he re-entered the Cauldron.

Bertram wrinkled his nose in disgust at the smell of horse shit. He almost gagged. Hopefully, Rae wouldn't keep him waiting long. Laying his cloak in the hay of a clean stall, he unbuttoned his vest, grinning at the delights Rae promised.

Rae sauntered into the stall, unlacing her shirt slowly, her gaze never leaving his. She did that cute thing she always did and bit her lower lip.

'Quick, Bertie, I have little time.' Then she was on top of him, trying to tear away his shirt.

'Easy, Rae, don't tear the buttons off. It's the only shirt I have here,' he said, trying to stop her.

'Fine. You undo the buttons while I wait down here.' She slid her shirt down over her hips, lying down on his cloak.

Bertram had trouble removing his shirt as Rae, becoming impatient, unlaced his trousers. As Rae busied herself, Bertram gave up on the remaining buttons and leaned back against a post to enjoy the sensation that was overwhelming him. When he was close to letting go and climaxing, Rae kissed her way back to his face.

'You really like that, huh,' she said, laughing, as Bertram could do nothing but nod his agreement.

Rae turned away from him, lifted her skirts to back onto him, letting out a slow growl of enjoyment as they moved together in unison. When Rae had climaxed, Bertram turned her onto her back, lowered her to the straw, and climbed on top of her, kissing her deeply. He was about to climax himself when he heard a voice.

Chapter 2

'What have we got here, then?'

Unable to stop himself, Bertram came with a surprised grunt.

Rae slid out from under him and quickly dressed while Bertram attempted to pull up his trousers as he looked for who had spoken. A dark-haired man with glittering green eyes leant against the stall door with a sneer on his thin face. Beside him, a young woman with immaculately coiled blonde hair was trying to smother a laugh with a hand.

'Did you see his face when he came while knowing their love play had been interrupted, Samual? And his lily-white ass is whiter even than yours.' She laughed again, then turned her large, brown eyes on Rae and looked the girl up and down before turning back to Bertram, who had now finished dressing.

'If you would like to ride a real woman, not some tavern whore, come find me later tonight,' the woman drawled as she walked away.

Rae's face had turned crimson. She wouldn't meet Bertram's eyes as she tried to open the stall door, but the weight of the man still leaning against it held the door closed. The man was leering at the two of them.

'Can you please move so I can leave?' Rae begged, then fixed her eyes on Bertram, her darting eyes showing desperation.

Before Bertram could speak, the man swung the door open, bowing to the waist.

'My apologies, sweet lady.'

Rae hurried away, leaving Bertram alone with the man.

'Do you normally take such enjoyment in watching others make love?' he spat as he left the stall.

The man fell into step beside Bertram.

'Is that what you call it? All I heard was a lot of moaning, like a calf in pain as we stabled our horses. Naturally, we investigated only to see your bare ass pumping up and down a moment before you came and pulled the most horrific face. It was a sight to see, although I wish never to have to endure it again, I'm afraid.'

Bertram stalked off, the man's next words following him. 'I must say, though, you sure know how to treat a woman. Very classy indeed.'

Chapter 3

Back inside the Cauldron, Bertram ordered another double of devil's breath, which he shucked down in two swallows. He saw Rae, but she either didn't see him or ignored him, so with another drink in hand, Bertram found a seat close to the three entertainers as they set up for their performance.

An abnormally tall man with a brown beard greying at the temples pushed back his mop of hair as he set out three harps—two were small enough for him to hold in his arms, the third he set up against a stand. The beautiful instrument matched his height, its polished hardwood laced with gold filigree patterns of vines, while the second man sat plucking a lute cradled to his chest like a lover. The final musician stood back to the crowd in a long, green hooded cloak, one fine blue boot idly tapping a tune. Bertram saw the two players nod at the third musician. The musicians then motioned for the crowd to be silent.

Slowly, the crowd obeyed. A humming came from the cloaked figure, who slowly raised its arms as the humming deepened. Mutters of magic weaved through the gathered patrons as the air about the stage darkened. Slowly pinpoints of silver blossomed above the performers, glittering softly; two moons took shape, one red and the other white to signify Aspre and Tamul. The red rays of Tamul illuminated the two players while the white of Illume fell on the cloaked figure. Anticipation built as the delicate notes of the largest harp floated through the tavern.

The cloaked figure began swaying side to side as if struggling with something. A sharp note from the harpists rang out. Head thrown back and cloak flaring, the figure on stage morphed into a red bird. Flames danced over it as it gave one loud wailing cry and then burst into a shower of falling blossoms to vanish before they hit the floor. A woman appeared amongst the falling flowers. She had lustrous, dark hair to the waist decorated with silver combs. Her delicate, pale face was highlighted with hues of gold. Then she began to sing. Her powerful voice soared to the highest notes, weaving the return of magic to the world. The tavern crowd was left stunned when her words trailed away with the harp's last notes.

Compared to the performers who normally graced the seedy tavern with passable performances, this trio captured their audience with one song.

After thunderous applause, the singer clapped her hands once before plunging the stage into darkness. The lute began playing a tune that reminded Bertram of rides through the woods. A rectangular shape appeared beside the singer, a door, its edge lit by a golden glow. There came one long, discordant note from the harp, then the singer reached out, turned the handle, and flung the door open.

For an instant the golden light within shimmered and then shapes boiled out: fairies, goblins, and pixies all laughing, shouting with glee as they charged into the audience to disappear with fading giggles. The pale singer sang of the fae gates once again opening to the world, allowing them to wreak havoc on mortals once more.

The crowd cavorted and danced to the shrieking instruments that accompanied the tale. When it finished, there was barely enough time to take a breath before the musicians launched into a joyous, upbeat tune that sent the patrons wild with delight.

Inhibitions now washed away with the devil's breath; Bertram joined in with the press of bodies around him. As he moved,

Chapter 3

Bertram spotted the two strangers who had spied on his coupling with Rae. The woman had referred to the eccentric man as Samual.

Who were they?

Bertram watched the two dance body to body, hips grinding, hands wandering. The woman was the shorter of the two, gazing up at Samual's face. The need in the woman's eyes struck Bertram as she moved seductively, her sole focus Samual revelling in the attention, but instead of returning it, he played a cruel game, taunting her with just enough attention to keep her beside him. A glance here, a smile there, a squeeze here, followed by moving just out of reach, then when she tired of the game attempting to twist away, he enfolded her in his arms.

As the song trailed off, Samual whistled his appreciation. The woman pushed up onto her toes to brush her lips against his, earning only an annoyed glance. Samual pushed her away, shattering the adoration in her eyes, breaking her smile, leaving her looking lost among the throng of patrons.

Bertram had to admit it. The man, Samual, had a certain charisma to him, a predatory grace as if he would snap into motion at any moment. It reminded Bertram of a serpent as he himself stood transfixed by the strange man's presence, which drew Bertram away from his surroundings, diminishing them. This man was dangerous.

Bertram felt a jolt of surprise ripple through his body as he realised Samual was staring back at him. The man smiled so wide it seemed to cover his whole lower face, revealing teeth of gold, a touch of malice.

Bertram looked away hurriedly, his heart beating abnormally fast. Samual certainly unnerved him, but besides the encounter in the stables where Samual had actually done nothing wrong besides showing himself to be a pervert, Bertram couldn't pinpoint any reason to feel this alarmed. So why did he feel threatened by the man's attention?

A group of staggering men vacated a table by an open window. Bertram slumped into the comfortable chair, enjoying the escape from the crowd. Cool air soon dried the sweat on his brow.

Bertram watched patrons come and go from his window vantage point, purposely avoiding looking in Samual's direction. When he once again turned back to the main room, he saw no sign of Samual or his girl among the dancing. Scanning the room, Bertrand felt himself visibly jump again when his eyes alighted on a table only two away from him, occupied by the two strangers.

The musicians stopped playing for the time being to slake their thirst as tankards banged on tables for more. When they realised this wouldn't happen, the crowd about the stage headed for the bar for their own refreshments.

Bertram pretended to be interested in anything but that table with the two strangers. Through his peripheral vision, Bertram watched three others join the table of interest. A tall, too-thin woman, all bones with pasty, tight skin that reminded Bertram of a corpse. She took a seat at their table, looking awkward and out of place in a white dress that stopped just below her knees, revealing a myriad of sores on her lower legs. Bertram couldn't see her face clearly through the long, black strands striped with grey. The man that took the seat beside her was straight-backed and clean shaven, with short blond hair. He sat facing outward lazily, taking in the surrounding scene with watchful eyes. His whole demeanour screamed warrior. The worn pommel on the long sword he lay against the table confirmed this was the case.

The third and final stranger arrived with a handful of drinks for his companions. Only the warrior sat without a beverage before him as the man ushered the slim woman farther along to take his own seat. This man was the most curious of them all, thought Bertram. Dressed in the finest cuts of scarlet and black with high leather boots shined to perfection, matching the silver wolf head belt buckle at his waist. He moved with coiled energy, gesticulating with his arms and facial expressions as he interacted with the others at the table. Bertram couldn't help but notice the long, thin sabre at his hip and the coiled whip tied to the small of his back.

Rae appeared at Bertram's table, startling him. She giggled, tracing a finger down his cheek with a wink as she bent low. She followed Bertram's gaze back to the strangers.

'Does the girl from the stables catch your interest?' Rae asked with her hands on her hips.

'No, not her, but her companions. I haven't seen any of them around here before,' Bertram replied, feeling his face flush with embarrassment, though he had no reason to feel that way.

'She told you to find her if you wanted to experience bedding a real woman, Bertram, so she must fancy you,' Rae replied with a glint of amusement in her eyes.

'She called you a whore, Rae,' Bertram said as if this explained everything.

'Do I detect a touch of gentlemanly anger in you, Bertie? Could it be that you feel protective of me suddenly?'

Bertram met Rae's eyes, noting the twitch of a smile at the corners of her mouth. He smiled back as he realised she was jesting with him.

'You are much more than a common whore, Rae,' he whispered in her ear; he beckoned her closer while Rae wiped down the table. Bertram tried to nip her ear, which Rae nimbly dodged away from.

'And, yet here I am, an uncommon whore waiting for an uncommon man to make an honest woman of her,' Rae said with a wink before hurrying back to the bar.

Bertram leaned back against the window frame, only now noticing Rae had replaced his empty glass with a fresh drink from which he now gladly sipped, wincing at the strength of it. At this rate he wouldn't make it to midnight.

Munn weaved his way over to Bertram.

'Bertie, I forgot to ask. Did you bring the wraith?'

Bertram removed the pouch from his belt, holding it up for the big man to check inside. Satisfied, Munn pushed a pouch of coin from his own pocket to Bertram.

'No need to pay for it, Munn. You have saved me from many a beating in the past, which is payment enough,' Bertram told the big man.

Munn's serious visage softened. 'Jade is rarely cognisant these days. Though I hate to admit it, the wraith allows her moments of clarity to be with me, which I cherish. At least with this,' he said, waving the pouch Bertram had given him,' Jade won't die in the astral, and it gives me time to find a way to remove its hold on her.'

'Be careful, Munn. If it happened to Jade, then the wraith can also take you for its own,' Bertram warned.

'Sometimes I think that wouldn't be so bad, Bertie. At least then I would have a daughter again,' Munn said, shrugging. He pocketed the pouch as he walked away.

Bertram returned his attention to the strangers, now embroiled in a heated conversation punctuated with raucous laughter. A serving girl delivered another tray of drinks for them. As she went to leave, Samual said something to her, which made her turn to look at Bertram. A short time later, the serving girl appeared at Bertram's table with a fresh devil's breath.

'The nobleman there asked me to give you this as an apology. He requests your companionship at their table so you can stop ogling them. He also said to ask if you had balls big enough to join them,' the girl relayed to Bertram with a laugh.

Looking at the strangers again, Bertram saw the blonde woman from the stables waving him over to join them.

Chapter 4

Bertram leaned back in his chair, unsure if he should accept the invitation. There was something not right about the five of them he couldn't work out. They were dangerous but also, in a way refreshingly different, and he had come here looking for some excitement to escape the drudgery of his boring life. By the Infernal hells, he thought, standing up, what do I have to lose? Then he grabbed his drink and weaved his way over to the table of strangers, who turned to watch him approach.

The man in red and black jumped to his feet, clapping his hands in glee, then wrapped an arm about Bertram's shoulders. 'I told you he would accept. Pay up now, losers.'

Coins slid across the table before the man who ignored the groans of his companions plucked up the silver ketches, depositing them within a belt pouch before turning back to Bertram with a hand held out in welcome.

'We are known as the Lords and Dames, and I am Museo Valente, at your service. I just won a bet at your expense, for which I now apologise and hope you won't think any less of me.'

'Of course, I won't,' Bertram replied. Samual placed a hand on Bertram's shoulder.

'This fine man is Bertram. He has proven he has enormous balls not once but twice as earlier Nix, and I found him putting them to use within the stables.'

The five strangers laughed and clapped their hands in delight.

All Bertram wanted to do at that moment was to escape this sudden attention. Not wishing to be the target of more ridicule, he took a seat.

Samual watched him carefully for a moment as if sensing his discomfort, then began the introductions of his companions.

'I am Samual Hayter, a traveller, writer and all-round scumbag. You briefly met this lovely lady by my side in the stables, Nix Borello.'

The woman winked at Bertram. 'Hi again, Bertram, oh, and nice ass,' she said in a purring voice.

'Next to Nix is Angus, a serious warrior, pessimist, and constant bore,' continued Samual, which earned him a glare from Angus.

'The fop who introduced himself already is Museo, an amazing performer if ever there was one, but also a constant nuisance for any that know him.' Museo sketched a bow for Bertram, his twinkling eyes full of mischief as he played with his perfectly manicured moustache before introductions turned to the last member.

'Finally, this is Elspeth, a vain, power-hungry witch who prefers the dead to the living.'

Bertram nodded to the woman, who just stared back at him in a way that made the hairs on his arms and neck stick up. She reached a gaunt arm out to Bertram expectantly, and he took it, shaking it lightly.

'Charmed' was all she said. Bertram attempted to pull his hand away, but her grip was vice-like as she smiled at him, then turned his hand over to look at his palm.

'I see noble blood, an accident, a broken sword, an empty bed, and the two moons with five faceless hounds cavorting beneath them.' Then Elspeth gasped, looked at Bertram, then away again, releasing his hand.

'What did you see in the end?' Bertram blurted out, feeling uneasy.

'The hand of yours I held turned to bones on which a swarm of flies descended, buzzing furiously. The meaning that comes to me, dear Bertram, is that you will have a hand in your own demise. You have interesting times ahead, Bertram, very interesting.'

'Did you see anything else?' Bertram croaked as his mouth went suddenly dry.

As Bertram met Elspeth's gaze, he was sure he saw her eyes blaze brighter for a moment, though he couldn't be sure. The strange woman gave him a small smile, then turned a now-pitying look upon him.

'You are very perceptive, Bertram. The last thing I saw was something that I was hesitant to share with you. Some visions are better left unspoken.'

'Tell me,' the plea came out, a rasping croak that drew laughter from all the others at the table except Elspeth, who still held Bertram's gaze with her own.

'A beating heart pumping wildly. The flesh then tears open in six places to reveal gore-covered asps that have eaten their way out.'

The horror that Bertram felt at Elspeth's vision must have shown on Bertram's face for all to see as his new companions broke into laughter once again.

'Glad it's not my future Elspeth was reading,' Samual said, clapping Bertram hard on the back. Samual draped an arm about Bertram's shoulders, pulling him close. 'Don't worry so much, my new friend. Not all visions come to pass, although the last part fits in well with the drinks I ordered us all.'

'What do you mean, Samual?' Bertram asked, still feeling on edge.

Samual pointed through the crowd where the serving wench Delsa was winding through the throng with a tray high above her head, on which sat six smoking glass mugs holding a swirling red liquid that bubbled as if something alive roiled about within the viscous liquid. Inwardly, Bertram groaned. They were tails of the asp, highly potent, maybe even toxic drinks that people had died from if concocted incorrectly.

'Bertie, I didn't realise these folk were your friends,' Delsa said as she unloaded the six drinks to the table, revealing an incredible amount of bosom as she did so. Delsa was a known town gossip. News of Bertram and his new friends would be common knowledge come morning.

'One cannot have too many friends, Delsa,' Bertram replied with a wink and smile he didn't really feel.

'Stand for the toast,' bellowed Samual, the scraping of chairs on the wooden floor echoing his own.

Bertram hurriedly followed, raising his own drink.

'To our new friend, Bertie, fresh paths forged within fine company!'

As one they all gulped down the drinks, the slightly sweet liquor glazed Bertram's throat, leaving a spicy aftertaste. He left the smoking lump at the bottom of the drink like the others did until they finished giving off its fumes, then with a chorus of exaggerated hisses, the six of them swallowed that too. The lump was known as the tail, which was a type of fungi with a harder outside that hid within a soft flesh; it was known for a range of strange effects, from visions to temporary madness. The alcohol reacted with the hard shell, melting it away so its effects could be experienced. Few sane people ever dared imbibe the drink.

Bertram slammed down his mug alongside the other five to their cheers and caught sight of Rae hurrying by with a sour look and a shake of her head for him as she went.

Nix seemed to have seen the shared moment between himself and Rae. She leant across the table, grasping his hair in her hands, then thrust her tongue into his mouth, licking, kissing, and biting his lip painfully. 'I hope she saw that,' Nix said before pulling away.

Bertram glanced over to where Rae had stopped and was now staring back at him, mouth slightly ajar. Rae's hand went to her mouth before she fled behind the bar. Surely Rae had seen the kiss had nothing to do with him, he thought as he sat. Bertram noticed one tail of the asp still sat on the table before the big man Angus who sat with his bulging arms crossed before him.

'Unlike you fools, I prefer not to poison my body with nefarious concoctions that will rot my innards, weaken my bones, and cloud my mind. The body is a temple not to be desecrated like some common latrine!' the big man said, reading Bertram's look.

'Enough of the damn self-righteousness, Angus,' Samual exclaimed.

'We can't all be as pure as you or as boring,' quipped Nix with a grin before she guzzled down Angus's drink.

As they sat drinking from a second asp tail that arrived soon after, Bertram found that he was enjoying himself amongst the company of these strange people. They were interested in him as much as he was with them, showering him with questions about his life as the conversation flowed easily with banter.

'Samual, when you introduced me to these fine folk, you referred to yourselves as the Lords and Dames. Are you truly all nobles?' Bertram asked as he tried not to slur.

The five friends shared a look before erupting into table pounding and laughter. Samual fought for composure as he wiped away the tears of merriment from the corners of his eyes. Samual puffed out his chest as he motioned for quiet.

'It is but a name we have taken upon ourselves in mockery to the stations that certain powers would attempt to thrust upon man. Some of us have belonged to that elite group of society, but here among our own, our previous station in life counts for naught, although it has a nice ring to it.'

Nix came and sat beside him. Bertram watched the girl pull a vial of powder from one leather boot. She tipped some of the powder along the top of one finely curved bosom.

'For you, my dear Bertram, it's fae powder.'

He snorted it from her skin while the others chanted his name. The fine powder seemed to shake something within him, momentarily sobering the effects of all the drinks. While the feeling lasted, he thought it was a good time to relieve his bladder.

'I shall relieve myself first, then return with the next round, my Lords and Dames,' he said, sketching a deep bow.

As he turned to weave away, Nix blocked his escape.

'Do you need some help with that, Bertie?' she cooed. 'Earlier in the stables you looked to be having so much fun that since then, I have wondered what all the fuss was about and wanted to see for myself.' She put one of his hands on her shapely, firm ass.

'Not yet, Nix. The night is young yet for pleasures such as you promise. This is just a call of nature,' Bertram replied.

Nix trailed a hand down his chest. 'Don't keep me waiting too long,' she whispered to him.

Once Bertram had finished his business, he made his way to the bar, which was easy to reach now the musicians had begun playing their last round.

As Dixie served him at the bar, he slipped her a generous tip that quickly disappeared beneath her apron. 'New friends, Bertie?'

'Out of town, folks, nice too, even if boisterous,' Bertram replied.

'Just be careful, dear. I have never seen them here before, and well-off people like them rarely come here without some purpose.'

'Did Rae put you up to that? It appears my drinking companions also displease her,' Bertram said.

'Rae? No, she left a while ago, although she looked like she had eaten something sour. You could make an honest woman of her, Bertram?'

'I could do much worse than Rae. Please keep the drinks coming, Dixie. We won't be any trouble,' Bertram added as he carried the drinks back to the table, trying to ignore the soft faerie lights that had begun to light the surroundings.

Chapter 4

As he went, he could faintly hear Dixie's words carry after him. 'It's not me you have to convince of that, Bertram dear. It's Seth and Munn.'

Bertram's cursed bladder struck again not long after the first time, although when he staggered towards the privy, he realised the Cauldron was now over half empty. When did that happen?

Bertram was ready to burst. He got his trousers down just in time not to piss on his fine clothing. He leaned against the wall, sighing with relief, then pulled his trousers up and turned to leave, almost bumping into a man standing right behind him.

'So sorry, my friend, I didn't realise you were there,' Bertram apologised, then went to step around him only to once again find his way blocked by the stocky figure. Bertram saw the man wore stained-white clothes common to the servants of many manors in the area. It definitely wasn't one of Arlo's servants or Bertram would have recognised him.

The man's nose had once been broken, and his right eye peered off to the side as if unwilling to look at Bertram. This forced a giggle to burst from Bertram before he could stop himself.

The man grabbed him by the shirt and then threw him hard up against the wall, causing Bertram's trousers to fall down again as he grasped his assailant's arms, leaving him naked from the waist down.

'I saw you flaunting your money pouch in there for all to see with your upstanding friends, pretending you are better than the rest of us,' spat the man, his face close to Bertram's. 'Tell you what, Lord fucking Paxton, how about you pass me that pouch from under your tunic nice and slow so I don't need to smash your skull in, and we can forget this little meeting even happened?'

Bertram knew he should panic at his predicament. However, he felt strangely calm instead, most likely because of the fae powder.

His voice sounded distant and strange, disassociated.

'Do nothing you might regret. We can talk this through with nobody getting hurt, nice and decent.'

The punch stole the breath from Bertram's body as his assailant slammed his fist into Bertram's gut, folding him over as he toppled to the ground.

The man squatted beside him.

'Now I will ask only one more time. Paxton, give me the coin purse, now!'

As Bertram attempted to draw breath, he saw a figure loom behind his assailant. A hard leather boot lashed out and sent his attacker to the side. Bertram could see Samual, who then clambered upon the attacker before crashing a fist into the man's face three times, breaking his nose once again. The man cried out and covered his bleeding face, so Samual struck him in the chest and ribs over and over while grunting with the effort. The man lay groaning quietly now as Samual stood above him, wiped the sweat from his brow, and then began kicking the prone man in the face.

'What's happening out there?' came Munn's deep voice, and Bertram saw the huge man walking down the lantern-lit path towards them.

'Samual, stop now. He's had enough,' Bertram said, climbing to his feet.

Munn took in the scene in one quick glance, then turned his gaze on Bertram expectantly.

'Munn, I can explain,' Bertram began, but then Samual broke in over the top of him.

'This filth attacked Lord Paxton here while he was doing his business, a cowardly act that I happened upon, and, thankfully, being the outstanding man I am, I was able to assist my friend from further assault. As for his pants being around his ankles, that's something Bertie will have to explain himself.'

Munn scowled at Samual and then at Bertram.

'Munn it was as Samual says. This man tried to take my money pouch, and Samual came to my aid.'

'Is he even alive?' Munn growled, nodding at the body at his feet as Bertram hurriedly retied his pants.

'Who fucking cares,' drawled Samual, straightening his shirt, the lantern light reflecting the perspiration sheen on his face giving him a devilish look to go with his dilated, fae-affected eyes.

'I, for one care, and so will Dixie, the owner of the Cauldron. Nasty business for us if he dies here.'

Bertram knelt, felt for a pulse, and breathed out when he found a faint fluttering at the man's neck.

'Still alive, Munn. I apologise for the trouble, but you know me and know I would start nothing here that could bring trouble upon Dixie.'

'Okay, Bertram, best you and your friend get back inside now while I take care of this, and remember, you owe me one now,' Munn growled as he picked the fallen man up.

Samual placed an arm around Bertram's shoulder, then they strolled back towards the common room.

'You're welcome, by the way, Bertie. Nothing like a bit of fun, is there? The bastard didn't know what hit him,' he added with a wink. 'You know, you need to stop making a habit of it.' Samual laughed.

'A habit of what?' Bertram asked, confused.

'Having your pants down around your ankles, baring that ass whiter than Aspre,' Samual retorted, and they both broke into a fit of laughter as they went to join the others.

Chapter 5

Bertram and Samual returned to the table just as Nix was passing more fae powder around.

Except for Angus, the others all took some. Then they passed it to Bertram. 'No. I will pass this time, but many thanks,' he said, sipping from yet another devil's breath.

Museo leaned in close and put his arm around Bertram's shoulder. 'My friend, celebrating with us is like a contract that must be followed through to the end. This is the first crossing of our path with you, a moment that only happens once, which makes it a powerful event. As my people would say: Celebrate the beating heart.'

'Must be immune to the stuff. It just hasn't worked yet, maybe a bad batch,' mumbled Bertram, trying to appear nonchalant under the gaze of the five of them.

'All the more reason to have more,' responded Museo as he pushed the tray back over in front of Bertram.

At Bertram's hesitation, Samual leant back in his chair.

'Bertie, old fellow, this is how I see it. You had the balls to join us while knowing we were not just here for tea and biscuits. The Lords and Dames don't do things by half measures; it's all in or go home. Now, I would guess that you were looking for an escape, an alternative way to bring the brightness back into your life, if only for an evening, and guess what, this is it. This is your reason to forget the day-to-day existence that plagues us all, a way

Chapter 5

to take control of life instead of letting it lead you down a series of dead ends where one day you wake up and say to yourself, "If only I had done this." Bertie, this is the only moment that means anything right now, here with us. Don't waste the perilous delights it offers.'

Because his thoughts were becoming more disorganised, his vision becoming more distorted, Bertram reached down and took the tray, scooped up some powder in the spoon, and snorted it up one nostril to the cheers of his new friends.

'That's it, Bertie,' exclaimed Nix, kissing him deeply. 'Throw caution to the wind.'

Things only became more intense from that moment on. An older musician started the music again, and no matter how much Bertram wanted to sit and just relax, his body had other ideas. He joined the celebrations with abandon, dancing, drinking, and laughing until everything blurred. Later, he found himself outside looking up at the stars, not sure how he had gotten there.

A face hovered above him. It was Angus, looking concerned.

'You okay, Bertie? We thought you had escaped,' said the serious man, which sent Bertram into a serious fit of giggling at the sight of the man's face. His next memory was arm wrestling against Angus while the others cheered him on. Angus was also laughing, which gave Bertram a chance since the man was too strong for him. It turned out he just wasn't strong enough, and Angus finally beat him.

It was midway to dawn when the copious amounts of fae powder took full effect. Everything softened, lending his movements a fluidity as smooth colours burst around him, and he gasped in wonder. The room changed before his eyes. The long bar area suddenly sprouted vines that wiggled and twisted along its surface and up the walls. The ground in front of Bertram split open and continued to form a gaping hole in which he could see swirling golden light. Bertram shook his head and it cleared, returning his view to the normal surroundings.

Munn was at his side. 'Bertram, are you okay? I think it's time to stop the fae powder. You have had enough.'

'Sure thing, Munn. Thank you for helping me,' Bertram said, and his words felt disjointed and strange.

Munn's skin had turned green, and Bertram reached out to touch it as he tried to tell him what was happening. Munn brushed his arm aside and moved away, shaking his head.

Then someone was leading him outside into the cool, fresh air. It was Nix, and she was beautiful. Her hands were warm where she touched his; her reassuring voice mesmerised him, carrying away his anxiety. They sat on soft grass watching the night come alive around them. There were whispers and laughter in the darkness, but when Bertram turned to see where they originated, he only caught glimpses of figures ducking out of sight.

'Did you see that, Nix?' he blurted out.

She giggled, then covered his face in small kisses.

'Why do you think they call it fae powder?'

She laughed. 'It's said that if you have enough it opens a gate to the fae realms, and they will come through to see who has summoned them.'

Bertram lay back on the grass and closed his eyes. He felt wonderful, alive, and bursting with love for everything. When he opened his eyes, Nix was straddled above him. She had let her hair fall out of its bun and topple down over her shoulders. 'Have you ever fucked on this stuff?' she whispered in his ear, and all he could do was shake his head and stare at her.

Their lovemaking was neither hurried nor urgent. They knew each other's needs and met them with exquisite attention while two moons above stood witness to the beauty of the moment. Bertram wished with all his soul that this night would never end.

Chapter 5

Afterwards, as if a figment of his imagination, Nix melted away into the night, leaving Bertram mesmerised by the moons. He was still there when Dixie came to him. She made him sit up with the help of Munn and Sef, who looked worried, but he couldn't work out why. 'Here, put your clothes back on, Bertram. We are closed now, and it's time you went home.'

'What about my friends?' he slurred. He felt disorientated for a time, wondering where he was, and they stayed with him until Sef tipped a cold bucket of water over his head, which snapped him awake.

'What? Why are you all staring at me, and why am I wet?' he managed to say as he spotted the bucket in Sef's hands. 'You wet me, you bastard.'

'That I did, Bertie. You have been out of your skull on fae powder and tails of the asp. Now it's time to go home.'

'Sef, take him home in the cart. He can get his horse tomorrow,' said Dixie from his side.

'No! I want to walk. Just get my horse. I am fine now and know my way home.'

They stared at him like he was a child, but eventually, Sef walked away to return with his horse.

'Goodnight, Dixie, Sef, Munn. I apologise if I made a fool of myself. Now I must sleep.' Then he mounted, turned, and led his horse down along the road towards home.

Chapter 6

The surreal ride back out of town was punctuated by clipped visions of events from earlier in the evening, causing Bertram to shake his head to dislodge the confusing images. It didn't work. As he cut across the field past the wraith crop, Bertram noticed an area at the edge of the twisted trees that appeared as a perfect patch of darkness. He angled Kitty away to give it as wide a berth as possible but couldn't take his eyes off it. There was something menacing and yet enticing that called to him while shrieking for him to ignore it, but he couldn't, and though he didn't remember stopping or how long he sat there staring into the dark mass, It was before that dark mass that Bertram found himself when he once again became aware of his surroundings.

Whispers called to him. They knew his name, but how was it possible? He felt his mind go away again, washed away in confusion before returning him to the moon-soaked wraith field. He was dripping through with sweat and shivering uncontrollably. Beneath him, Kitty shimmied sideways away from the darkness, which Bertram realised in shock was only feet away from him. He could see a silhouette—tall, lithe, all hard angles bent the wrong way.

A rasping laughter rolled forth. Then it spoke his name. The shock was so great that he slammed his heels into Kitty's flanks and raced off along the road as fast as he could without looking back.

Chapter 6

He was racing along the road to the manor when he fell from Kitty, rolling and bouncing into the undergrowth. His fear propelled him onwards on legs fuelled with adrenaline, and he would have screamed if he could, but he was mute. Sounds came from behind him; unearthly, high, grating laughter punctuated with grunts and howls; up ahead loomed the guardhouse.

The new guard must have heard him approaching and stepped out onto the roadway before the gate with a lantern. Bertram almost knocked the young guard down, who dropped the lantern with a curse. Flames flared, followed by a scream, and Bertram knew the guard was dead.

Finally, he got the courage to look behind him. A thorny, hunchbacked creature crouched over the guard's body, holding an arm in its twisted hands. It grinned at him as it broke the arm with a snap. Stopping was the mistake that could cost Bertram his life. As he turned away, running, he could hear pursuit. Ahead, the manor shivered in and out of existence, a figure looming up before him, the statue of Erin. An inhuman howl of frustration sounded behind him.

Then Bertram collapsed.

Bertram opened his eyes as something crawled over his face. He brushed it away, wincing in pain as the movement caused aching pain to blossom through his skull. His mouth was dry, and the taste in his mouth was disgusting. Bertram sat up. He spat out some soil and a beetle that had wandered into his mouth.

His muscles resisted him. His chest burned beneath his torn shirt. Bertram managed to walk slowly, bent at the waist, nausea washing over him. He retched, overcame with need, fell to his knees and purged, which made him feel much better. He focused on the statue of his grandfather Erin standing proudly in the middle of the fountain pool. Bertram dunked his head beneath the water, ignoring the pondweed and the bright fish darting around him. Then he sat with his back against the stone lip of the pond to rest a moment.

The crunch of boots on cobblestones snapped Bertram back into the world. Images of the monstrosity atop the new guard flashed through his mind. The guard was dead, and now it was his turn; he wanted to scream and call for help, but instead, he prayed silently, though the gods had never been a part of his life despite his mother's deep belief in them.

Something grabbed Bertram in a firm grip, and in that moment, he surrendered completely to what would come next.

'Bertie, come on, wake up. Can you walk?'

It was Martin. Maybe the gods had heard after all. Bertram opened his eyes. Martin's face blurred before him. The words just tumbled out of him in a rush as he tried to explain what had happened, but all that came out was gibberish. He felt himself lifted as Martin's gruff voice reached him through the waves of nausea and exhaustion. 'Hold still, Bertie. I will get you inside to bed. Tess, get some cloths and bandages. Oh, and fresh water. Master Bertie is in a bad way.'

The distinct fragrance of lavender was the first thing to come to Bertram when he woke in bed dressed in a night robe. Shadows draped the room, daylight hidden by thick curtains. Bertram sat up, cringing from the pain in his skull. From a pitcher, he drank cool water, trying to ignore his body's chorus of aches. He was starving.

On bruised feet, Bertram crept from the bedroom. The last thing he needed was Arlo to hear him. Interacting with anyone right

Chapter 6

now was just too much. His stomach gurgled loudly, reminding Bertram that his sole purpose was to find food. Though the kitchen was empty, he spotted freshly baked loaves of bread and an apple pie resting on a window ledge. Silently, he thanked Nellie for the food, hardly tasting the bread as he forced it into himself. Halfway through a fourth mouthful, the urgent need to eat subsided some, and he chewed slower, this time lathering the bread with jam and drinking deeply from fresh milk in a jug.

What had he done last night? He remembered only up to the altercation at the latrine where Samual beat a man to the edge of his life for giving Bertram a hard time. Later he would return to the Cauldron to find out what happened last night and if he had anything to apologise for.

This was routine for Bertram, who seemed unable to have just a few drinks. When he drank he did so excessively, much to his father's disappointment, who saw this as an embarrassing habit not suitable for a first noble son. His mouth was filled with the next bite when Nellie walked in, jumping in surprise, almost dropping her armload of vegetables. 'Bertie don't scare my poor heart like that,' she scolded him, slapping the food bowl down on the long bench.

'Sorry, Nellie, I just couldn't wait ….' He motioned to the food he held.

Nellie came over and turned his head to face her. 'What happened to you, Bertie? You look like you have been at the gates to the Infernal lands themselves.'

Bertram rinsed his mouth with milk before answering. 'Big night at the Cauldron.'

'Really? I thought you would have outgrown this behaviour by now.'

'Enough of that, Nellie, you sound just like Arlo,' groaned Bertram.

'Well, your father has a point, Bertram. Some day you will take over the estate from him, and he wants you to be ready and for the manor to prosper so your children will also live good lives from all his hard work.'

Bertram visibly shuddered. 'Children. I would rather die.' He collected an apple from the fruit bowl. 'I'm going back to bed, so please tell everyone not to bother me,' he said, pausing and looking back at Nellie, then walking off.

'Guess I better bake some more bread for the rest of us,' complained Nellie loudly as Bertram left, making him smile.

Back in the bedroom, he managed to tip over the chamber pot and made a weak attempt at cleaning up his mess before collapsing back into bed.

Bertram could see the stars outside from the windows when he awoke, which meant someone had opened the drapes. Finally, his mind seemed back to normal now that he had long slept.

Somebody was leaning against the door watching him, and for a moment, Bertram knew fear as a memory of the darkness in the wraith field surfaced.

'Martin, is that you?'

'Of course, it is, Bertram. Who else would check up on you if not me?' said Martin as he came to sit on the bed. 'You look like shit. I was concerned about what happened last night. I paid Dixie a visit.'

This made Bertram groan as he turned back to Martin. 'What did she say?' At Martin's pause, Bertram sighed. 'No need to keep me in suspense, Martin.'

'Nothing good. You partied with five strangers who had plenty of coin and even more fae powder. It's a wonder your nose still works. Worse still, you rutted near the tavern in sight of others. Then later, Munn was present when one of your associates nearly killed a man. People are going to want answers and maybe even compensation if he dies, Bertram.'

They paused, both staring at each other, neither willing to be the first to look away.

Chapter 6

'Tell me more about these five strangers, Bertram. They could be dangerous.'

'Dangerous? They were just passing through. I don't expect to ever see them again,' Bertram replied.

'Lucas, the new guard, is missing. A bloodstain at the estate gates was the only sign of trouble. Could it have been these friends of yours? Did you see anything on the way home?'

'I didn't see any guard when I came through. Maybe he left.' As Bertram said the words, he lacked any belief in their validity. 'I can't remember much.'

'What do you want me to tell your new friends, Master Bertram?'

'Why would I want you to tell them anything? I just said.'

'I heard you the first time. Your five friends are downstairs in the greeting room waiting for you.'

'Tell me you are kidding,' gasped Bertram, standing up, still in his nightclothes.

'No, sir. I would not joke about this. I have gone to the trouble of selecting suitable attire for you. Dress, then come and meet with them to see what they want. You will need to send them on their way, Bertram. Your father won't want strangers here. You know how he is.'

'Just give me a moment and offer them tea to be polite. I will deal with this,' said Bertram, pulling on his clothes.

Chapter 7

Suitably attired, Bertram made his way downstairs, hoping he looked better than he felt. Through the windows that flanked the winding staircase, Bertram could see five horses tied off at the front of the manor. They looked well-bred even from this distance, and he remembered Samual referring to their group as the Lords and Dames, so maybe they were nobles after all. He felt it was something he knew, but he just couldn't remember.

When he entered the greeting chamber, the Lords and Dames were busy eating from a platter loaded with cured ham, fruits, and that beautifully baked bread. They had yet to notice him, so he watched them momentarily. Memories surfaced as he watched Elsie, a young, comely servant, pouring them wine. Museo, now dressed in a cloak that chased his heels, long, red trousers with a bone-white long-sleeved shirt and red hat to match, reached out and cupped her bottom, making her squeal and dance away from him nervously. The mysterious Elspeth who had read his palm, sat reading a volume from the bookcase as she ate fruit. She wore a grey dress, and a satchel sat across her knees. Angus, the most serious of them all, was in leather armour, and at his belt hung a familiar blade, Bertram's father's famed blade Soulcounter.

Angus was animatedly talking to Samual. 'Samual, this man in the painting is famous. He was a general in the king's army and retired injured with many commendations. This must be Bertie's daddy.'

'Never heard of him. I must say, though, this place is amazing. I could get used to this,' replied Samual, smiling. Samual looked the part of the noble in high, black leather boots; tight, brown trousers; and a glittering belt from which hung a rapier below a royal-blue shirt beneath a black vest. His long hair was tied back into a tight ponytail, a fashion that had yet to be accepted in this part of the world.

Seeing the final of the five, Nix, brought back a memory of her naked body atop his, which made Bertram blush. If only she could stay and the others leave, this might not end badly.

It was Nix who noticed him first, and she leapt up with a squeal and ran to him. Her slim, tan trousers and tight corset accentuating her breasts immediately caught his attention.

'Bertie, you are here at last. I was just fearing that the invitation you extended to us was just a figment of my imagination.' Nix stood on her toes and kissed him deeply, bringing a deeper blush to his cheeks that threatened to set him on fire.

'It's good to see you again, Nix,' said Bertram, waving at the others to stay seated. 'Don't get up. Enjoy the food and wine. Elsie, be a darling and pour me some of that red, will you?'

Elsie hurried past Museo and had to weave away from his groping hands. She looked positively distraught as she handed Bertram a goblet of the wine before fleeing the chamber.

With wine in hand, Bertram joined his new friends around the table. Samual wrapped him in a tight hug, then jabbed him hard in the ribs, which momentarily winded Bertram, but he tried hard not to show it.

'Bertie, first, on behalf of the Lords and Dames, I would like to sincerely thank you for extending your hospitality to us strangers, although after last night, not so much strangers now, are we?' said Samual enthusiastically.

'So nice of you to drop in to say goodbye. Where are you headed now, out of town?' Bertram swallowed his wine in one gulp.

They all turned to look at him, almost comically as if surprised, and then Samual burst into laughter. 'Oh, you beast, jesting with us like that.'

'I don't know what you are talking about, Samual,' replied Bertram, perplexed.

Elspeth poured herself more wine and then another for Bertram. 'I believe our noble friend has forgotten the whole conversation we had last night about staying here for a while,' she said, eyes twinkling with amusement.

'I said that?' asked Bertram, feeling the anxiety within him growing.

'Not only did you say it, Bertie, you put it in writing,' said Elspeth, leaning forward and gazing at him with a stare he didn't like, a stare that promised trouble should he do the wrong thing.

Museo produced a folded parchment with a flourish, cleared his throat, and then read.

'I, Bertram Paxton, do hereby authorise the Lords and Dames temporary residence at the family Paxton manor until their business in this area is concluded, whenever that may be,' and it was definitely his signature at the bottom.

'Well, that's that then,' he said, giving a little laugh that was on the shrill side.

'Problem solved then. Now we can celebrate,' said Nix, clapping her hands together. Bertram caught himself staring at his sword still hanging from Angus's belt. Another problem, he thought, wondering if he could somehow get it back.

The man stared back at him, then his mouth twinged into a smile.

'If you are wondering why I am wearing your sword, it is because you lost it to me fair and square arm wrestling. Can you even remember that Bertie?'

Bertram could remember the arm wrestling with everybody around them cheering on, but not the sword.

Chapter 7

'Partially,' said Bertram, feeling sick.

'Truly a magnificent weapon and well used. I would assume that it was passed down to you by your father, the famous general Arlo Paxton.'

'You have heard of him, then?'

'Only this morning that brute from the Cauldron, Sef, I think it was, came to our rooms to ask politely for the sword back. Naturally, I had to refuse though, since I won it over a bout of honour between two gentlemen. Sef told me the importance of it as a family heirloom. Sorry, Bertram, a bet is a bet, and I like the measure of the blade: well-balanced, sharp and expertly crafted. Rarely have I seen such a fine blade.'

'Can I at least ask you to keep it out of sight of my father? Its loss will upset him greatly.'

Angus shrugged as if this was a minor request. 'Yes, I can do that for you, Bertram.'

'So where is this famous general father of yours anyway, Bertram?' said Angus. 'Does he still spar? I would love to pit myself against a true warrior, even if only one of the distant past.'

'Angus, you insensitive barbarian,' cut in Nix. 'You must have heard Sef say that Arlo was injured while on campaign, the nerves to his legs destroyed in battle.'

'Oh, sorry, I forgot all that dastardly detail. It must be hard for him. Is it, Bertram?'

Bertram got the feeling that Angus was playing with him and had indeed known of Arlo's accident. He decided then he really didn't like Angus.

Nellie came in and clapped her hands together, looking about with a huge smile. She loved cooking for guests; these days, Paxton Manor had few of them.

'Master Bertram, will your friends be staying for dinner?'

'Yes, they will be Nellie, and can you tell Tess to prepare two of the rooms for them? They will stay awhile until their business in town is concluded.'

'Yes, Bertram. Should I also inform your father?' she asked, turning to go.

'I would appreciate that and tell him that we will see him at dinner.'

The wine continued to flow, and when the fae powder made its appearance, Bertram quickly repulsed any suggestions for him to take some. 'I lost my father's sword, signed a contract to let five delinquents move in, and was involved in a near murder, so this time I will have to refuse.'

'Such a shame. Guess it's more for me,' said Nix a little sulkily as she loaded another spoon of the powder and snorted it.

'Can I ask what business you are here for?' Bertram said to Samual.

'We are waiting for a friend to arrive. He was supposed to be here two days ago, but there is no sign of him, so we left messages in town saying that he can find us here.'

'Who is this friend, and why is he so important?' asked Bertram.

'Uh-uh-uh, Bertie, don't be too nosy,' laughed Samual.

'Sorry, I didn't mean to pry, Samual. Now if you come with me, I will show you to your rooms so you can freshen up for dinner.'

Chapter 8

The dining room was Bertram's favourite place in the manor. A memory swam to the forefront of his consciousness each time he entered it. He had been young when the sounds of laughter called him from his dreams. Mother was home. Still in his nightclothes, Bertram rushed downstairs into the dining room, straight into his mother's arms. Her long, red hair tickled his nose as he nuzzled against her breast, fighting tears.

'Bertram, you silly sod,' she cooed, kissing his forehead as she kneeled in front of him, Arlo grinning behind her.

'With father leaving on the campaign today, I was scared you wouldn't be home in time, and I would be alone.'

'You don't have to worry about that, Bertram. I am here now. I have something for you all the way from the Scented Isles.' His mother held up a small, red velvet bag with a strange symbol on it. When Bertram pulled open the drawstring, a silver figure fell out. It was a fox head.

'In the Scented Isles, these fox heads are used for protection against misfortune or bad luck. It is very special, but you must always wear it to work. Can you do that, Bertram?'

With the calming pressure of the fox's head against the skin of his chest, Bertram ran his fingers along the thick mahogany table with its stump base. The chairs were newly covered with fresh leather, their earthy, fresh scent comforting. Portraits of the family decorated the walls, all painted by his father. One depicted

Arlo in uniform from his days in the military, standing proud yet showing the ravages of war clearly in his features. Another was of Bertram's first time atop a horse, long hair splayed back in the wind and beneath him a fine white mare that had been his mother's. The one he loved the most was his mother. Arlo had captured her carefree nature perfectly, looking back over her shoulder in a turquoise gown. Bertram wondered not for the first time what had become of her, to where she had fled when she had left both him and Arlo.

The table had been set for eight places: Bertram, Arlo, and the Lords and Dames, but who was the eighth place for? He mused. Bertram poured a generous amount of wine for himself to settle his nerves, which were jangled. He was dreading the meal and the Lords and Dames meeting with Arlo.

Arlo was the first to arrive, carried in by Martin, whom Bertram noticed had dressed for duty in his leathers with a sword on his hip, which was unusual since he never wore blades within the manor nor attended meals. The eighth place must be his. Looks like I'm not the only one who doesn't trust my guests.

Arlo didn't even acknowledge Bertram as they entered the dining room. Bertram placed the thick cushions on the seat at the head of the table so Martin could put his father down. Arlo gestured for wine before finally turning to Bertram.

'Martin, kindly give us a moment, please, and should our guests arrive, keep them outside until I have finished talking with my son.'

Bertram passed Arlo the wine and pulled up a seat next to him. Once robust and athletic, his father had been known as the bear because of his ferocious fighting ability and strength. His height had enabled him to tower over most men, but he had lost the use of his legs to a sword blow that should have killed him. His legs, now useless, had shrivelled to become nothing more to him than an inconvenience. Though his body was broken, his father was not

Chapter 8

one to sit and wallow in his misery. He kept his upper body fit with daily exercises, maintained a strict diet, and turned his attention to other pursuits, such as his art.

'Martin told me about our guests.' Bertram went to speak, but Arlo silenced him with a stern glare.

'If I may say so, I am disappointed that you didn't consult me first, Bertram. It's not that I don't trust you, son. You have shown me a side of you over the last cycle that I have rarely seen. You have run the estate extremely well while I have been preoccupied with other pursuits. These are your guests and are your full responsibility. Should anything untoward happen, I will hold you accountable. Do you understand me?'

'Yes, Father, I do. They are only in town awaiting the arrival of a colleague, so they will stay a few days at most. Now can I let the others in?'

'I haven't finished yet, Bertram. They can wait. Your behaviour last night, by all accounts was not merely abysmal but downright embarrassing. After all the sacrifices I have made fostering an excellent reputation for this family, this type of behaviour will destroy it. That I cannot allow. Should you wish to maintain your freedom from my attentions, then act like the noble son you are. Now let them in so I can eat, I'm famished.'

Martin opened the door for their guests. Museo was grappling with Samual, Angus was thumbing smoke mixture into a pipe, which he lit from a lamp as the door opened, and Nix was dancing with Elspeth in spinning circles. If it weren't his responsibility to behave, Bertram would have laughed out loud at the sight of his father's jaw falling open like a fish.

Samual stopped, then smiled broadly. 'The pig trough is finally open.' Then he sauntered in, only to be stopped by Martin's firm glare and outstretched arm.

'What is it, old man? I thought we were guests here,' he said, shoulders stiffening.

'And so you are, but here we use our manners. Now introduce yourself to the master of the house, Arlo Paxton, or have you forgotten such civilised practices on your travels?'

Samual glared back at Martin and then sighed, throwing his hands up theatrically.

'Master Paxton, I am Samual Hayter. I hail from Stormwatch but spent much of my childhood in Cavere. I am at your service.' Then he took a seat opposite Bertram.

Next was Elspeth, whose fake smile mocked the whole occasion. 'Elspeth Quince at your service, Master Paxton. I am a practitioner of the arts but have no fear. I will not put my talents to use within your home.'

Next was Nix, who curtsied low with practised ease. 'Master Paxton, I am charmed to meet such a distinguished man. You must tell me all about your war stories. I am Nix Bordello, a noble's daughter who goes where the wind blows.'

Angus entered next, giving a shallow bow, seemingly unimpressed by Arlo Paxton or the dining room. 'Angus,' he simply stated, then sat down.

Museo bowed and then saluted. 'Master Paxton, or should I call you general? I am a musician who travels the path of the blade. I have heard of your mighty deeds and am honoured to share food with you. Thank you for having us all in your home.

Bertram's father addressed the guests.

'Welcome to my home. I must admit we are unused to visitors here, and I require you to conduct yourself with a measure of decorum. While any friend of Bertram's is a friend of mine, I will repay respect with respect. I hope you enjoy your stay. Now raise your glasses and let us drink to our health.'

Servants began filing into the room with platters of vegetables, fruit, meats with gravy, bread, and pitchers of ale. The Lords and Dames tore into the banquet with the same abandon as they had celebrated at the Cauldron. Martin took the last seat beside Arlo.

He ate sparingly as he observed the guests, expecting trouble, and when it didn't come immediately, he relaxed back into his chair and even managed a smile at some of the outrageous jokes told by Museo and Samual.

As they sat eating fresh apple pie and drinking a dessert wine, the conversation turned to Arlo.

'Arlo, you are famous in these parts for the service you gave to the king of Scuttle. Do you miss that time?' asked Samual as he swirled the wine in his glass.

'Well, that was a lifetime ago, Samual, but as they say, you can take the man out of the war but not the war out of man. Since I was a soldier for over thirty cycles, then, yes, I guess I do miss some of it.'

'It is told that you were quite the swordsman, Arlo. Last night I heard tales of your exploits from the townsfolk who talk about you as if you are a hero. It is a pity that you cannot fight now. I would have loved to test myself against your skills in a sparring contest,' said Museo, leaning forward on his elbows.

'I just did what I needed to do to survive. There were never any thoughts of glory, just getting me and my men out alive,' responded Arlo with a faint smile.

Samual ran a finger around the rim of his empty glass. 'Who did you spend most of the military time fighting, Arlo?'

'Mostly against the forces of the emperor of Cavere and also protecting the coast when the flotilla of the Maelstrom tried to take our lands. While fighting in Cavere, I had my accident,' reflected Arlo, as his eyes took on a distant look.

'Was it while you were burning the villages of innocents, poisoning the waterways of the grasslands, or when the great fires all but destroyed that beautiful nation?' asked Samual. A hush fell upon the table.

'Tell me, Samual, what do you know of war?' said Arlo.

'I know enough to see that while some so-called heroes get fame and fortune for committing atrocities, calling it warfare, others truly fight for the right reasons. Scuttle was the driving force behind the attempted destruction of Cavere. Its people suffered for the dreams of a madman you called king,' said Samual, slamming his fist down on the table.

Martin was on his feet in an instant, sword in hand.

'Martin! Sheath your blade, I will not have the blood of guests on my conscience within my home,' Arlo said, voice ringing with authority.

Martin sheathed his blade but moved around to stand on the other side of Arlo between him and Samual.

'Samual, as a young man, I had a thirst for blood, glory and service for my country. Like most, I believed the lies fed to me to inspire my willingness to perform terrible deeds, all on behalf of Scuttle. As my service wore on, I both committed and witnessed atrocities that would give you nightmares. I now know a common grunt like I was then had no chance of changing things. Even when promoted up through the ranks, I was naïve enough to think I could make a difference, stop the slaughter of innocents, and protect my men. In all these, I was wrong. So, your claim is true in that I am not a genuine hero and never claimed to be. By the Infernal Lands, I hate being thought of in that way when I did only what I had to do, no more. Yes, Scuttle brought death and destruction to Cavere, but we can say the same about both sides in a war. For instance, the emperor of Cavere allowed the kidnapping of three envoys on a diplomatic mission. They were tortured for months before being put on display for all to see. The reason for all this was that the precious emperor felt insulted over the suggestion of a shared border garrison between our two nations. This was why we invaded the Cavere grasslands,' replied Arlo, thrusting his index finger at Samual.

The tension was thick in the dining room now, and Bertram felt ill at the thought of violence. Martin was involved in a tense, staring duel with Angus, who had flicked back his cloak, revealing his own sword.

Chapter 8

'Well, this is fun. I love a squabble,' Nix said with a laugh as she continued eating.

Museo poured himself wine, then placed his feet up on the table.

Martin fixed Museo with a glare. 'Take your feet from the table. We don't abide by such behaviour here. If you prefer, you can go dine with the sows. They might be of your own level.'

'Mind your manners, Martin, I truly don't think you can handle me if it comes to a duel,' Museo snarled, but he removed his boots.

Bertram saw Elspeth had used her wine to create a symbol on the tablecloth that, though faint, seemed to move as if alive. Magic! Is she going to use magic? he thought, getting scared. They did not know what she was capable of, and while most people avoided the pitfalls of magic since its return, Elspeth, as she had said, was a student in the arts.

Her eyes looked glazed as her mouth moved silently. Fearing what she would do, Bertram stood to reach across the table, purposefully knocking over a large jug of water, which washed over the symbol and then onto Elspeth. The effect was immediate as with a gasp, Elspeth snapped from her state, looked at the symbol with a soft curse, and then looked over at Bertram.

'Sorry, Elspeth, I am clumsy. All this unnecessary hostility made me nervous.'

Nix stood, suggestively licking the rim of her wineglass while staring at Arlo. 'Dear Arlo, I just want to know one thing,' said Nix as now she leaned forward across the table to whisper something.

Though she whispered, she may well have shouted the next words because everybody heard them.

'What I really want to know, Arlo is if your dick still works. Does the little soldier still salute?'

Arlo hurled the contents of his drink into Nix's face. 'You whore, think you can come here and insult me, do you?'

Nix actually looked surprised by the attack, shrinking away from Arlo's anger. In a blur of movement, Angus drew his sword and scooted past Samual as Martin drew his blade again. The two stopped, facing off against each other.

Museo was now standing on the table. He had drawn his sword, which he had levelled at Arlo while Samual still sat cool as a summer breeze, unconcerned but highly amused at the scene unfolding around him.

They all froze at the sound of the entrance door banging open, revealing five warriors all armed with crossbows now trained upon the five guests.

'Leave the weapons alone if you value your lives. One more movement towards Arlo or his son Bertram and my men will fire upon you,' Martin said. The five crossbowmen stood with weapons sighted on the guests, waiting to see their reactions.

Samual's laughter cut through the uneasy silence. 'You must forgive my dear Nix. She can't hold her drink at the best of times. Nix, you need to apologise to Arlo, my dear.'

'For what?' she replied, her voice reminding Bertram of a spoilt child.

The change in Samual's appearance then seemed extraordinary to Bertram. His eyes narrowed, and his neck cracked horribly as he turned to stretch it. He fixed a hostile sneer upon Nix, and Bertram could see the man's left eye twitching as if he had developed a tick. His mouth opened wide in an obscene grin that revealed a complete set of golden teeth.

'Nix, do we have to go through this again later?' he said in a threatening tone. Then he turned to Museo, visibly shaking with anger. 'Museo, get down from Arlo's fucking table, we are not barbarians.'

Museo slowly sheathed his sword while the crossbowmen watched his every move, then he nimbly jumped down from the table.

'Angus, for god's sake, sheath your weapon too unless you want to sprout arrows,' said Samual next, without turning.

Chapter 8

The blade slammed back into its sheath.

'That's better behaviour, Angus. Now return to your seat like a good hound,' said Martin with his blade still aimed at Angus.

'Don't push it, old man,' replied Angus, but he turned and slumped down in his seat.

'Nix, we are all still waiting for your apology,' snarled Samual.

'I was curious, that's all. Why should I have to apologise for that when I bet I'm not the first woman to wonder?'

Samual merely continued staring at Nix until she rolled her eyes, then turned to face Arlo.

'Arlo, I humbly apologise for my rude behaviour while under your roof. I did not mean it to cause anger or upset you.'

Arlo was practically shaking with anger. His face had gone beet red, alarming Bertram considerably.

'I don't want you,' he began, then he stopped talking, put a hand to his head, closed his eyes, and started speaking again. Except none of the words made sense and came out as garbled nonsense. Arlo's mouth dropped open, eyes flickered, then rolled back to show the whites, his body began twitching as tremors spread over his upper body.

Bertram couldn't remember getting to his feet but was there alongside Arlo at the same time as Martin.

'Father, can you hear me?'

Arlo began drooling as he lost consciousness, his body now tense with jerking movements as he was overcome with seizures accompanied by the sharp smell of urine.

'Martin, get him out of the damn chair and onto the ground so he doesn't hurt himself.'

The five guards had now lowered their weapons as everybody watched the scene unfold, their conflict forgotten for the moment.

They placed Arlo on the floor as he continued to spasm. Someone laughed loudly, but Bertram didn't know who or care at that moment. He just wanted to help Arlo get through his latest seizure. It had been so long since his father had suffered one that it had taken Bertram by surprise.

They used the five soldiers to help move Arlo from the room once his seizure appeared finished, leaving the five guests alone. As they carried him away, snippets of conversation trailed after them.

'Did you see that? I thought he was going to die right before us.'

'The old fool still didn't even answer my question, so I'm guessing it doesn't work anymore,' were the last words Bertram heard as they left the dining room.

Chapter 9

Arlo was safe in his bed, sleeping now. He looked frail, skin pasty beneath salt-and-pepper hair that draped the side of his face. Bertram closed the bedroom door and then went to where the apothecary was waiting.

'It has been so long since he had an attack, I was hoping he was past that now,' Bertram said, suddenly weary.

The apothecary, an old friend of Arlo and now retired, continued to help the town locals if needed. 'Bertram, these attacks may well plague your father's health until his death, long may that be. I have tied belladonna above his bed and given him a dose of valerian root to help him sleep. I was lucky to have recently acquired some Cranius humanus powder, which needs to be added little by little to his drinking water over the coming month until it's all used. I have also left powdered mugwort for teas, and it will help with Arlo's fatigue once he comes out of this latest attack.'

'Cranius humanus?'

'The medical colleges are all proclaiming its healing properties regarding such symptoms.'

Powdered skull. Bertram had indeed heard of this remedy while in Stormwatch before the battle of the Elemental Tower. A physician there had labelled it a gross display of malpractice, nothing more than a superstition. Bertram took Grant's hands in his. 'I am so thankful to be able to call on your extensive knowledge of medicine. How can I ever repay you?'

'Well, maybe a bottle or two of that vine vintage red wine you know I just adore. That would be sufficient payment, Master Bertram.'

Bertram saw the apothecary out before returning upstairs to his father's room, where Martin waited outside with two of his men who now guarded the chamber.

As soon as Bertram saw Martin, the man pulled him into an adjoining room.

'Bertram, this is not good. You need to get rid of these scum before anything else happens.'

'I can't, Martin. I promised they could stay until their business is concluded,' Bertram said and began pacing.

'By the gods and the Infernal Realms, Bertram, Arlo is your father, and this is his and your home. It's time to show some strength son before things get worse. These idiots are not the type of friends you need,' said Martin, stepping in front of him to stop Bertram's pacing.

'I know, I know, alright? I just need to think about this.'

'There is nothing to think about, Bertram. You are lord in Arlo's absence, so start acting like it instead of a foolish child!'

The words hurt Bertram deeply. He had done everything for Arlo and the manor. He didn't deserve such criticism.

'I said I will deal with it, and I will. Now get out of my face, Martin, or by the gods, you will regret it!' yelled Bertram.

'That's more like it, Bertram, now get rid of them. If you need me or my men, we will be ready. I have posted them throughout the manor. I will stay close to you should you need me.'

Bertram returned to the dining room, where Nellie and Tess were busy cleaning up the room. Food was everywhere, even caked on the portrait of Arlo on the wall. The fine floor rugs were soaked with wine, and the tabletop had three words carved into the fine mahogany surface. Lords and Dames.

Trying to contain his fury, Bertram drank deeply from a decanter of wine.

Old Tess looked over at him. 'Master Bertram, who are these animals you bring into this home? They have no respect.'

Bertram didn't reply. He turned with a decanter in hand, the wine in his system emboldening him as he stalked downstairs.

Bertram found the Lords and Dames in the library. They were deep in a heated conversation. Bertram stopped just outside the door, out of sight, to listen.

'Where is Witter, anyway? He was meant to meet us at the Cauldron, and now his absence puts our entire mission in jeopardy,' Angus was saying.

'He will be here within the day, I'm sure. He has never been one to dawdle,' replied Museo.

'You vouched for him, Museo; this is on you. We had other choices, but no, you had to insist on using Witter!'

'Are you questioning my loyalty to our group, Angus? I would have thought by now that I have proved myself.'

'Not your loyalty, Museo, but I am questioning the damn choices you make that affect us all. Tamul waits for no man, and it will be four long cycles before the red moon once again overshadows Aspre. Time is of the essence.'

'We will wait until nightfall. If Witter hasn't arrived, we will have a choice to make and may need to find someone else to help us,' drawled Samual.

'It's not like he has an important part in our mission, anyway,' Bertram heard Elspeth say. 'We could use anyone who can hold a blade and carry equipment.'

'That is not true, Elspeth! I agree with Angus on this. Witter is a seasoned warrior known to us all, and we all trust his abilities and wisdom. At this advanced stage of the mission, we cannot let anything at all go wrong,' countered Nix in her high voice.

'All I'm saying is that once we arrive at the location, then Witter's role is a lesser one. Anybody can fulfil that role,' retorted Elspeth.

'Elspeth, I think all the time with your head in tomes and meditating on symbols and the like has addled your brain. Witter is the only one with an extensive knowledge of the local area. Without him, we might become lost or fail to find the entrance,' broke in Angus.

'It looks like we might just have our first serious problem then,' said Samual.

Bertram's mind was racing. Mission, location, hidden entrance. What were they planning? Then he had an idea. He took a long pull of the wine. With a deep breath, Bertram walked into the library with as much poise as he could muster.

'I have a solution to yours and my problems, 'said Bertram as the Lords and Dames turned to look at him.

'Why don't you run along, Bertie dear, and let the adults talk. Maybe you could rustle up some tea for us,' said Museo in a voice thick with condescension.

'I'm not going anywhere until you hear me out, Museo. Don't think you can order me around in my own house. After the deplorable behaviour at dinner, I should be having my men escort you off my land, but I am a man of my word, and I said you could stay here until your business is concluded,' said Bertram, crossing his arms across his chest.

'Continue, Bertie, dazzle us with your clever ideas since you already have the floor,' said Samual, putting down the book he was perusing.

'I couldn't help but hear your conversation when I was on the way down here to tell you to leave my home. I know you must think I was spying on you, and I can only state in my defence this is not so. You are waiting for this Witter fellow who obviously has not shown, and that leaves you short of one man for this mission of yours.'

Elspeth started to speak, but Samual waved at her to be quiet and for Bertram to continue.

'You said Witter was the one with local knowledge and without him you will have trouble finding the location of what you seek. I have lived here all my life. I know the surrounding lands like the back of my hands. Yes, I am not a great warrior, but I can handle a blade.' At a snicker from Angus, Bertram glared at the man. 'I have been trained by my father in swordplay. No matter how much you mock me, I can hold my own with a blade. I will allow you to take what you need from our stores to help with your mission, and in return I ask for just one thing. That you leave my home and allow us to live in peace. I must not put my father under the constant strain that your being here will cause him,' finished Bertram.

Nix stood and sauntered over to Bertram, suddenly grabbing at his groin, and he had to push her away, hoping the blush he felt rising on his face did nothing to diminish his confidence. 'I like the new Bertie. Let's bring him along, if for nothing else but the fun of it,' she said, licking her lips and smiling at him.

'Nix, sit down. We are not interested in whose pants you want to be next. Just sit down and shut up,' said Samual, his tone showing he had lost his patience with Nix.

She did what he said and sat down to sulk.

Samual came fluidly to his feet. 'It seems, fellow Lords and Dames that we have a vote on our hands. Should we allow our young, expressive friend here to join us and give us the required number for our mission, or do we ignore him and his own request for us to leave his home? Voice your thoughts now.'

'A body is a body. Like I said earlier, it doesn't matter who we take as long as we can find this damn place,' said Elspeth as she examined her nails. 'I vote yes.'

'It's a damn no for me. The boy can't even defend his own family honour, and I doubt he has any skills that would prove beneficial to our cause,' snarled Angus.

'You have all made it plainly obvious that my input doesn't count for anything, and to tell the truth, I couldn't care less either way,' said Nix sullenly, without looking up from where she sulked.

'Yes, for me. I like Bertie, and who are we to judge him when we know not of his abilities? After all, he has a point when saying he knows the area better than any of us,' Museo said, studying Bertram intensely.

They all looked toward their leader, Samual, expectantly.

'Yes, we will take Bertie with us, but only if Witter still hasn't arrived by nightfall. And yes, Bertie, we will leave you to your invalid father. A hero deserves better treatment than what we have shown here tonight.' The words were said in such a way that Bertram knew Samual was politely insulting his father.

'You idiots, mark my words. We will come to regret including him in our plans,' said Angus, spitting out every word.

'Great! I will be by my father's side. If you require anything, then ask my men, and if you need me, they will come get me,' said Bertram, and then he strolled out of the library when he wanted to run.

Back inside Arlo's rooms, Bertram sat by the window alternating between watching for this mysterious man called Witter to arrive and watching Arlo as he slept. His father looked older, more vulnerable than Bertram had ever seen him before.

Arlo was so strong of will and body that Bertram had never really felt concerned for his father. Seeing him have that attack tonight had really shaken Bertram up, which had not become clear until after he confronted Samual and his cronies. Now alone with his father, the full weight of the evening's events descended upon him. Bertram couldn't shake the worry he now felt from his mind. What would he do without his guidance and trust when Arlo died?

As much as Bertram attempted to shake the morose feelings, he found they wouldn't leave him. He had brought strangers into his home who had caused Arlo to have an attack. This was all his fault. He would lead them away from here, help them locate the place they

Chapter 9

sought, then he would be free to return to the family manor with his honour restored to find his father recovering.

When night fell without Witter arriving Bertram trudged wearily downstairs. The only one of the Lords and Dames awake was Samual, who reclined on a seat that sat just outside the front door of the manor facing the direction of the road. Bertram packed his pipe with sweet tobacco, lit it, and offered his pouch to Samual, who nodded his appreciation and did likewise. They sat in silence with only the crickets as company.

'Doesn't look like your friend Witter is coming,' Bertram said.

'By the sound of your voice, Bertram, I would say that makes you happy. I warn you, though, that the mission we are embarking on will be dangerous and is not for the fainthearted. The risk is solely on your shoulders.'

'Don't treat me like a child Samual. I will only tolerate that from my father,' replied Bertram as he puffed away at his pipe.

'How is he, anyway?'

Bertram laughed softly. 'He is okay, not that you care anyway,' Bertram said, watching the man beside him.

Samual shrugged his shoulders. 'You are right of course Bertie. I don't care.' Samual tapped the ash from his pipe and stood, stretching his arms out to the side. 'We leave early, so be ready just after dawn to help stock our supplies. I have a list of what we require packed in saddle bags for us to travel.' Then Samual returned inside the house.

Chapter 10

Bertram was up before dawn, as told to do. He sent for Martin, who he knew slept little these days to meet him at the stores. The list that Samual had given him was rather extensive, and Martin grumbled at every item as they packed it in five new saddlebags.

'Bertram, it's well and good you giving these mongrels food, clothing, and general stores, but it's not wise to hand over any of our weapons. They don't even need them; you know that. Another thing is that last night when I was facing off against Angus he had a sword I swear I recognised. Your father's blade was given to you as the first son. Do you have Soulcounter, I don't see it hanging at your belt?'

'I lost it in a competition with Angus, and before you say it, yes. I am a stupid fool and regret my actions while blinded with drink and fae weed. However, I will get it back, I promise you.'

'That would be wise, Bertram, before your father finds out, you know how he treasures that weapon.' Martin pulled Bertram into a hug.

'I love you like my own son, Bertram. You know that. Be careful with these five. They are kin to the Infernals themselves. Lead them to their precious location, then hightail it out of there and back here to safety. If they come here again, we will meet them with our blades and this time they will not find us wanting.' Martin helped him load the horses of the Lords and Dames as Bertram

Chapter 10

saddled his grey-speckled horse. Kitty was still missing since the trip home from the cauldron.

'Did you find the young guard, Martin?'

'We did. Dead, broken apart in the woods. I have seen nothing like it, Bertram. In death, the boy's face was contorted into a scream.' Martin actually shivered as he recounted the event.

An icy fear wound its way down Bertram's spine as images sprang to mind of an unusual patch of darkness from which whispers emanated, and the silhouette of a strange, thorny creature near the gatehouse. Bertram shook his head to try to dislodge the unwelcome images. Absurd imaginings were all they were. What could you expect with so much fae powder?

The sun was just climbing up to peek over the horizon when the Lords and Dames came out of the manor.

'Seems like it's all here, except the crossbows, bolts, four swords, a longbow and two quivers of arrows,' questioned Samual as he inspected the gathered stores.

Bertram was just about to answer, but Martin beat him to it. 'We don't have enough weaponry to cover what you ask, Samual. Arlo is not willing to leave the manor armoury empty.'

'You're a loyal dog, aren't you, Martin? An able soldier too, I expect, wasted here looking after a cripple whose time has passed him by. You want Bertram to be safe, then how about you accompany us instead of him? I would pay you handsomely to find the place we seek. Think of the gold that would secure your retirement, old warrior.'

'I would rather skin myself alive than spend any more time than necessary with you pieces of carrion,' said Martin.

Samual leant from his saddle then spat a gobbet of spit on Martin's boots. The slap from Martin nearly tore Samual from the saddle with its force. When Samual regained his composure and settled on his horse, a trickle of blood was winding its way from one nostril down his chin. Samual reached up to dab at the blood with a finger, managing to smear it over his cheek as he struggled to contain his fury.

'If you harm Bertram, then make sure you check over your weak shoulders because I will come for you.'

'I will give you that one for free, old dog. The next time you dare touch me, you die. Pray we don't meet again,' hissed Samual.

Bertram watched as the Lords and Dames trotted past him. He nodded at Martin before glancing up at the window of Arlo's bed chamber. Though he knew his father was bedridden, Bertram still expected to see Arlo standing there at the window, staring down at him. The absence of his father shaded the drab, overcast day with a darker grey of gloom.

Once away from the outskirts of Fallon's March, Samual pulled out a map, indicating a small circle. 'Have you heard of Vixen's Dell?'

'It's a half day's ride northwest from the coast where Saffron Isle can be seen by land. It's a village near the forest, avoided mostly by the locals who say a devil that lives there haunts the forest. There are many stories about why the place is to be avoided. Most are simply put down to superstitious country folk. It is told that fires won't burn in the nearby forest, wine sours in the skin, and sleep only brings nightmares. The locals leave regular offerings to placate the spirits that inhabit the surrounding dells of which Vixens Dell is but one,' replied Bertram.

'Sounds like a delightful place,' muttered Angus from behind them.

Elspeth moved up alongside Bertram to look at the map. 'Why is it referred to as Vixen's Dell? Information on the place is very hard to find, and nobody in Fallon's March would even discuss it.'

'It was once common to see red foxes right through this country, all the way to the coast. Their numbers became so many that the villagers, sick of losing livestock and fearing the diseases the beasts carried, gathered at Vixen's Dell where most of the foxes roamed and culled the beasts.'

Chapter 10

That day they rode southeast, towards the Middle River and the coast. The farther away from his father, the better, Bertram thought, though with each step a new tension fell over him as they wound closer to Vixen's Dell. Only fools would dare enter the dell. The Lords and Dames had proven themselves such fools, dangerous ones to be sure that would not let him slip away until he had delivered them to wherever they intended to go. Damn it! He had thought it a good idea to lead them away from all he held dear, but now he could almost feel the strands of his promise wrapping themselves around him. He could flee, though he knew without a doubt Samual would never forget his betrayal. Just deliver them to the Dell, then by the Infernal hells get out of there.

Museo sang as they rode, the strumming of his harp accompanied by the many songs they had all grown up with, songs sung in the inns and taverns throughout Scuttle that had them all singing. They rode through a small village called Liedel's Mill where the folk stared at them with blank faces and hard eyes.

'Do you ever wish for the excitement of the city rather than these small hovels of simple people?' asked Nix from beside Bertram.

'Just because someone comes from the country doesn't mean they lack in intelligence or knowledge, Nix.'

'Do you really believe that Bertram? It's in the cities where a man stands on the precipice of knowledge, where innovators invent, scholars discover through academic pursuits, not shovel shit or thrash crops.'

'City people are reliant on what these country folk do, Nix. Can you blame any who seek a simpler life away from crime, corruption and the machinations of the crown or its noble families?'

'Guess the romantic notion of adventure got the better of me. You never hear about the long days of travel far from a bath or fine food in the ballads or tales.'

Angus snorted rudely. 'Maybe you should have stayed, spread your legs and reared children, Nix. The only problem is that you would never know who the father was since there would be so many candidates.'

'Guess it wouldn't be you, Angus. We all know your tastes lean towards young boys!' Nix snapped back at the warrior.

Samual turned in his saddle. 'Now, now, play nice. We are all friends here. We can't have Bertie thinking we are not civilised folk, like him.'

'So, when do you fill me in on the details? If I am to go to Vixen's Dell I need to know more about what I'm looking for, Samual.'

'In time, Bertie, just get us to the dell.'

It took a day of hard riding to reach the coastal cliffs where Saffron Island, one of the many Perfumed Isles, could be seen. From there Bertram led them inland, sticking to the hills and thinly populated forest. It was almost nightfall when he spotted the smoke of a small village he knew lay near the dell.

Samual removed a hand-drawn map that was covered in messages and small drawings. 'This is all I have to go on. I am assuming the village below us is marked here on the map.'

Bertram confirmed it was so.

'We shall camp here until the eclipse. Ready your gear, get some rest, and remember, no fires.'

They chose an open place hidden by a large outcrop of rocks. While the others set up tents, Bertram found Samual sitting at the rocks, looking down over the village.

'Why don't we just stay down there tonight and then set out at dawn tomorrow?' asked Bertram, who didn't see the point of messing around out here in the wilderness.

'We must wait for the eclipse. Only then can we be sure of our path.'

'I have completed my part of our bargain, Samual. You make fine travelling companions, but I must return to my home now.'

'No, Bertram, you agreed to lead us to Vixen's Dell. I know Vixen's Dell is within its boundary of the forest. I need you to lead us to its entry.'

Chapter 10

Bertram looked at Samual in alarm. 'You mean to enter the cave there, the supposed home of the Vixen?'

'You are a bright man, Bertram. No wonder you call yourself a scholar. We are hardly here to pick berries.'

'But the tales say…'

'Just tales, as you said, Bertie. If you are right, you have nothing to fear.'

'Nobody enters those caves. Ghosts haunt them. Worse, the Vixen who is said to dwell there won't tolerate intruders. I will not go!'

Bertram felt the point of Samual's sword against his chest.

'Easy, Samual.'

'Don't test my patience, you fool. I have come this far and will not be denied. You will enter the dell and the caves with us or I will gut you here. Your choice!'

Bertram nodded as understanding came over him. Samual had played him once again. 'Wise choice, Bertram. There are distant kin of the Vixen who live in this village, and they are an inbred, secretive lot. As you mentioned before about leaving offerings to the spirits, well, that is what they do during the eclipse. We wait until they take their tithe then follow them into the dell. This is the perfect location to watch the village without arousing any suspicion. Failing that and if we cannot see anyone set off with offerings, then you can find the place for us. For the tithe to be delivered, the layers of magic that protect the place will lower and then we can find the cave,' finished Samual, sitting back on his haunches.

'If the tales are true, the Vixen is powerful. Many have tried to kill her or loot her lair, and all have failed.'

'I seek an item of power that rests in the dell that was stolen from my kin. I intend to have this item, and nothing will stop me from doing that. Tonight, during the eclipse is when the Vixen, if she does indeed live, will be weakest. This item will be like a beacon, able to be tracked by magic, which is where Elspeth comes in. Her power will cut through the protective spells and show us where we will find it.'

'It would appear to me that such an item would be carefully guarded. We are going in there blind, not knowing who or what awaits us. Expecting just to walk in, gather what you want and leave is sheer stupidity.'

'Supposedly, the lair has lain empty since the return of magic, whereupon the denizens fled to somewhere safer. The Vixen being an unnatural creature returned to the Infernal or Celestial land it came from.'

'That is a big risk, don't you think?' Bertram asked. 'What if they are still there?'

'That is why I have brought Angus and Museo, two great warriors, and of course, you can add another blade if needed. For now, we just need to track the villagers when they leave to take their offerings.'

'It will be easy to miss them leaving from this distance, Samual. They might approach from a different direction, and what then?'

Samual pulled a tube from his pack, and Bertram recognised it as an eyeglass that had magnified glass within, allowing the user to see a greater distance.

'The eclipse is a time of celebration during which the villagers refuse to sleep until it is over. We watch and can hopefully see enough to know how to proceed. Follow me but keep low.' Samual crawled around to the top of the rock formation where he jammed himself between two rocks, and Bertram joined him there. They had an unobstructed view down over the village, and when Samual passed him the eyeglass, Bertram could see the villagers had set up a pyre. They had decorated all the houses in red-and-white cloth, tables had been set up for a feast, and somewhere below faint music played. Children ran back and forth around a semi-circle of wagons, the opening facing northwest from the middle of the village square.

Chapter 10

When they returned to the small camp, Elspeth sat deep in meditation. Angus sharpened Bertram's blade while Museo lay on the grass, his hat covering his face. Bertram slumped down on the grass, trying to push away the feelings of dread.

Nix came and sat down next to him. 'You are so tense, Bertie. Relax while you can. Here, let me get the knots out of your shoulders,' she said and began kneading his tight neck and the surrounding muscles. Nix confused Bertram. She was certainly attractive, childlike in ways, but cruel as he knew from when she had insulted his father.

He pulled free of her hands. 'Not now, Nix. I prefer just to talk.'

'Still carrying a grudge then are we, Bertie?'

'You expect me to forget the way you all treated my father in his own home? Until you arrived at the manor, I had thought you were my friends,' he replied.

'Don't be such a dullard, Bertie, it was fun that got out of hand, that's all,' she said with an incredulous look.

'Maybe for you. Maybe you think insulting the very ones who give you shelter is fun, but to me, it's just disrespect. After I lead you to the lair, that's me out, and I hope to see none of you again,' he said, unwrapping his sabre and cutting stone to sharpen it.

Nix tried to continue the conversation, but Bertram pointedly ignored her, so she eventually got the hint and moved away.

After honing the sabre blade to a sharp edge, Bertram climbed into his bedroll and lay down to watch the moons already high in the sky.

Tamul's red light was creeping over Aspre's glorious white incandescence. Down in the village someone had begun beating a steady rhythm on a drum that sounded like a distant heartbeat. Samual had returned to his post between the rocks using the eyeglass as all the others except Angus rested. Angus sat with his back to a rock peering out into the darkness. Occasionally he regarded Bertram, and when their eyes met, the warrior would sneer at him or spit into the night.

It was close to full eclipse when Elspeth came to Bertram with a board on which she had mixed red and white paint.

'I need to anoint you with this paint, Bertram. If we are spotted, the villagers will take little notice of you and will think you are of their own.' Bertram allowed Elspeth to daub the paint on his cheeks and forehead. She chanted as she worked, and he might have imagined it, but he thought he saw strands of her dark hair turn to grey and her skin take on a sickly pallor. He was the last to be anointed, and Elspeth then stood, arms outstretched to the moons above. She slashed one of his palms with a sharp knife then tightened it into a fist, the blood dripping down into the soil.

'Tamul, it is your time. Grant us passage through the trial ahead and hide us from the common sight.' She then knelt with her head on the earth. 'Mother, I have paid the blood price; fill me with your power.'

When she rose, she seemed to Bertram to be more alive, filled with vigour and energy. Her hair, though, was definitely lighter and grey in places.

Elspeth saw him staring and grimaced. 'Your hair,' he said to Elspeth.

'Since magic has returned, things have changed. The power required is directly from the Mother and has physical or mental repercussions for the practitioner. It is as if the Mother grows stronger now instead of before the Severing when she nearly died due to the misuse of power. Now the cost of power is higher than most are prepared to pay. Look here,' she said, pointing to the grass area around where she had meditated. Bertram could see the grass had grown longer by a foot and flowers had grown compared to the bare, patchy earth that made up the rest of the area.

'What place do the two moons have then since the Severing?' he asked.

Chapter 10

'Tamul and Aspre are the only other way for mortals to gain power. You could say that the moons have replaced the gods as both have a substantial priesthood now. Aspre obviously represents all that is good while Tamul represents evil and darkness.'

'So that would make you either a mage or priestess of Tamul, wouldn't it?'

'I serve Tamul and no other. Since the Severing, the red moon has always been in my life, showing me the way on the path of power.'

'I find this all very fascinating,' replied Bertram. 'I have a recent copy of a study compiled by sages who say that since the Severing each person now has an affinity for one element which is decided by the time of one's birth month. To have the knowledge of somebody's birth month can give an enemy a serious advantage. The current season will bring those born under that element more power, while those in the opposite or waning element less,' explained Bertram.

Elspeth looked surprised at Bertram's knowledge on the subject. 'There is more to you than just a noble fop, isn't there, Bertram? Here is a bit of information you may not know and is only talked about in certain circles. There is a fifth element, spirit, just like the elemental tower has five spires that represent the five elements, but little is known about its role and how it relates to the other four elements.'

Aspre and Tamul continued their paths into eclipse, the former white moon falling within the crimson of Tamul, painting the land a nightmare shade of red. Below them in the village, the celebrations were intensifying as those taking part danced with unceasing energy, the hallucinogenic brew Bertram knew they would have imbibed pushing them beyond the normal limits.

Bertram waited with the Lords and Dames crouched behind the rocks.

In less than a chime Aspre's white halo would totally disappear when the celebrations would reach a crescendo. They watched as those in the village cavorted about the fire. Nix's eyes were glassy as she gazed down with longing at the wild celebration below, Angus picked at his teeth with a stick, Museo's knee jigging up and down, Samual pacing. Only Elspeth, who sat back against a rock, showed no sign of anxiety or impatience. In her hands she held an amulet crafted from a green-tinted metal he had never seen before with a large emerald set on its surface. As Bertram bent to get a closer look, an eye opened on the gem, glaring up at him, which startled him so much that he stepped back, tripping.

Behind him, he heard a low chuckle and turned to see Museo watching him. 'You saw her astral eye, did you not? Luckily, you didn't stare too long, or it can capture your will. Careful where you pry, dear Bertie. We are people not to trifle with,' said Museo, his face lit by the glow of the pipe at the corner of his mouth.

When Elspeth stood suddenly, it startled Bertram. 'Prepare yourselves, it's about to happen.'

The villagers had harnessed one wagon laden with supplies to two horses. The night sky began to darken, bleeding a deeper red as a young girl and boy were chosen from the revellers. Bertram picked up the eyeglass from the rock beside him and Samual. The dancers were draped with coloured ribbons, the boy given a sword which was strapped across his back and the girl a crown of glass. They climbed up onto the wagon as the sky lit up with small explosions of colour as the village fire master set off the fireworks.

'That's our signal,' said Samual, scrabbling back to them through the rocks. 'The wagon is ready to leave now. We will await them in the valley behind the copse of trees there and follow at a distance. Elspeth, prepare your spells.'

Bertram couldn't be anything but impressed at how easily the Lords and Dames worked together when they needed to. They rode quickly to beat the wagon to the cover of the trees that intersected the trail the wagon followed, where they tied their mounts before hiding in the long grass near the trail.

Chapter 11

A blade of grass tickled the inside of one of Bertram's nostrils. He cupped a hand over the offending organ to stifle the sneeze he felt building. Damn, grass always played havoc with his nose. Beside him, Angus gave him a look that threatened broken bones.

The trundling of the wagon drew closer. A torch fixed on the wagon enabled Bertram to see that the drivers were children barely ten cycles old. The young girl sobbed, tears wetting her cheeks as she sat straight, stiff as a board. The boy slipped an arm around her shoulder as the wagon halted.

'Don't worry, Maize, all we have to do is deliver the wagon, set the signal, and leave. By dawn, we will be home safe and sound in our beds again.'

'Sorry, Harle, it's just that I'm scared. You know the tales as well as I do.'

'Yes, Maize, I have had nightmares thinking about this night. My da shared something with me before I left. Do you want to hear it?'

'Yes,' came back the tremulous voice.

'Da said that the Vixen will not kill those who deliver her tithes because then there would be no more deliveries. We will bring good luck to our village and families for the next cycle. That's why tonight is very important. Do you understand?'

Maize wiped her eyes on her sleeve, sitting up straighter.

'Then why don't our parents do this? Why does it have to be children like us?'

'Dunno, maybe the Vixen doesn't like grown-ups.'

'So, she likes us, I mean children, then?'

'I would say so. Every cycle our village sends children to bring the wagon, and each time they come home just like we will tonight.'

'Do you promise, Harle?'

'I don't like promises, Maize. Da always says everything will get better, never does though.'

Bertram followed the Lords and Dames as they crept behind the slow-moving wagon, Samual in the lead. When the wagon stopped at a clearing, the Lords and Dames hid in the long grass again. Museo pulled Bertram down beside him.

'Here, hold the reins, Maize, while I light and wind the lantern.'

The boy scrambled up onto the wagon, searching through boxes until he found a large lantern with small glass panes etched with symbols. With the torch, he lit the oil wick of the lantern, then reached into his pocket for a small handle, which he slipped into place.

'Are you ready, Maize?'

The girl nodded. Then Harle turned the handle.

Shutters on the devices' sides opened and closed, having a strobing effect on the light emitted by the lamp flame, while the base of the lamp also turned slowly, accompanied by a chiming that hung in the air.

Bertram squatted, transfixed, watching the scene's strange beauty. He tried to turn away but couldn't remove his gaze from the lantern with its eerie music; tried to cover his ears, but his arms ignored him. Bertram's eyelids became heavy as the chiming drew him down. The last thing he felt was his face hitting the soft grass.

'Bertie, wake up, dammit, we have work to do.' Samual was crouched over him shaking his shoulder.

Chapter 11

'The sound of that strange lantern put me to sleep,' he replied, struggling to speak as a yawn overcame him, quickly smothered by Samual's hand.

'You were not the only one. Luckily for us, Elspeth had protection against the enchantment.' The wagon was still nearby but now empty.

'Two hooded men unloaded the wagon and took the packages farther into the forest,' Samual explained, reading Bertram's look.

'How long was I asleep?'

'Like us, maybe half a chime. This long grass and Elspeth's magic were the only things stopping us from being discovered. If we are to find this entrance, we need your tracking ability, Bertie. You will need to be at your best. Failing me is not an option. Tamul's power is already receding, which leaves us precious little time. Now move.'

Bertram easily found the tracks of the two men. They had been barefoot with strangely elongated toes, he surmised as he squatted, inspecting them. They must have been strong because there was no drag sign of the crates from the wagon, leaving the only possibility that they had carried them by hand. Bertram followed the tracks silently; the tracks became harder to read as the woods were littered with leaves and pine needles that ended with a fallen trunk crossing the way.

'What's taking so long?' whispered Samual just behind Bertram.

He took a small of satisfaction by simply ignoring the man.

Scanning the area before him, Bertram searched for any sign of the two men's passage.

No broken twigs or scuff marks on the fallen trunk's bark, but there must be something.

Then he saw a broken spider web with one side of the insects' construction blowing loosely in the cool breeze just past the fallen tree.

'They went this way,' he said, scampering over the trunk, noticing a broken twig up ahead. The trail was heading deeper into woods that would become Scuttle Forest to the west, but the ground became rockier the further north they went.

The tracks sloped down into the deepest part of the dell, which wasn't as impressive as the name Vixen's Dell suggested. Just beyond the right embankment, the slope became the start of a long outcrop or rock. If there was a cave, it would be here.

Sure enough, when Bertram moved to the other side of the dell, he found signs of broken branches and compressed grass as if someone had placed something heavy there, presumably the stores from the wagon.

Bertram turned to Samual. 'The tracks stop here. The entrance cannot be far.'

Finding the entrance turned out to be significantly easier than any of them had thought and revealed why it had to be done during Tamul's eclipse. As they cut away foliage around the cliff, the red light of Tamul lit up the top rock of the cliff, revealing the faint outlines of an opening. Illusionary magic, Elspeth surmised, then removed a container and used a brush to paint a thick powder around that edge that revealed symbols.

'Stand away from me,' Elspeth said as she stepped away from the symbols.

The guttural words of the incantation hurt Bertram's ears. Those foul words grated and sawed at his sanity. The others didn't seem likewise affected and busied themselves checking each other's armour and equipment. Museo put himself through a series of deep stretches that looked like a slow dance. Bertram rotated his neck, then stretched his shoulders, trying to shake free the roiling of his guts. He wiped clammy hands on his trousers and accepted a water skin from Nix.

Elspeth's words when they came were almost a relief.

'There.' She pointed to a nondescript area on the wall about six feet farther along the top of the cliff. 'This entrance is a trap. That is the real one.'

Angus easily climbed the small cliff, then pulled the others up after him. With the illusion now broken, it revealed a small

Chapter 11

passageway disappearing into the foreboding darkness. Bertram slumped down in relief. He had done it, helped them find the cave.

'Samual, my part is finished. I trust you will act the gentlemen and honour your part of our agreement,' Bertram said, his voice hollow around them.

Angus snatched Bertram by his neck, moving quicker than anyone Bertram had seen before. The big man's other hand held Bertram's hand tightly where it clasped against the pommel of his sword. Angus pulled Bertram closer to him. 'Bad news, Bertie. You are the one leading us inside. Now pull yourself together.'

'I can't do this, caves, enclosed places. I can't breathe in them.' Bertram felt the panic well up inside him as he thrashed in Angus's grip. The man slapped him, which caused blood to fill Bertram's nostrils, making breathing almost impossible. Bertram coughed blood that spattered across the front of Angus, who threw Bertram away from him in disgust. Bertram turned to run and tripped over himself, got up, then tried to run again, only to run into Elspeth.

'Destaile!' Elspeth said and slapped a palm against Bertram's chest.

Instantly, Bertram's fear dissipated, and his breathing steadied.

Elspeth cupped his cheeks in her hands. 'You are feeling the effects of fey magic, designed to make you fear the worst. Now, be calm and focus more than ever. You will lead us deeper,' Elspeth said, her voice soothing.

Bertram couldn't believe what he was hearing. 'That was not the deal. 'I was to lead you here, that was all, and you all know this. Samual, we had a gentleman's agreement!'

Angus laughed drily. 'Ha, a gentleman's agreement. Oh, dear, dear, Bertie, do you really think our Samual is a gentleman?'

The others were all laughing now except Elspeth, who stood wearily rubbing her shoulders, her posture looking a little hunched. She moved with short, scuffing steps, breathing hard. Angus helped her sit down.

The magic is weakening her, Bertram thought.

Samual went to Elspeth, leaving the way clear to the edge of the cliff and woods below. Bertram thought he might have an opportunity to escape, only to find Nix in his way. She looked wild and excited, her feet braced on the rock. In her hand rested a sickle blade that she twirled effortlessly.

'You can't leave us, Bertie. Don't you want to protect me?'

Bertram gaged the chance he had of getting past her.

'Try it, Bertie; c'mon, see if you can escape. I will only cut you a little.'

Bertram gulped and turned away from Nix, defeated. He was well and truly trapped now.

'If I refuse and you kill me here, my father and Martin will hunt you to the ends of the world,' he said through clenched teeth.

'I would love to see that,' said Museo, smiling. 'An old warrior and a cripple. Such a dangerous combination. Grow some balls quickly, Bertie. You asked to come along, and we accepted. Now, just like for the rest of us, you are in up to your scrawny neck, so stop the blubbering already and prepare yourself.'

They waited half a chime for Elspeth to regain some energy. She had deep bags gathering under her eyes, and Bertram could swear she had more wrinkles at the corners of her eyes.

'Is it worth it? The power, I mean, when it does this to you? You will be a crone before this damn quest of yours is through.'

She just stared at Bertram blankly before turning away, but he saw a flicker of what may have been unease in those haunted eyes.

'Enough time wasting,' said Samual, who had a feverish look to him now. 'We are so close. I can feel it. Bertie, you are first. Angus, help our spoiled brat into the cave.'

Bertram had no other choice but to do what Samual said. The hard looks of his companions proved that. He allowed Angus to boost him up to the ledge, then dropped himself into the stone

Chapter 11

tunnel, which was clear of debris. Normally this might have been reassuring, but it now hinted that the tunnel was well used and whatever used it was waiting for them, and he was the bait.

Angus passed him down a burning torch, and the smell of pitch in the confined space made Bertram feel dizzy. Once they were all crouched inside, Bertram called back to Samual. 'Do we have a map?'

'Follow that noble nose of yours, Bertie, and you can't go wrong,' returned Samual, which got a chuckle out of the others.

Bertram started forward, the tunnel allowing crouching room only. He scuttled forward to a drop of maybe ten feet; the torchlight settling on the many bones littering the dusty stone floor below. A narrow ledge circumvented the hole, around which Bertram moved carefully with his back to the wall. His foot slipped as the rock below it crumbled, making him almost topple down into the hole, but he clawed himself back against the stone wall and found the next safe step and the next until he reached the other side to safety. Bertram sat gasping for breath as he watched the others circumvent the hole.

Samual motioned Bertram to continue, and with no other choice, Bertram crept farther into the unknown.

As they continued forward, they entered a stone tunnel reinforced with timber. Unlit hooded lanterns hung from the rafters at regular intervals that once lit dispelled some of the darkness. They found the tithe crates in the first chamber they came to, along with a chest and saddle bags. There must have been another entrance to get here, Bertram realised, noticing the drag mark of the crates along one wall. A secret door maybe.

Tracks in the sand showed the same two sets of footprints Bertram had tracked through the woods. One left by the exit to the west and the other north. The cargo was unopened, and further drag marks led to the west. As Bertram checked the prints, something clattered loudly down the semi-lit passage before him. Bertram froze where he was to peer down the passage as he drew his sabre.

'What was that Bertram?' said Samual, moving up beside him.

'Something is down there. I heard it moving,' he replied, still looking down the tunnel.

Bertram felt a sharp prick in the small of his back, smelt the sour breath of Samual near his ear. 'Keep moving, Bertie.'

Bertram's blade felt heavier than he remembered. Steadying his legs that were threatening to collapse beneath him, he inched forward again.

Bertram licked lips that had become dry with dust. He would have killed for water. Ahead, the pungent stench of urine was overpowering. Bertram pulled his shirt up to cover his nose and mouth, then continued on. The tunnel turned left. In the lantern light, Bertram noticed something strange about their shadows cast on the wall. They had stopped, and now Samual was whispering something to Angus. Samual's shadow moved differently from what Samual was doing. It unfurled itself into something bigger, sinuous, crouched, and ready to spring.

A low growl up ahead tore away Bertram's attention. He wiped perspiration out of his eyes, then crept forward to peer around the corner.

A naked man sat chained to the wall, dirt and worse crusted his skin, the skin around his wrist manacles chafed raw. As he saw Bertram, he cried and gibbered. 'Leave now, don't go any farther. Is your life worth losing here, far below the earth, away from your loved ones?' The man turned to look down the passage behind him, chains rattling. 'Go quickly! They will come soon.'

Chapter 12

Bertram continued forward cautiously. 'Keep quiet. Can you tell me what is up ahead?' Bertram asked the captive.

The figure nodded vigorously between sniffles, motioning for Bertram to go back. Behind him he could hear Samual calling out to him, which he ignored. As he scuffled forward, the man disappeared, leaving in his place a broken skeleton with smashed ribs slumped against the wall in chains. It had been an illusion. Bertram looked around frantically, shaking his head. First the damn shadows, now this? What's real, what's not?

Ahead was a chamber. The smell that wafted from it made Bertram, as well as at least one of the Lords and Dames, gag. Before Samual prodded him, Bertram continued forward, revealing a circular room from which carcases hung from three iron meat hooks. The meat looked healthy enough, though the stench told another story.

Nix prodded a carcass with her blade, then retched as rotten flesh fell to the floor, writhing with worms. Bertram turned away, thankful he hadn't eaten recently. He sidled between the carcasses with the others close behind him then crept into another chamber, this one stocked with tools of slaughter. An impressive range of butchering knives, leather aprons, and hooks lay upon a large wooden tabletop. There were no exits from the chamber.

'The star ball is close,' Elspeth said.

'There are no exits from here. We need to turn back,' Bertram whispered after drinking from a water skin. They backtracked, searching the walls for hidden passages, and it took a frustrating amount of time before Angus detected a draft along an area of the wall.

A shriek came from somewhere. Angus turned towards the direction, cursing when he realised nothing was there. They couldn't find any doorway to open and were forced to go farther back to the western branch they had bypassed earlier.

The way west took them to an iron-reinforced door. With no other option, Angus pulled out the axe strapped across his back and began hacking away at the timber. It took the big man longer than it should have to cut the timber down because of magical wards etched in the door frame that lit up with a red glare every time the axe struck the door. Finally, the door collapsed inwards, only left hanging from one hinge.

'This is not a good idea, Samual,' Bertram croaked as a wave of nausea rolled over him.

Samual roughly grabbed Bertram by the arm propelling him forward through the doorway. A bowl of sun-blazer fish lit the chamber in shades of indigo; a long mural draped the wall above a bed depicting a scene of three people with strangely long limbs standing on a cliff looking down over a village. The one exit from this room led into another, larger chamber. From where Bertram stood, he could see some sort of altar draped in garlands. There was a pale, white statue behind the altar of a man chiselled with muscle and only partially visible in the gloom. Behind him, he could hear the others searching about.

'At least the bed is comfortable,' Nix said giggling.

'Samual, look at this. There is a hidden area behind the painted canvas,' Bertram heard Museo say.

'Nix, go with Museo and explore that. Here, take this lantern to help see,' replied Samual.

Bertram continued forward, mesmerised by the strange scene in front of him. The statue was immaculate workmanship, so lifelike.

Chapter 12

A gust of wind rushed through the chamber, then swept up into Bertram, blowing back his hair, extinguishing the torch, and plunging the chambers into almost total darkness.

'Samual,' he called, noticing the waiver in his voice. 'I need light up here now!'

'Here, Bertram, take my lantern,' grunted Angus from behind. Bertram took the second lantern, lifting it high, then stopped to face Angus behind him. 'You will be right behind me, won't you, Angus?'

'I am now, ain't I?'

Bertram turned back, facing the altar. The statue had disappeared; now there was just the flower-draped altar on which sat a collection of gems that caught the light spectacularly. Something chortled to his right, and Bertram felt his bowels evacuate. He spun in a half circle towards the noise as he retreated, crashing into Angus. 'Forward, you fool,' grunted Angus, halting his advance as they crashed together. The contact knocked Bertram off balance. Bertram grunted as pain lanced through his left knee, making his leg give way. He reached out to the wall, bracing himself as the swinging lantern in his other hand illuminated a hulking man, all muscle and gleaming teeth moving towards him. Strong hands snatched Bertram from his feet.

'Angus, help!' The cry came out as a weak mewl.

The man began shaking Bertram, who glanced back to see if Angus was coming to his aid. The chamber was empty. They had left him. Bertram dropped the lantern as the hulking man pulled him up level with his face, fixing him with an iron glare, hissing in anger. 'You dare break the pact on tribute night?'

'I don't belong here. They forced me to come here.'

The man's eyes widened almost comically. 'You have come here to hurt the Vixen, to steal her power. You can't have it. Leave us alone!'

When Bertram still didn't answer, the man shook him harder, then threw him, and he bounced off something hard with a crash and then fell to the stone on his side. The lantern was still intact, lying on its side, the hulking man standing near it looking into the next chamber.

Bertram slowly climbed to his feet, intending to run, but the man turned, then charged at him, cannoning into Bertram with his shoulder, which spun Bertram away. Somehow Bertram stayed on his feet, and he ran towards a torch-lit passage, his breath coming in gasps, sharp pain shooting up from his injured knee.

He heard the sound of running just behind him. Bertram snatched up a torch, turned, and swung it with all his might in one movement. The torch struck the man across the face with a thud. Bertram was grabbed again, the torch knocked from his fingers as he was carried back towards the altar. The man struck Bertram repeatedly in the stomach and face, grunting terribly with each hit. Bertram was blubbering now. He didn't want to die.

A white face twisted with hatred filled his vision.

'Why do you want to hurt us when we help the people?'

Bertram's hand found his sabre hilt and he managed to slide the blade free, which angered the man even more. He snatched Bertram's sabre, the sharp blade cutting fingers and dripping blood to the floor, then tried to tear it away from Bertram's grasp. 'You want to kill us, but then who will protect the villages when threatened? There are worse than us, much worse.'

Bertram got the blade free then, but because he had no room to use the blade he swung the pommel which struck the man below the eye splitting the skin.

A fist rammed into his lower abdomen so hard it folded Bertram over, then the man struck him on the back of his spine, making an awful cracking sound. All energy drained from Bertram as he lay there, staring up at his attacker. To Bertram's horror, he saw the man's face had undergone a transformation; the jaw and head had elongated and long canine teeth slathered drool as it growled

Chapter 12

at Bertram. His body betrayed him then as he pissed himself and simply passed out.

When Bertram came back to consciousness, the fallen lantern had been stood back up. The stone was cold against his back and the side of his head. Need to move, to get out of here. But the rest of his body felt disassociated and wouldn't rally to the thoughts of running away. He was wet or lying in something, a puddle maybe, and the thirst was upon him, driving his senses wild. Water, he needed water. How long had he been unconscious? Tuning his head was difficult and felt strange, restricted like his spine was fighting his every movement to do so, but sheer determination won over, and when he saw the strange altar before him, he wished he hadn't bothered trying. The altar had a scene painted on its side of a group of villagers abasing themselves before a woman with long, red hair who was handing out wrapped parcels to a line of children.

From far to his right Bertram heard screaming and the sound of frantic chanting. Elspeth, it was Elspeth. They were still here, which meant he still had a chance to get out of this death trap. Trying to collect his thoughts, Bertram concentrated on learning about the state of his body. He attempted to wiggle his toes. There was no response or feeling. Before he could panic, he worked his way up his legs, willing his muscles to respond. When he got to the arms, they thankfully responded and he could feel around, though he dreaded doing so. His hands found a wound to his stomach, just below his sternum. He managed to move his ripped shirt and ball the material over the small hole there. Moving upwards, his throat was intact, leaving his breathing uninhibited. His face seemed unmarred, but blood caked his mouth, and teeth were missing on one side.

Even with the fear and horror coursing through him, he tried to stay positive. Could be worse. Arms work and I can breathe fine. The unresponsive legs were the big problem and pointed to a spinal injury. Would he be a cripple, just like his father? The self-exploration had proved exhausting, so Bertram shut his eyes to rest. He was so tired. The sounds of boots on stone brought him back. They came from behind him. Not knowing who was approaching was the worst feeling.

Samual's face came into view, blood now spattered his face. His golden teeth showed as he grinned manically.

'Water, please,' croaked Bertram.

'Nix, pass your water bottle; Bertie is thirsty,' Samual said.

'We may need it for us, Samual.' But Bertram heard the lid being loosened and then the bottle being brought to his lips. Cool water flowed down into his mouth too fast, making him spit most of it back up.

'Are we going home now?' Bertram said.

His question was met with low chuckles.

'We are leaving, but not you, Bertie. You are now a hindrance, and we can't carry you instead of all the treasure we have.'

'But I helped you, just like we planned. I did my part, Samual. Don't leave me here, please!'

'You did well, Bertie, much better than I ever expected, but now our paths must split,' replied Samual, his face swimming back into Bertram's view again.

'Samual, I thought we were together in this. I thought you and I had worked things out. I thought we were okay,' Bertram said through the pain.

Samual began laughing, and his breath smelt terrible just above Bertram's face. Samual stared down at him.

'Don't worry, Bertie, my friend. We're golden, you and me, we're golden.'

Samual's face disappeared to be replaced by Nix and the sound of the others moving away.

'Bertie you don't look good. I really liked you, Bertie. Don't worry, it will all be over soon.'

Chapter 12

'Nix, come on, we're leaving,' came Samual's voice from behind them, and Bertram began to cry.

'Nix, please. I will do whatever you want. Just take me with you.'

Nix didn't reply. She reached down and kissed him on the lips. 'I will tell your father how brave you were, Bertie. I won't even mention how you cried like a baby. Goodbye.'

There was nothing else he could do but lie there, broken, listening to the Lords and Dames walking away from him.

'Can you believe that? He was crying like a baby,' he heard Angus say with his voice thick with contempt.

'At least he served his purpose and distracted the guardians,' said Museo, laughing.

Chapter 13

It was silent now. The last of the lantern's oil was almost gone and would soon plunge the chamber into darkness. A movement caught Bertram's eye up on the wall in the chamber's corner above the altar. Impossibly, there was a woman crouched there, long legs and arms braced against the two walls. Thick, red rope-like strands of hair hung down over most of her face except her eyes, which blinked slowly, owl-like, as she began crawling down the wall to the ground. She had some sort of tail of gold-and-white fur that spread out behind her like a fan. From this angle it seemed like more tails than just one. She moved in utter silence, which was more terrifying than if she had come screaming in fury.

Bertram held his breath. Maybe she hadn't seen him. He would have prayed if he could remember the words, but they had deserted him, and so he sat there helpless and waited to see his fate.

The woman creature with tails stopped briefly beside Bertram, then sniffed deeply. He stared up at her. She was beyond beauty in a feral way, and intelligent eyes glittered in the dim light.

'I will be back, manling. You better pray that my sons are alive. If not, make peace with yourself and with death.'

Then she was gone.

It wasn't the knowledge that he was broken or the difficulty in reigning in the plethora of thoughts that descended upon his fragile mind with their whispers of death, regret, and loss that were the worst. As Bertram lay there, it was the silence that truly bothered

Chapter 13

him. It lay him bare, body and soul, at the complete mercy of the world around him, a world that he clung to that was threatening to shake him off with a mere shrug into the unknown.

Priests and scholars claimed to know what came after death; they knew nothing, and this state of realisation did nothing to console Bertram. When the lies created to make one feel better about their own mortality would have helped him come to terms with his own demise faded away to the stark reality that he was alone he began to weep. He lay there in a state free from the pain that his severe injuries must have caused him, alone and afraid as scenes of his too-brief life filtered through his mind, giving firsthand clarity of the person he truly had been, and Bertram wished he had been better. A better son to Arlo, who did everything to provide him with a good life, to keep him safe. It was too much, and Bertram realised he now just wished for the end to be upon him to free him of his pitiless self-importance, to end any suffering and take away these last moments of realisation that he wasn't a good person after all.

At some point, Bertram did what all mortals must do and simply surrendered to a greater power, death. As it came for him, arms outstretched, he was suddenly ripped away from its comforting grasp.

'Manling, wake up!'

Eyes so nearly turned inwards forced themselves open. The lady with red hair knelt over him.

'You don't get to go so easily, manling. My sons are both dead because of you and your wicked friends, and you think I will grant you release? Only after I have shredded any sanity your small mind has left, then dismembered your body, burnt your bones, drunk the sour blood of your mortal prison will you get that, and only if I finally feel some measure of pity for the gutless swine you are.'

Bertram felt himself drifting away from the voice again, and something hit his face over and over until he opened his eyes again.

She was still crouched above him, crying great sobs. 'You kill my children, steal my soul, and try to leave. Now your friends have power over me. They will make me do things against my will. I swore it would never happen again and foolishly thought your kind would protect me, just as I did them. Now all I have is you to repay for the atrocities you have delivered upon me this day.'

'Don't kill me,' he managed to say, and she turned swollen, red eyes upon him.

'You dare to beg for mercy? What about my sons? Do you think they had a chance to beg, a choice when attacked in their home, a place of safety?'

'You need me,' Bertram replied.

'For what, manling? I have nothing left. It has all been taken from me, thanks to you. Why would you help me when you came here with them?'

'They lied to me. They never told me why we had come here. I can help you get back whatever you have lost. Get revenge for those who left me here. They never told me why we were here, and now I realise I was nothing but a distraction so they could get what they wanted while I kept your sons busy. I, like you, am nothing but a victim.' He coughed and felt blood well up in his mouth while the woman stared down at him blankly.

'So be it. It is a fitting punishment, far better than what I had in mind, but you owe me a debt and believe me, you will not thank me for this!' snarled the woman. She changed, her snout elongating, teeth reforming and fur appearing over her beautiful features. Almost gently, she lowered her mouth down to his neck, and he couldn't breathe as skin split beneath tearing teeth, and Bertram was granted his long-awaited release.

There was a battle, and Bertram found himself in the thick of it. It was a battle for his soul. He found himself above his body

Chapter 13

looking down upon its broken form—gutted, twisted in a posture of death, and yet here he was fully aware of what was happening around him but void of the bodily sensations. The woman was there, and Bertram saw she was now part woman, part wolf—no, not wolf, but a fox with red fur that matched her hair and the bushy tail with nine separate sections. She seemed to sense him there above her and turned to look up, gore covering her snout. She slinked away, and Bertram felt himself pulled down into his body again. Except it felt different now. He wasn't alone.

Something pushed against his awareness, alien and feral, that tried to dislodge him and push him away, and Bertram could feel hatred emanating from it that terrified him. He wanted to flee, but he knew with total certainty if he ran and gave in to whatever fought against him he would lose his soul and cease to exist. So, he fought with everything possible in his awareness as the alien entity attempted to dislodge his consciousness and take him for itself.

How long the silent battle for his soul lasted, he couldn't say, since he was between time where nothing mattered except holding on. Eventually, he became exhausted and so was the intruder within him, and they both existed there, aware of each other yet unable to defeat the other, forced to coexist.

The first time he woke up still in his physical body he was lying in a bed, poultices covering his chest and abdomen. He felt so weak it was hard even to open his eyes. He was dimly aware of the intruder inside of him, but he was still too exhausted to fight.

The woman came into view, carrying a steaming bowl. She no longer was part fox, and he remembered the legend and the name Vixen's Dell. This woman was the vixen. He knew that now.

'You wake, manling? I feared you had lost the battle.'

How did she know? Bertram wondered, then remembered that if the legends were true, she had been here for many natural lifetimes. One per tail if you believed the legend. That, he realised, was the significance of the nine tails.

Bertram wanted to talk, to ask what was happening, except he couldn't muster up the energy to do so. All he could do was lie there as she tended to him.

'Now listen to me carefully, manling. I will say this just once, and then it's up to you to use that knowledge to survive the battle you have only just begun. You are undergoing a transformation brought on by my bite. Now my blood mingles with yours, making you possibly more than a man or a mere beast, depending on whether you can defeat the intruder inside you.'

The nature of the intruder will always try to overthrow your consciousness. If it does, you will lose yourself until it lets go again. You need to keep the beast under control by feeding on the right foods to keep it sated. Wear it out through physical exertion. Only when you allow it to build strength within you will the intruder fight you for supremacy. Your senses will become enhanced, and you will easily be able to hide when the moons are full, but beware, because when Aspre is full you will be in control, but when Tamul is full, the intruder will rise up against you and at those times it is better you are somewhere where you cannot do anyone harm.

Finally, beware hounds. They will know you are fox kin now and will attack without a second thought. Then she wiped him down with a damp cloth before ladling warm broth for Bertram to eat. His immediate needs now sated, Bertram slipped into sleep.

Chapter 14

With the sun painting the land in summer hues, Bertram thundered down the manor road, his childhood home looming up ahead, warm and welcoming. It was good to finally be home. The regrettable business with the Lords and Dames was at an end, though the terror imprinted on his mind would never truly leave him. The feeling of freedom as he rode, hair streaming back in the wind, was overwhelming now that he knew he had another chance to fix what had been broken.

The front door to the manor swung open as Bertram pulled Kitty to a stop, vaulting out of the saddle as Martin emerged carrying his father. Tears traced lines down Arlo's cheeks.

'My boy's home. Bertram is home,' Arlo cried out, his fists raised as if in victory.

Bertram held his father's head against his chest, as Martin beamed a smile.

'Outstanding work, Bertram, you are a dutiful son.'

From behind Martin came a low growl. Skulker, the old wolfhound, crept into view, the grey hackles raised, ears pulled back as he bared his fangs, tensing as if to pounce at Bertram. 'Skulker, you silly mutt, it's me, Bertram.' What was wrong with his hound? Skulker loved him, and he had raised the hound from the litter.

'C'mon, boy,' he said, kneeling and stretching out his hand. 'Skulker, it's me. Bertram,' he said again as Skulker continued to bare his teeth and growl low in his throat. Then Skulker struck, teeth tearing into Bertram's hand. He snatched it back a touch too late, which tore the skin more. Bertram meant to scream in pain, but all that came out was a howl. He felt the ripping of flesh, the swelling of bones, and the popping of vertebrae as he fell to the ground on all fours. As Skulker attacked again, Bertram darted to the side, the wolfhound's jaws tearing fur from his flank. Then Bertram fled, Skulker in close pursuit, chasing him away from his home. His acute hearing picked up his father's words.

'My boy is a monster.'

Bertram was lathered in sweat. He was still secured to the cot as the red-haired lady soothed him, stroking his head and face. Putting the damp cloth down, she held his head up, then slowly poured water down his throat. As Bertram lay gasping, the remnants of the nightmare already fading, the red-haired woman sang a lullaby as if to a sick child.

'Thank you for your kindness,' Bertram managed to say.

'I need what's mine returned, and for that, you must be alive. I don't do this out of kindness,' she replied, then stalked away.

Bertram tried his hardest to stay awake. He sang songs, yelled his anger at his betrayal, even twisted his body in such a way that pain lanced through his injured knee, but at least it kept him from falling asleep where the dreams waited. Against his will, he fell asleep anyway.

The hearth cackled as flames licked hungrily over the dry timber, bathing the cottage in a soothing glow. Two lavender candles spread Rae's favourite fragrance through her home, and rose petals made a trail from the door to the bed. The key turned in the lock. Bertram smiled in anticipation as Rae stepped into her home, dropping back the hood from her head and smiling.

'Now I could get used to this, Bertram. You even made a petal path,' she cooed, following it with exaggerated steps to the bed's edge where Bertram sat. She stopped a few feet from the bed, peering at him.

Chapter 14

'Why is it so dark around you, Bertie? I can't see you well.'

Bertram smiled, then moved forward, thinking this was a part of the game.

Rae shrunk back from him, her hand going to her mouth. 'Your eyes, they are golden.'

'Don't be daft, Rae,' Bertram meant to say, but all that came out was a growl. He could hear her heartbeat from here, the pale flesh of her neck bulging slightly as she gulped back her fright.

'Bertie?'

Rae ran for the door screaming. Bertram felt the intruder rise up, pushing him aside. It leaped after her as she swung the door open, then dragged her back inside with a guttural laugh before pulling the door closed.

Bertram awoke, screaming until his throat was raw.

Days passed him by as he lay there, falling in and out of that unnatural sleep, where his dreams warned him constantly of the changes that had befallen him. It was too late now; he realised in those rare moments of clarity when they came. He could feel the differences already, and with the intruder sharing his mind now, Bertram knew life could never be the same for him.

It was dark, and his clothes smelt of stale sweat. To his right came the sounds of tearing, chewing, and sucking. Something struck the stone close to Bertram. A bone sucked clean. The thought of food caused his stomach to react painfully. From its corner in his mind, the intruder rose. Bertram could see the intruder in his mind through inward-seeing eyes. It was a gaunt, furred creature, only its abdomen free of fur where ribs protruded through thin skin. It stared back at him, sniffing the air.

'It hurts, needs food.'

Bertram pushed away from it in disgust. His mouth was watering, the smell of rich meat wafting to him. Bertram tried to sit up but found his wrists and ankles restrained with iron manacles.

'Vixen. I need food,' he said.

She strolled from the darkness, the fading daylight giving her form as she chewed at a haunch of meat, another held in her free hand which she placed on the floor before the window, then sunk down with her back against the wall.

'Then come get it!'

'Take these off, please,' Bertram said, holding his arms up to show the manacles.

'No. It's time you learned to fend for yourselves. Bonds, unless magic, cannot hold us. Find a way between you both to get free. You might both battle for the same body, but together you become the latest of my brood. You will become Golden.'

Bertram tested his restraints calmly at first, then desperation overcame him as his senses went into overdrive, the smell of meat so close shut all else out. He thrashed against the cot, bucking his body until it ached, and blood welled up beneath the iron shackles where it chafed skin.

The Vixen rose, a look of disgust marring her pretty face, then left the chamber.

The intruder howled inside him. 'She is letting us die. I will tear her limb from limb.'

Bertram felt the surge within his mind, a transference of strength as he struggled to break free and get to the meat that was so close. Something cracked in his arm, sending pain shooting along the nerve up to his neck. If they kept this up, his body would be broken by morning.

'No, we must stop. There has to be another way,' Bertram snarled, focusing on the intruder who stopped, cocking its head to the side to stare back at him. Then it threw itself forward without warning, jaws snapping close to his throat, forcing him to snarl his fingers in its fur, pushing it away. They fought against each other until exhausted, then both slumped down, breathing hard. The intruder lay down panting, long tongue lolling from its jaws, watching him warily.

Chapter 14

Bertram stared at it lying there, looking more fox than man, its ribcage rising and falling as it panted, and it took him a moment to realise he was panting too, in time with the beast, could feel its tongue against the cold stone, the hunger within its guts, and he pulled back, scared.

What is happening to me?

The intruder watched for a time, then its eyes closed, its breathing regulated. Bertram quested towards it with his mind somehow passing into it. Images of woods shoved their way into his mind, the sweet tang of tree sap, movement from the bushes, a rabbit. He scampered after it, his ears pulling back, uncovering a myriad of unfamiliar smells.

A howl close by snatched him from that strange state back to the real world. He was still on the bed, manacles loose about his paws.

Paws? Looking down, Bertram saw he was a fox. The total surprise ended with the rising of the intruder, who howled with glee.

'Free, we are free! Food, now.'

They slunk from the bed to the haunch of meat and feasted. Feeling eyes upon them, Bertram glanced up at the window where a large red fox stood staring in. It seemed to smile.

Chapter 15

Wonderfully satiated following the fresh meat, Bertram returned to the cot, allowing the promise of sleep to draw him down into its embrace. His body was healing, which required as much rest as he could get. The intruder slunk away to the corner of his mind, content for now.

Bertram awoke to golden eyes regarding him in the darkness. A large, red fox sat staring at him. As he watched, its form shimmered with soft, orange light. Then the red-haired woman sat there. This was the first time he had been clear of mind and seen her up close. She had slightly oval-shaped eyes, thin eyebrows, high cheekbones, and a pale complexion with close-set eyes of faded jade. A short scar at the corner of her mouth gave her the appearance she was smiling even when she wasn't.

'I see you are in control of the intruder again. Fresh meat will help subdue its power, so will vigorous physical exertion. As you learned yesterday, you can meld together with it, which is how you changed form, but remember it can meld with you. Take your form while you stay helpless in the background. Not until one of you triumphs in the battle for your soul will you merge and become golden.'

'What does being golden mean?' Bertram asked.

'It's ascension beyond man, beyond beasts, where strange and wondrous powers open up to you.'

'Powers. Like what?'

Chapter 15

'That depends on the type of beast spirit within you. Traditionally in the Scented Isles, there were thirteen types that mimic aspects of nature. I know not if it will be different for you, because I have never sired a pup in your lands.'

On the fifth day, Bertram awoke in his usual place on the cot, except this time the Vixen was tying him down with leather straps.

'What are you doing?' Bertram asked, suddenly nervous.

'The swollen moon is upon us, and you are too weak to resist its lure. Your spirit will attempt to travel, and the intruder will do its best to dislodge your control.'

Bertram watched her finish the complex knots that secured him to the pallet, then she began stuffing the leaves of a plant beneath the mattress and around the bed.

'Wolf's bane,' she murmured as she worked. 'It will keep you from taking any other form than that of a man.'

'My mother used to tell me a story about the Vixen. In it she had many tails, and each tail represented a human life span. Each new life slowly changed the colour of the vixen until it turned gold and ascended to the spirit world. Your tail is golden and white, yet you are still here,' he said, watching her.

'There are many tales about my kind, Bertram, and most hold some truth to them, but most are simply fiction or rumours spread to make others wary of us. What else did this mother of yours say about me?'

'That if the vixen was to be killed or driven off the people would suffer all kinds of problems, for the fox people are benevolent allies of man, bringing good luck and aiding the unfortunate whenever they can. With the fox people gone, man would be even more vulnerable to the insidious powers that wish to destroy him.'

'This mother of yours interests me. Did she give you this?' The vixen held up Bertram's necklace of the fox head.

Bertram nodded. 'Yes before she abandoned me and my father. Can I have it back?'

'Maybe in time,' she said pocketing the trinket.

The vixen had finished securing Bertram and now sat watching him with a glazed look in her eyes.

'Your mother was a wise woman to know about me. However, never forget not all of our kind are benevolent. There are some that prey on man, driving them insane with cruel trickery before murdering them.'

'Please tell me your name,' Bertram said, then wondered if he had gone too far.

She was quiet as she checked the restraints one last time before answering. 'My birth name is Kasumi, but my sons called me Kassy. You can too,' she replied.

'You are from the Scented Isles where there are many types of spirit folk, aren't you, Kassy?'

'I was born there, yes, but circumstances conspired to make me leave my ancestral home. Once the people worshipped me almost as much as their gods and welcomed me to the lands of Scuttle. For centuries we coexisted peacefully. The villagers swore to keep my presence secret in return for my protection. Someone could not keep their mouths shut, and now my two sons are dead. I shall protect them no more and abandon their lands.'

'You can't blame the villagers for this, Kassy. Eventually someone, would have found you. The Lords and Dames are the ones to blame.'

'A curious name. Why do they call themselves that?'

'They are all from noble heritage, but the title is more a mockery than anything else. We will get back what you lost, Kassy, and I will have my own revenge,' Bertram said, trying to reassure her.

'Yes, we will, Bertram. Never forget your promise to me, for that is the only reason you still draw breath,' Kassy said. When she turned and went away, Bertram found himself wanting her to stay.

Chapter 15

Even though Bertram couldn't see Tamul, he could feel its effect thrumming through his whole body. He attempted to stand and only then remembered the bonds that Kassy had applied. Struggling against the bonds proved futile, and he fell back panting hard when he longed to run just run through the night, feel the wind tickle his nose, ruffle his fur. On one level he was aware of this absurd thought as a man. I am more than a man, less than a beast, Kassy had told him, turning his attention inwards to the intruder who sat regarding him. As he focused on the intruder it responded with a snarl.

'Move aside, Bertie,' it quipped with a wine. 'Let me out. Just for a while, the night calls to us. I know you can feel it.'

'We are bound. The wolf bane won't allow us to change, even if I wanted,' responded Bertram.

'Call her then. She created me; call her and beg her for our release. We are not animals, and together you and I can dominate, take the life that meets both our needs. You don't need to fight with me, Bertie. You need what I can offer. You are too soft, too forgiving, and I am the weapon we will use to get your precious vengeance. Or have you forgotten already?'

'I have forgotten nothing, and what do you know of my life? You are the intruder. You are not me,' rallied Bertram.

'But I am you, Bertram. I am all the things you will never be, I am you and you are me. Together we are a force to be reckoned with, not to fight against each other.'

'If that is to be so, then we need to trust Kassy. She knows what she is doing, and this is new to us, so obviously she fears what will happen if you are released. I don't think you will allow anybody, even her, to control us. I am sure she will allow us freedom once we are ready,' replied Bertram.

'I can't wait. It hurts to be trapped when the moon calls. The night is ripe with opportunity, and I long to feel it around me, to look upon the moon, hunt, and know completeness. We will never have that while we allow her to control us. She is turning us against each other.'

The intruder retreated soon after, but more than ever Bertram could feel it there, and its exasperation at being thwarted. There was nothing more to do except rest.

When the next surge came over him, Kassy was beside the pallet beside him. Her eyes had turned golden, and she was naked, lithe, and beautiful to behold.

'I know the pain you feel, and it hurts me to have to make you go through this, but if I let you out now, you will lose yourself to the intruder forever. Our pact is too important for this, and I need my spirit ball back. Without you, I fear I am too weak to achieve that.'

Before his eyes Kassy seemed to melt and change, falling to the ground into a crouch, fur sprouting over her body, and then she sat there, golden eyes regarding him. He saw what he might become, a fox kin, and though he didn't truly understand what that meant. Kassy had explained that one of her sons she had changed had never taken the fox form and instead

been blessed with its cunning and strength while the other flowed effortlessly between the two forms but was weak in man form and sickly.

She left Bertram like that, wracked by needs he didn't understand yet, while the intruder howled from within.

The cool soil beneath his paws felt good. The night was free of any wind, and the moon Aspre seemed to dominate the sky. Sounds carried to him of men singing and food roasting that made his stomach turn with hunger. The longing for juicy meat led him by the nose as he slunk through the woods to the top of the hill where below a small camp lay. There were three of them—men, his nose told him, and they had cular lizard mounts, not his desired choice of food but slow and easy to attack, and if you could pry away some of the thick hide, sweet meat awaited. A guard sat facing where he lay in the long grass with a weapon, and he had felt the bites that those weapons delivered with no wish to experience that again. That was how his pack had died. Something broke to his left, bounding through the undergrowth, and he took off low to the ground after the easier prey soon lost in the chase. He could feel the rabbit's fear, and it drove him on; he swatted out a paw just as the rabbit changed direction, catching it. He leapt upon it, grabbing its thin neck, crunching bones and holding while it struggled uselessly in his grasp and fell still. Then he crouched on his haunches and feasted.

When Kassy returned, she brought with her two rabbits, which she skinned as he watched. Then she fed him the fresh meat in titbits, and where once he would only eat meat well cooked and despised any sign of blood he revelled in the raw meat. Even the intruder within him became less prominent as it slunk lower in his awareness, for the time sated.

'You are linked to me like I am to you, and though here, you accompanied me for a part of my night. Remember that skill; it will help keep us both safe.'

So not a dream but riding her experience.

After she fed him, Kassy sat on the pallet beside him. She looked weary, and he could feel the worry that consumed her.

'Tomorrow we leave the dell,' she said, curling up beside him.

'Leave your home? Why?'

'I have no choice now, Bertram.'

'But I am not ready. I still don't understand what i am now and what about the intruder?'

'My spirit ball calls to me, and if I am too far from it for too long, I will die. I think your friends know this and know I need to come to them, then they can use me as they wish. You have run out of time and must adapt to your new world or perish.'

'What about the people, the villagers, whom you have protected for so long? What will become of them?'

'I have already discussed that with you,' Kassy snapped. 'It will force them to fend for themselves. I am now powerless to help them. Everything must be about self-preservation and that of my pack.' She yawned.

'Pack? I thought you had no pack now your sons are dead,' replied Bertram, looking at her.

'I have you now, Bertie. Together we are pack.'

'Can't you change others and build the pack up?'

'I can, though I am loath to change one unless they come willingly. You asked me to save you and I did, but I will not do so to any innocents or they will turn against me. Now sleep, Bertram, for tomorrow I need you to lead me to Fallon's March, and then we can plan this vengeance against our enemies.'

Chapter 16

Rae pulled on her shawl. Grabbing the wrapped-up portion of meat and fresh bread, and scanned the kitchen to make sure all was in order. Happy that it was, she stepped out into the night, pulling a large key from her apron to lock the door.

'Eating alone then?'

Startled, Rae dropped the key. Turning, she saw Sef's large form leaning against the wall, pipe in hand.

'You scared me half to death, Sef,' Rae admonished, stooping down to pick the key back up.

'Don't worry about locking up. I've got a few things to do, then I will close. We could eat together, Rae, and then I could walk you home.'

'That's sweet of you, Sef, but all I want is to put my feet up by the fire. No need to walk me.'

'You have been coping well with all the stress you are under since Bertram's disappearance. Why don't you take a few days off? I know Dixie wouldn't mind.'

'Being busy is the only tonic that takes my mind off it, Sef. Don't worry, I will be okay. I just need some sleep.'

'Until tomorrow then. Goodnight Rae.'

Rae set off along the path to the streets of houses that clung to the hillside down into Fallon's March, smiling to herself at Sef's concern. He was like a father to her, and it was nice to have someone looking out for her, especially since Bertram had gone missing.

It had been almost one month since Rae had last seen Bertram. That night she had planned to tell Bertram that she was pregnant but had not been able to after he partied throughout the night with the five strangers that had visited the Cauldron. Rae had not liked them one bit. There was something off about them in a predatory way that had screamed danger to her. After a week of Bertram not showing up drunk at her door or harassing her while she worked her shifts at the Cauldron, Rae had gone to the Paxton residence to ask after him.

Arlo, Bertram's father, had filled her in on some details that had surprised her. Bertram had invited the strangers to the manor, which had caused quite a bit of trouble, and then left on some journey with them. Throughout the conversation, Arlo did not act his usual chatty self. He looked old now and those eyes that usually showed a hint of fire now were dull as if the life was draining from them.

'Are you okay, Arlo? Sorry, stupid question. I know Bertram's disappearance must be driving you crazy with worry like it is me,' she said, resting a hand on his shoulder. After visiting Arlo, Rae had nearly collapsed when she had been about clearing tables one night and turned to see the Lords and Dames walk into the Cauldron. Bertram was still missing, and the five strangers had returned to Fallon's march without him. Rae just couldn't accept that Bertram had just up and left without coming back to look after his father or help run the manor.

Though he complained constantly about these duties, it was not like him to neglect either of them.

The morning sickness had already begun before Bertram's disappearance, along with her moon blood stopping. Rae had wanted to deny it and even hid the fact that she was pregnant from those closest to her, but Dixie, her employer, had seen right through the facade.

Rae took a deep breath, fighting the tears that threatened to come. This child would not be fatherless like she had been.

Chapter 16

Bertram would come home, and together they would marry and raise the child together, as it should be.

Emerging from her thoughts, Rae found she had stopped walking. She stood at the mouth of the alley that led to her home. The alley ahead felt somehow wrong, odd, misshapen. Thick shadows created an unearthly presence of darkness that to Rae waited, poised to drag her down into its depths to smother her and her unborn baby.

Her eyes caught a movement in that darkness that caught Rae's breath as she paused, willing herself to utter silence. A growl, low and dangerous, emerged from the alley.

A flash of grey broke the barrier of darkness. A cat burst into view, running towards Rae. Close behind it came a dark shape, foaming jaws and wild eyes, its teeth snapping at its fleeing enemy barely missing its target then yelping as it came to a sudden halt, chains chinking loudly as the beast's restraints halted its chase. The cat howled as it weaved around Rae into the safety of the streets.

Rae settled a hand on her chest. A nervous laugh escaped her.

There was nothing to fear here. It was only Sturm's hound scaring away a cat, silly. A hound she had petted many times, even thrown sticks for.

'Good boy Chase. It's only me, Rae. Good boy,' Rae said, walking towards where Chase sat by the gate of its owners' home. The way Chase now stared at Rae unnerved her. There was no usual wagging of his tail or excited wiggling of his body that he usually gave when Rae approached. Now he stood braced as if to attack, hackles raised, tail pointed straight out behind him.

Rae stepped closer and Chase's lips pulled back, showing his sharp canines in a silent growl. His eyes bore into Rae's, scaring her with the hint of intelligence and malevolence she saw there. Rae moved to the far side of the alley, giving the hound a wide berth.

I'm nearly home. Gods be damned if I will let a stupid hound ruin my night.

Chase jumped and although his chain was too short for him to get anywhere near Rae, his growl and cracking of chains pulling tight propelled her into a mad sprint down the rest of the alleyway into sight of her small home where it backed onto the forest.

'Chase, you stupid mutt, shut the hell up or you going to get another kicking,' came the addled voice of Sturm through the darkness.

Rae raced the rest of the distance to her door, her key already in hand, and easily found the keyhole. She twisted the key, breathing quick shallow breaths that left her feeling dizzy. The click of the lock came. Rae pushed the door. It didn't budge. She grunted, pushing again with the weight of her body behind it. Nothing.

It was a feeling more than instinct that made Rae turn around. Her eyes were instantly drawn to a figure within the alley's depths draped in shadows. It was hard to make out the details but there was someone there and they were watching her. Rae turned again, throwing her shoulder into the hardwood of the door, grunting in pain as it refused to budge.

Must get inside, now!

Rae could sense the danger behind her closing in fast. She didn't need to see this with her own eyes when, with every inch of her body, mind, and soul, she knew the darkness was coming for her.

Rae rammed her body into the door, once, twice, and on the third time the door fell open, sending Rae sprawling into her home. Her food flew from desperately reaching arms, attempting to stop her fall, attempting to protect her baby. She fell onto her knees and palms, skin shredding on the timber floor.

A small price to pay. Considering the danger she had sensed.

The door was still open. Rae launched herself at it, slamming it shut, and then dropping the latch into place. She fell back against the door, still fighting for air as her short wheezing breaths

Chapter 16

continued with a power of their own as if Rae was no longer in control of her own body. Her vision was blurring now, tears streaking her cheeks as her heart thumped wildly in her chest, prompting a kick from her belly, bringing pain and clarity that cut through the fear enveloping her. Rae steadied herself back to deep, normal breaths, sucking in valuable air, pushing away the fear. When Rae had regained a sense of normalcy, she realised she wasn't alone.

Somebody was sitting in Rae's favourite chair by the fire clapping their hands.

'That's what I call an entrance,' came a woman's voice, tinged with amusement. Rae tried to peer through the gloom to see who had invaded her home but could see nothing but a seated figure beside the flickering flames of the fire.

Rae grabbed the cudgel she kept by the front door. Hefting in with both hands, she approached the woman.

'Whomever you are, get out of my home.'

'Come now, Rae, don't be a poor host. I have been waiting here for you to arrive home. We need to talk.'

'I don't even know who you are. If you don't leave now, there is going to be trouble.'

'You are a feisty little thing, aren't you, Rae? The woman waved an arm and the area about her lightened. The woman had pale skin, long dark ringlets of hair, and wore a dark red dress. Rae recognised her immediately. It was one of the Lords and Dames, Elspeth.

Rage flowed through Rae. She raised the cudgel threateningly.

'You! Get out. I don't want you or your damned friends anywhere near me.'

Elspeth flowed to her feet from the chair and walked slowly towards Rae. Beautiful and terrifying.

'What do you plan to do with your little piece of wood, dear? Hit me? Well, this is your chance.'

Rae tried to swing the cudgel. It didn't move. She found she could move nothing but her eyes and mouth as Elspeth stepped close to her, their faces almost touching. Elspeth flicked a hand lazily at the cudgel and Rae felt her fingers loosen, causing the weapon to drop to the floor.

'There, that's better. Now we can be civil. You have been sticking your nose into our business, Rae, and that is not a wise idea.'

'Bertram left Fallon's March with you and your friends. What did you do to him?'

'Bertie is a man capable of his own choices. He went with us of his own free will. When our business concluded, he left while we returned here.'

'No. Bertram wouldn't have done that. He has obligations here that I know he would never leave unattended. The manor, his father, and me. Bertram would not just leave. I know this and nothing you say will change that.'

Elspeth leaned in, her lips so close to Rae's ear that she could smell the woman's sickly, sweet sweat.

'You think you know Bertie so well? You were nothing more than a convenience to him. He bedded Nix after you that night at the Cauldron, did you know that? Bertie was tired of his droll life here in this small, stagnant town. He was sick of wiping his father's ass and the stupid little girl games you played trying to win his affection. I guess the lure of Stormwatch with the pretty maids and his scholarly dreams were too much for him to deny. You are a pretty girl, Rae. I'm sure you will find another prospective husband.' Elspeth ran a hand down Rae's cheek.

'Don't touch us!'

Rae realised her mistake immediately after the words had left her mouth.

Elspeth frowned. Then her eyes widened.

'You are pregnant, aren't you?'

Chapter 16

'No. That's not what I meant,' Rae blurted out.

Elspeth lowered her hand onto Rae's belly.

Rae fought to pull away. She couldn't. Tears of frustration and pain wet her cheeks as Elspeth moved her hand over her abdomen chanting softly.

'It's not too late to get rid of it, Rae. I could stop its feeble heartbeat with the squeeze of my hand,' Elspeth said, holding an open hand up for emphasis.'

'Please. Don't hurt my baby,' Rae choked out.

'That is entirely up to you, Rae. If you insist on meddling in our affairs and drawing attention to me and my friends, then I will return here and kill both of you. Do you understand me?'

Rae didn't answer fast enough. The hand on her belly grew painfully hot. Rae could feel her skin blistering, could feel the baby's answering kick of fear.

'Yes, I understand,' she yelled.

'See, I am very reasonable Rae, but if you push me, I will destroy you and all you love. Now, I will leave you to your pathetic little home.'

Elspeth rearranged her dress, pushed her hair back from her face, then left Rae's home. It was some time before Rae's movement returned to her body. When it did, she collapsed to the floor, shaking with fear, talking lovingly to the growing baby within her.

Chapter 17

They left under the cover of nightfall, carrying packs filled only with the necessities that Kassy was unwilling to leave behind.
Though Bertram felt stronger, his wounds still ached with the exertion of the fast pace that Kassy set. He guessed it was at most a month since he had been dealt the almost fatal wounds in the cave, and he was amazed at the short recovery time from his wounds. The intruder briefly fought against him, but with no food or having the strength of the full moon Bertram easily brushed it away its efforts.

Mist curtained the crisp night, alive with sounds and smells as they plodded through forest and hills. A calm had descended upon Bertram and his intruder as they enjoyed the sensation of being away from the confined cave that had been Kassy's den.

That first night they moved carefully, twice altering their direction to avoid villages and the barking of hounds that protected them. The one thing that Bertram noticed that had changed for him was the feeling of being in nature. Where before he felt uneasy and in constant danger, now he felt a part of that nature, accepted and no longer seen as a threat. As if reading his thoughts, Kassy waited for him to catch up to her.

'The Mother is everything to our kind, Bertram. Where once we feared to move about freely, now it is man who fears nature more. The return of magic has seen nature turn against man, and it has become dangerous for mankind to be found alone in the deep

Chapter 17

forests or grasslands. Now it is as it should be, and the races must appease the Mother to benefit from her many gifts.'

Only chimes before dawn they came to a farmhouse. There were no hounds to chase them away here, and a man sat on his veranda tossing grain to chickens who fluttered about uneasily as they sensed Bertram and Kassy.

'Go to him, Bertram, and ask for shelter. I have gold to pay, and we just need the use of a barn or spare room for the day.'

Bertram moved forward slowly, stopping when the man saw him. He removed his pack and lay it at his feet, then showed he was unarmed as the man snatched a longbow he had beside him and nocked an arrow.

'Who are you who comes under cover of darkness to my home when the good folk are all a bed?'

'We are two travellers seeking a place to rest. Our mounts were stolen by bandits, and it has forced us to travel by foot. We wish you and yours no harm, and can offer gold in return for shelter,' replied Bertram.

'You said you are two and yet I only see yourself. Where is this companion of yours?' said the man, looking around nervously.

'My wife is back behind me, good man. We are tired. Are you willing to help us?'

'How long are you expecting to stay?' the man asked.

'Just until nightfall, good man, then we will be on our way. We have our own food and will be no bother.'

The farmer watched him intently. 'Bring forth this companion of yours, so I can see them before I decide,' he said.

Kassy came forward to stop beside Bertram.

'This is my wife. It is just us two, like I said.'

'I have the barn that is free from any beasts. Two gold cetas and if you step forth from the barn, our deal is over. In return, I will leave you to yourselves and keep my family away from you.'

We're Golden

'May we approach then, good man, to pay you?' Bertram asked, and when the farmer nodded his affirmation, they approached.

They paid the farmer, who led them into the barn, and they quickly settled down. Soon after there came a knock at the door and the man entered carrying a bowl with fresh fruit, meat, and still-warm bread.

'From my wife,' he said simply.

When they left early that evening, there was a pack near the barn door filled with food and some blankets. A note read: safe travels, Mother Vixen, may you smile upon this family.

'How did they know?' asked Bertram as they set off.

'I have lived for centuries. The old families know of me, and the red hair or gold eyes usually give it away.'

The next two days were like the first as they headed for Fallon's March, sleeping during the day and paying for a roof over their heads. People, of course, were suspicious at first, but the power of Kassy's gold won through.

They were moving through heavy woods late one afternoon when Kassy suddenly sprinted away from Bertram's side. Her voice carried back to him. 'Come on Bertram, catch up. You must learn to use your senses. Focus on them and open to the new world you are now a part of,' Bertram groaned then broke into a run. Soon his legs tired. His breaths turned to ragged gasps with Kassy always in sight just ahead, her mocking voice and laughter goading him onwards. Bertram saw an intersecting well-worn path ahead, he followed Kassy onto it and cursed as she turned sharply left back into the woods. Ahead Bertram noticed the path turning left and thought if he stayed on the path it would allow him to close on Kassy. Forgetting his fatigue Bertram drove himself harder, he could catch her. Bertram's foot struck something hard just beneath the soil. There came a sharp cracking noise and then a terrible pain

Chapter 17

in his lower leg and Bertram was falling. He came to a sudden halt as something pulled taunt and fresh pain shot up his leg drawing a scream of pain from him.

Bertram struggled into a sitting position to see his leg and was shocked by the metal trap clasped over his foot and ankle that had torn the flesh and splintered a bone. Shock washed over him, Bertram began to hyperventilate and his vision blurred.

Kassy jogged back to squat beside Bertram. She studied him with a look lacking in sympathy and layered with anger and disappointment. Kassy grabbed both jaws of the trap, pulling it apart and nearly causing Bertram to faint. Her strength was incredible. She carefully removed the trap from Bertram's leg. Rummaging in her pack, she drew forth a cloth with which she pressed to the gaping wound to help staunch the bleeding.

'If you had listened to me this would never have happened.'

'You didn't say anything,' Bertram said between gasps.

'Don't be a child, Bertram! I told you to use your senses. If you had done so you would have smelt the scent of a man and the rusted metal trap. You would have seen the scuffed soil covered with leaves on a path free of debris. If you don't use your new senses then you won't be long for this world.

Kassy carried Bertram deeper into the forest away from the path before setting up a camp with a small fire. She gave Bertram some leaves to chew which would help with the pain before foraging for herbs to make a poultice. Bertram watched her work as darkness settled around them.

'My foot and ankle are destroyed,' he choked out.

'You are not like other men anymore. You will heal quickly from this painful lesson.' Kassy was right. By midday the following day he could walk on it although it still pained him. Bertram marvelled at the difference in his wound when Kassy unwrapped his bandage. The skin was knitting back together, the bone had mended and popped back into its rightful place when he began to take steps.

'Will my wounds always heal this fast?' Bertram asked.

Wounds to extremities heal faster than ones to vital areas. Only with rest will your accelerated healing take place, so never be so foolish as to think you can't be killed.'

Just before midnight on the fifth night, they reached the ridiculously large hill that overlooked Fallon's March. Kassy began to skirt its base, which would add another chime or more to their destination.

'Kassy, we need to go up this hill. It is one of the many natural marvels around Fallon's March.'

Kassy eyed Bertram suspiciously, then continued onwards. Although the last five days had allowed them time together to get to know each other, he knew she still nursed a deep hatred for his involvement in the death of her family. There would be little or no trust now, and maybe forever.

'We have come this far together. Let me show you what my people call Heaven's Reach,' Bertram called after her as he began heading up the hill. When he glanced back, he noted with a smile Kassy had fallen in behind him.

They plodded slowly to the summit, where Bertram slid the heavy pack from his chafed shoulders. Below them spread out Fallon's March, alight with firefly glows from the many houses. Aspre was in the last quarter moon visible above them. Bertram watched Kassy stand at the summit, staring first up at the moon and then down over the town far below. Then her face broke into the first smile he had seen her offer.

'It's better on full-moon nights when the moon seems close enough to pluck like ripe fruit. My mother showed me this spot when I was younger.'

'So, this is Fallon's March. It's so alive and beautiful,' she said, inhaling deeply, then stiffened.

'I can feel it. My spirit ball down there. There is confusion surrounding it as this Samual is not sure how to use it against me.'

Chapter 17

'How do you know that?'

'It's been almost a month since it was taken. When they learn how to use it, I won't be able to resist the call. I pray they will not figure it out soon.' They stayed on Heaven's Reach to share a meal of cold fowl, fruit, and the remainder of the honeyed wine, eating in silence. Bertram had that light-headed, energetic feeling he got when returning home from his travels, but this time would be different. He didn't know what he was returning to. Kassy had confirmed that the Lords and Dames were still within the town, so what did that mean for his father? Could he be in danger?

As Bertram sat looking down at his hometown, his mood became morose as the thought kept drifting to the change he had undergone.

'You are thinking of your family?'

'If I have learned anything over the last few months, it is that my life could never be what it had been before. I long to see my father, but I worry what his reaction will be when he finds out his only son is not only less than his expectations but now not even a man. Do you think when this is all over I can go back to my life?'

'For a time, yes. Until those close to you begin to notice the differences. Your increased strength, fine-tuned senses, disappearing for days at a time, and how you are affected by the moon, to mention only some. Eventually, you will be forced to leave,' Kassy replied, eyes glowing golden in the night.

'I could explain…'

'No, Bertram. People fear what they don't understand. It is better you leave them with fond memories of you.'

'Magic then. I could find someone to reverse my condition. Will you help me?'

'I am only interested in getting back what is mine. Once I have the spirit ball, I will be gone from here, maybe even back to my island home, where I will rebuild my pack. I know now we were too weak and won't make that mistake again. What you do means little to me,' Kassy said, cold eyes on his as she flung a bone off the summit.

'You said we were pack!' Bertram said, trying to keep the anger out of his voice.

'Yes, I said that, and it's true if you submit to me, acknowledge my leadership. Maybe even join me where I'm going. If not, then I will abandon you.'

Bertram lay back on the grass, attempting to sort out his muddling thoughts. The conversation had done nothing to halt the gloom he felt settling upon him.

The intruder stirred behind his eyes with a soft laugh.

'She doesn't care about us. She will use us, maybe even be the death of us, unless we act. We only have each other, Bertram.'

Bertram couldn't say how long they stayed there beneath the stars and was only roused from his rest when Kassy crept over to him.

'We need to find a suitable lair; can you suggest anywhere?'

The ideal place came to mind immediately.

'The adjoining estate to my father's lands is owned by old man Dufell, who is nearly dead. His family is long gone, and he lives there alone. There is an old windmill with a cellar that is partially damaged. The mill itself doesn't work but has two chambers atop one another. I think this might be our best choice. It is close to my home too, which will allow me to check on my father.'

They skirted the town before dawn could awaken its occupants. The mill was situated beside the Gelded River with an uncleared field behind it that stretched to the forest's edge. The mill was old and run down, but that mattered little to Kassy, who was delighted with the cellar that still had a functional door that could be bolted from within. Too tired from their travel to explore farther, they bedded down with the rats and slept until morning. The next day the repairs began in earnest. Bertram had never been a hands-on man, but he easily finished the repairs on the inside of the mill. He

Chapter 17

found plenty of tools still in the mill as well as fairly good timber stocks, and together they built a viewing platform from which to see anyone approaching the mill. Then they began the most important change, a hidden exit from the cellar so they wouldn't become trapped in there should enemies find them. Before the change, Bertram would have been easily exhausted with the physical work. Now he easily carried timber or dug away soil for the tunnel without tiring.

While searching for other valuables they could use in this new den, Bertram found the jagged piece of a mirror, and he used it to examine himself. His hair was longer now, and a dirty-blond colour had a silver streak behind his left ear, which is where he had taken a hit to the skull. His skin, always which had been pale, was now a more almond colour, and his eyes had a slight golden tinge. He had been quite lean; now his body had taken on more muscle. If any similarity to his old self remained, it could be said he was a distant relative of Bertram, nothing more. This gave Bertram an idea that he could use to enter Fallon's March without his true identity being discovered.

They used black dye found in the store to colour his hair. Unfortunately, the silver streak remained since the dye wouldn't catch, so they left it, but cut the hair short, making him appear older. When he looked in the glass again after they had made the changes the image of himself blurred, then another seemed to materialise, this one with facial hair, strange, elongated ears, and jagged teeth. Bertram tore his eyes away. The intruder filled his mind with laughter.

They finished the escape tunnel within another three days, disguising the exit point with a small wooden shed. During this time the intruder appeared content to sit back within Bertram's mind as he worked, hunted, and helped turn the mill into their makeshift home.

Chapter 18

'I need to go to my father's manor just to look in on him. Nothing more,' Bertram said, as Kassy sat mending her clothes. 'I won't talk with him or the servants, but I need to see he is okay before we start our plans.'

Kassy searched his face and stared at him blankly.

'Is there anything I could say that would dissuade you in this, Bertram?'

'No. I need to know my father is alive and well, and that will be enough,' he replied.

'And if he isn't?'

The question caught Bertram by surprise. 'I had not considered that,' he confessed.

'It's settled then. I will come with you,' she said, 'but it's only to see how your father is. Then we return here no matter what. Is that clear?'

They left after midnight when the awareness of most people would be at its lowest. Kassy took her fox form as they meandered through the fields and onto Arlo's land, approaching the manor from behind near the small barracks Martin kept for his guards. On any night that Bertram could remember, soft music would be heard coming from the barracks, along with the sound of jesting. On this night the barracks were dark and silent, which brought a sense of foreboding to Bertram that he tried unsuccessfully to shake off.

Chapter 18

'There should be men in there, my father's hired guardsmen,' he whispered to Kassy. She motioned for him to bypass the barracks and head to the manor, where light from the dining room, library, and Arlo's room showed, but the rest of the building was wrapped in darkness. They skulked forward, and Bertram also noted the absence of the hounds his father kept that roamed around the manor freely. Their absence this night may be a good thing, he thought, since now they were a danger to him.

He nodded to the manor and motioned that he was going to approach the window that looked in at the library on the ground floor. Kassy loped beside him.

At the side of the window against the wall, his now-keen hearing detected voices from within—muffled, but they were there. Cautiously, Bertram peeked into the room and could just see between the drawn curtains.

A figure pranced into view, and Bertram almost gasped out loud. It was Museo, naked from the waist up and wearing Arlo's generals cap as he slashed around with a rapier.

'You always said you wanted to bed someone famous, now you can. A true general not like that piece of shit Arlo upstairs,' Museo said, performing a perfect riposte with the blade.

Then Bertram saw Nix. She was drunk and unsteady on her feet as she came forward and hugged Museo from behind.

'My general, you are so brave, and yet you perform one duty so poorly. Am I to bed the common men that guard this manor when it is a general's tactics I desire?'

Museo turned around, breaking free of the grip Nix had caught him in, then lifted her onto the map table, scattering books, scrolls, and maps to the floor.

'I guess a brief break from warmongering would be quite okay, my lady.' He giggled, then tore the dress from her upper body. With a squeal, Nix lay down.

Bertram had seen enough and turned away, slipping down the wall to a sitting position, his mind reeling.

Kassy was by his side. 'Bertram, someone comes. Quickly move back here,' she said and practically dragged him back behind a hedge.

The door opened out onto the back porch and the tall figure of Elspeth emerged, dressed in a long, white gown. The darkness gave her a ghostly look.

As he stood peering out into the night, Bertram could see Elspeth looked weary. He noticed then she held a long knife in one hand as she knelt on the earth near the porch, then slashed the blade down her palm, letting blood pool in the soil beside her. 'Mother, I pay you the blood price, sustain me with your own.'

As they watched Elspeth, tendrils of green elongated from the nearby plants and wrapped around her arms, causing her to gasp as if in pain, which then turned to moans, not unlike those of ecstasy. Her skin coloured, bringing back a rosy blush to her cheeks, and the bags beneath her eyes vanished. Even her hair took on a new lustre.

As suddenly as they had come, the plant tendrils shrank away again, leaving Elspeth kneeling there. She stood, gown now soiled at the knees, and turned as someone else emerged from the manor. It was Samual. He placed an arm around her shoulder.

'Sit with me, Elspeth.'

She nodded, and they sat side by side, silently looking at each other.

'You pay a high price for your sorcery, El.'

Elspeth shrugged. 'It is the cost of power now that the Mother no longer gives her power freely, but I knew this before I made my choice,' she replied with a wan smile.

'When will you forge this pendant you told me of, the one that will allow you to be youthful again?'

Chapter 18

'I need certain ingredients that are scarce. With Arlo's wealth, it will be easier. What do we do now that we have the spirit ball?'

'There is just the matter of getting Arlo to sign his lands over to me, a distant nephew now that his beloved Bertie is no more. The old fool insists we give him proof of his son's demise before he does anything.'

'The Vixen will come. She cannot ignore the pull of the spirit ball. When she finally lays herself at my feet begging for her life, then we can strike against our enemies. Nobody will mock me then. This is our home now, El, and I will build you a sacred temple for your studies. We will recruit our own men and be a power to reckon with.'

'Master Samual, the food you requested is ready,' called a feminine voice from just within the door. A maid came out onto the porch. One side of her face was grey and yellow with bruising. She stood holding the tray, looking down at her feet nervously.

'We will eat inside, dear girl,' said Samual, helping Elspeth up with a hand. The three of them disappeared inside, and the door closed and bolted behind them.

'This is enough, Bertram. It is dangerous for us to linger here,' Kassy whispered to him as the intruder also spoke in an urgent tone.

'Seize the moment, Bertie, kill them all while they are not ready for us. We wait we die,' the intruder hissed.

Bertram followed Kassy in a crouch, ignoring the intruder's mocking laughter.

'We need to check the barracks to see if Martin and his men are still alive,' Bertram said, catching up to Kassy. 'There is death here,' whispered the intruder as Bertram tested the door. It was unlocked. Bertram entered slowly with his sabre ready. His keen night vision took in the twelve immaculately made cots, the weapons hanging on hooks, and the row of boots beside a wall. The barracks were empty of guards. Some smell drew Bertram in from a corner near the last cot, the smell of old blood, and he located a stain on the boards beneath the cot, which seemed to confirm his worst thoughts.

Outside the barracks once again, they set off through the field behind it. Up ahead, Kassy stopped and whined, which drew Bertram's attention. When he approached her, he saw what she had found, a ditch from which a godawful smell came. Fresh soil lay in mounds along the ditch, and Bertram used his sabre to scrape away some of it to reveal what lay beneath. A scrap of blue clothing showed through the disturbed soil, and Bertram reached down, seized it, and pulled it from the ground. Then he fell away with a yelp; it was attached to a body. The man had his head almost severed at the neck and the worms had eaten his eyes. Bertram stumbled away to vomit, then they set off again with him realizing that the chances that Martin lived were very slim. The Lords and Dames must have killed them all.

Back at the mill, safely in the cellar, they made hot tea to take away the chill that the night's events had left them with.

'The mage, what was her name?' asked Kassy.

'Elspeth. What about her?' Bertram said as he sipped his tea.

'She has an affinity to the earth,' she replied, looking at him as if expecting him to realise something.

'And, so what,' he replied, shrugging.

'So what? I bet that the earth is her birth element, and she only draws power from it around those she can trust, which means we now know her strengths and her weakness, which is a hell of a thing when it comes time to defeat her.'

'You are right, Kassy,' Bertram said.

'All mages have a key element which, when it matches the corresponding season, means they are at the height of their power. They also have an opposite element, which is dangerous for them because during that season their power is weaker and harder to recuperate. But it's autumn, which is the earth season, so how does this help us?'

Chapter 18

'Knowing her key element allows us to plan for the type of power she will bring against us. Or find an ally who wields the opposite power to hers.'

'I need to get my father out of there before they kill him. While he stalls on signing over his land they will keep him alive, but how long for?'

'Let's summarise what we know then. They are holding your father ransom for the land and manor. They killed all the guardsmen and have taken control of the manor. The mage, Elspeth, has earth as her birth element, and that knowledge gives us an advantage over her. Bertram, it is time for you to recruit some allies.'

Chapter 19

'Don't stay too long, Bertram. Be back by nightfall.'

'Yes, I know, and stay away from hounds or people I know too well,' Bertram finished for Kassy. He took the gold that Kassy gave him and then set out for town.

Alone now, Bertram couldn't banish the feeling of nervousness. Will somebody see through my disguise? What if I see Rae or bump into one of the servants?

'You are not alone. You have me. We are free from Kassy now. We don't even need to go back to her,' the intruder said.

'Be quiet. We need her help to save my father.'

'Kassy doesn't care about your father, you fool. She just uses us to help regain her power. We should leave while she is weak.'

'I will not abandon my father or break my vow to Kassy!'

The walking soothed Bertram, allowing him time to think about his problem and the allies he could draw to his aid. He was wise enough to realise that until the unpleasant business with the Lords and Dames was completed, it would be foolish to become involved in his old life and approach his father or friends as himself.

Fallon's March was a medium-sized town that was spreading itself at an alarming pace. There were various buildings that were being constructed, another inn, and a small military outpost at the orders of the king. The one that he was interested in was the new trader's post. Here he bought grain, crossbows with bolts, two new sabres of decent quality, coils of rope, and a collection of common utensils and anything that would make this new home more attractive and comfortable. The next stop was the tailor, where he was measured up for new clothes to replace his tattered ones. He also found a finely woven white scarf, which he purchased for Kassy.

'Oh, so now you are buying her gifts like a lovesick pup?' the intruder chortled.

Obviously not able to use his actual name, Bertram went by the name of Wren Sorenson, a name he had often used in his personal writings of fiction that nobody had ever read but himself. Bertram was tempted to go past the Cauldron but decided it was better to leave that for another day. His last part of business was at the tanners, where he came across a sign announcing two old horses for sale. He haggled a cart into the price by paying the gold right away. With the two horses and the cart loaded with supplies, Bertram started out of town towards the coast, then backtracked along the potted, little-used roads to the old mill, arriving late afternoon.

They ate a dinner of vegetables and fish that he had purchased and then sat around a small fire in the bottom room. Sated from the food and feeling for the first time comfortable since moving to the mill, Bertram lit his pipe with its new mixture.

'I have a gift for you, Kassy.'

She seemed surprised and took the package, smelling it, which made him laugh.

'Go on, open it. It won't bite you.'

Kassy tore off the wrapping and withdrew the scarf, smiling in delight at the soft wool. Then she placed it back in its wrapping and pushed it back to him.

'Don't you like it?'

'I love it, Bertram, but I don't want gifts from you now or ever.'

'It's nothing, really. I just saw it and thought it would suit you and that long, red hair.'

'We are allies by necessity, nothing more, and I don't need niceties for you to ease some of the guilt you have over the murder of my sons.'

Bertram attempted not to feel hurt by Kassy's refusal of the gift and failed, leaving them both with an uncomfortable silence during which Bertram tried to ignore the jibes of the intruder.

'I told you, idiot!'

'If this plan is going to work, you need a persona,' Kassy said breaking the silence.

'I already have done that when I went into town yesterday,' he said with a smile. 'My persona is Wren Sorenson, a distant relative of old man Dufell, whose land we are hiding on.'

'That's dangerous mentioning him to anyone. What if they check with him?'

'He lives alone and is mentally very sick. The last time someone tried to talk to him, he shot them with a crossbow. People prefer to avoid him when possible.'

When Kassy slept, Bertram sat out on the viewing platform, smoking his pipe. He was deeply worried for his father, but he realised running in there to attack the Lords and Dames would only end in his own and Arlo's death. No, he would do this the right way, and every one of them would pay.

Bertram was all dressed in his new clothes; deep-blue trousers and jacket with a long, black cloak, high, black riding boots, and a pale pink shirt. He wore several valuable rings that Kassy had given him, and a large purse hung on his belt.

'Be careful, Bertram, and don't start a fight. Just gather information on whichever Lords and Dames arrive,' she said, ignoring the low bow he gave her.

Bertram arrived by horseback using one of the old mares he had purchased with the wagon. The Cauldron was already half full,

Chapter 19

and the musicians had not begun playing yet. He headed for the entrance and Sef stepped in front of him, his ridiculously big arms crossed over his chest.

'Haven't seen you around here before,' the big man said.

'That's because I'm new in town. Is that a problem?'

'No problem, as long as you keep your hands to yourself, pay for drink and food, and don't start any fights. Is that a problem?' countered Sef as he stepped forward into Bertram's personal space.

'Look, whatever your name is, if you don't want my patronage, I will leave and tell my sponsors that this town needs another inn because the Cauldron treats customers in the worst way, and it will be easy to take their customers. Your choice, my friend. Is that a problem?'

Sef stared down at Bertram, then laughed and clapped him on the back. 'Go on inside, friend, and yes, we do welcome new guests. It's just that we are more discerning who enters after some recent problems with strangers.'

Once inside, Bertram strode confidently to the bar, pulled a gold ceta from his pouch, and tapped it impatiently on the bar top.

Dixie turned and stared at him, then purposely ignored him to serve someone else. Finally, she came over to him with a cloth and began polishing the surface of the bar.

'You keep tapping that bar top and you will never get a drink,' she snapped.

Bertram feigned indifference. 'My apologies, miss. From where I come from that's how you get the bartender's attention.'

His politeness took her back a moment, and her stern face softened. 'Well, here in my place I don't like it. Now, what can I get you, and what place in this world allows such rude behaviour?'

'I would like a fine wine, preferably red, if you have one. To answer your other question, I hail from Karfael, which certainly must be the rudest city in this miserable world. '

'Karfael? Are you a tribesman, then, because you sure don't look like one?'

'Actually, I am originally from Stormwatch, and have just returned from Karfael where my family moved some cycles ago.' He held out his hand to her. 'I am Wren Sorenson. What might your name be?'

'Folk around here call me Dixie. Now what would drag you back to this small town when you are so used to big cities, Wren?'

'Old man Dufell. Do you know him, Dixie?'

'Of course, I do, though he rarely leaves his home these days,' she replied as she polished glasses.

'Well, believe it or not, I am his nephew and have come to help him.'

Dixie's mouth literally fell open. 'Nephew? We thought he had murdered all his family long ago. Sorry, I shouldn't have said that,' she apologised. Then she looked at him again. 'I can't shake the feeling that I know you.'

Bertram sipped from the garnet-coloured wine and raised his drink to Dixie. 'I would be a lucky man if I did know you.' Then he turned on his heels and strode over to a table.

He was still sitting there alone two chimes later when Nix and Angus strolled into the establishment. At their entry, a man two tables away from Bertram whistled loudly.

'Angus, you whoreson, get me an ale and bring the rest of that purse here so I can win it from you,' shouted the man sitting behind Bertram.

At the bar, Angus grinned. When he had the drinks, he took a seat at the table with the man. Nix meanwhile stayed at the bar looking around. After a time, her gaze settled on Bertram. She sat watching him and he pointedly ignored her, so she then came over to his table.

'Hi, do you want some company?' she asked, sitting opposite him.

'These seats are taken,' Bertram replied, not meeting her gaze.

'Can't see anyone hurrying over to keep you company. I, on the other hand, am free.'

Chapter 19

'I have no money for a whore,' Bertram said, as he motioned her away with a wave of his hand.

'I am no whore, you piece of shit!'

'Well, stop acting like one,' Bertram spat back at her. Nix regarded him for a moment, then stormed off to the bar again.

Bertram needed to be rid of Nix, which was why he had been so rude. Not only had it felt good to treat her like that, but it left him alone so he could overhear what was going on at the table behind him where Angus sat.

By the considerable amount of gold on the table Bertram realised they were playing cards for big money. Angus did have a vice then, a contradiction to how strict Angus had been about living a clean life in order to hone his warrior self. From the bar, Nix was talking with Dixie, and they were both looking over at him.

He wondered where Rae was tonight. It wasn't often that she wasn't working. Laughter, then a shout of dismay came from behind him, and he turned to look. Angus stood, hands clenched in victory, as he dragged a pile of coins towards his seat.

'I'm thinking you have cursed me, Angus. Otherwise, you're a cheating dog.'

There came the distinct sound of steel being drawn, and as Bertram watched Angus lay his blade at the other man's throat. Others in the room had noticed now and turned to watch.

'Never again call me a cheat and expect to walk away from me alive.'

'I'm sorry,' stuttered the man apologetically. 'I don't take kindly to losing, friend.'

'Maybe you should find another hobby, friend. If you can't handle losing, then stop playing,' Angus snarled. He sheathed his sword, and Bertram noticed it was still Arlo's blade that Angus had. Angus collected his winnings and went to stand over with Nix, who finished her drink. Then, with a glare at Bertram, she followed Angus out of the Cauldron. Bertram followed them. He acknowledged Dixie with a curt nod, then trailed slowly behind them. As he waited for a servant to bring his horse, Bertram listened to the conversation between Angus and Nix, keeping himself out of sight.

'Are we going back to the manor now, Angus?' asked Nix hopefully.

'Not yet, Nix. The night is young, and I have much coin to win. I'm going to the blacksmith. Earl is having a few rounds.'

'C'mon, Angus, let's go back to the manor…'

She stopped suddenly as Angus turned on her. 'Look here, Nix, I'm not your man or your father. Just fuck off back to the manor for all I care or come and make yourself useful,' he growled at her.

'If I come, can I keep some of the winnings? I can show some thigh and much more cleavage and make sure all the men have full ales in front of them,' she asked clasping her hands together in front of her.

'Yes, of course you can come Nix, and I'm sorry I raised my voice, but this entire trip is getting on my nerves, and I long to be gone from here. Samual, as you know, has other plans.'

'Here is your horse, sir,' said the stable boy, making Bertram flinch because he was concentrating on trying to hear the rest of the conversation between Angus and Nix.

Bertram made a show of trying to mount his horse, pretending to be drunker than he was, and the stable boy helped push him up onto the beast, only for Bertram to fall over the other side. He couldn't go yet until Angus and Nix had moved away.

Out of the corner of his eye, Bertram saw Sef lumber over, laughing. 'Let's get your sorry ass up on that horse there, friend. We don't want your sponsor to think we took ill care of you. Have you got a problem with that?'

'The only problem I got is that you are looking mighty fine for an ugly woman,' Bertram said, affecting an excellent imitation of a slur.

'Touch my ass and I'll kill ya,' Sef said with a laugh. Then he slapped the horse's rump, and it took off, nearly running down Angus and Nix, who jumped aside.

Chapter 19

'Bloody fool, watch yourself!' Angus yelled after him, and Bertram cursed at how close he had come to an altercation with the warrior, which he couldn't afford to do just yet, or it would ruin all their plans.

Bertram let the horse carry him away out of sight, then he doubled around back to the smithy where Earl, who had served with Arlo, lived. He knew Earl loved to gamble, and as Bertram tied his mount to a tree behind the house, an idea formed in his mind about how he could deal with Angus.

He hid, listening to the small talk of the men already gathered for the gambling. There were five local farmers and Earl, and they laughed at how they would show this traveller up and take his gold and how city folks didn't know the real specifics of the game they were going to play. Bertram stayed there until he heard voices approach along the road, then positioned himself to listen as Earl greeted Angus and Nix.

After the introductions, the man spoke again. 'The girl cannot sit here beside you, Angus unless she is playing.'

'Nix, you heard the smith. Make yourself useful and bring the drinks when we need them,' Angus said with a touch of dismissive arrogance in his tone. 'That is, if it's okay with the rest of you, of course,' Angus said.

'Will give me more time to separate you from your gold, stranger,' Bertram heard Earl say. 'There is a spiked barrel of ale inside the back room there, as well as spare ale pots.'

'I don't know who you men think you are, but I'm not some serving wench, you know,' came Nix's voice and the sound of stamping feet walking away.

Bertram knew he needed a better position to see what was going on. He climbed the tree that huddled over and around the shed, behind which he hid. Ever so slowly, he slid up through the branches until it afforded him an unobstructed view of the game.

'Fiery lass you got there, Angus. Sure you can handle her?' one man asked.

'Ha, you think she's with me? Nothing more than a travelling companion, my friends—a pretty one, to be sure, but that's all. I have a wife waiting for me back in Stormwatch who would cut the nuts from my body if I was to go around bedding other women.'

This brought a ripple of laughter from the men.

'So, you're telling me that this pretty Nix with you is free for the taking?' asked one man.

'Yes, but let me tell you about her, friend. She is a feisty, jealous filly who loves being bedded, but if you try to tie her down and marry her, then she is the wrong girl for you,' warned Angus.

'You make her sound better and better by the word, Angus.'

'I hope you gentlemen are not talking about me,' said Nix as she strolled back to the men carrying a tray of tankards, allowing a view of her cleavage as she bent over to place the drinks before the men. 'You know it's rude to talk about someone when they are not around to defend themselves, right?'

The ale flowed, the cards were dealt, and by the reactions of the other men, Angus was doing very well from the start. The ale dulled wits, Bertram, who had to try harder to keep quiet in his uncomfortable hiding place, now saw the scheme take another turn. As Nix delivered more ale or removed empty tankards, she would take a glance at another player's cards, and then, while retreating to the house, send quick hand signals to Angus that Bertram couldn't understand, but the meaning was obvious.

One farmer flung his cards down on the table, then followed that with a handful of coins.

'That's me then. Angus has masterfully destroyed my savings, and now I must return home so my wife can kill me,' he said and then stumbled away.

Soon, it was just down to Angus and Earl. The others were out too, and one was trying his hardest to pry Nix away into the

Chapter 19

house, but she kept dodging away playfully. It was easy to tell that the smith was losing the game from the simple, relaxed image of Angus, who almost looked bored. Earl, meanwhile, was biting his lip, and one leg moved up and down as he tried to outplay Angus.

Nix stood behind Earl and suddenly grabbed the farmer, who had been harassing her. She pulled his face down into her bosom and leaned forward to see Earl's hand, then made a quick hand gesture to Angus as she giggled from the farmer's muffled cries. Earl turned to glare at Nix and the farmer.

'Do you two bloody well mind? I am trying to win my gold back from this soulless leprechaun!'

As soon as Earl turned away, Angus shook his left sleeve, and Bertram saw cards fall into his hand. So that was how he was doing it. He had an extra deck, which could only mean that for the scam to succeed, he needed to use his own cards.

Bertram had seen enough. He climbed down the tree without giving himself away. Once on the ground, he turned to sneak back to his horse and saw a hound staring at him, its tail straight, ears pricked, hackles rising. It was not much older than a pup. Bertram circled away as the pup slinked closer, sniffing the air and whining.

A whistle came from near the house. 'Here boy, come back here,' followed by three more quick whistles. The pup whined again, looking from Bertram to the house, then back. Bertram knelt and picked up a clump of wood which he hurled at the animal, striking it on the back leg. The pup gave a yelp and then took off back to the house, allowing Bertram to retrieve his horse and ride away. That had been close, and if the pup had been an adult, then Bertram could have been caught. He needed to remember the danger hounds now provided him.

'It was only a pup, no match for us,' came the unwanted commentary from the intruder.

'I know that! If we killed everything like you seem to want, we would be found out. Now be quiet.'

Chapter 20

As he neared the mill, Bertram could see Kassy crouched up on the lookout; long, twisted locks of red framing golden eyes. They drank hot tea while Bertram filled her in with the details, trying not to leave out a thing as she watched him intently. When he had finished his retelling, she regarded him coolly, and he felt she was not happy with the night's events.

'You play a dangerous game, Bertram. These people, as we both know, are not the type to be trifled with or treated so casually.'

'I was of the opinion I was going to the Cauldron to make the acquaintance of whichever Lords and Dames showed up as Wren Sorenson. They have seen me, nothing more. Was I wrong then?'

'Cut the spoiled brat tone, Bertram, and wipe the sour look from your face. Tonight was to observe only. To find a weakness that could be exploited, that is all!'

'Well, I achieved that and more, Kassy. Now I know that their best warrior does indeed have a weakness for gambling, and he is damn good at both it and the art of deceit. I watched the little scam Angus and Nix played out as they won the savings of the farmers and the smith. So, what is your issue?'

Kassy threw her hands in the air. 'What would have happened if they had found you out or if the pup was a full-grown hound?'

'But none of that happened, Kassy. I am here, safe, and well.'

'I was just worried, Bertram. Like it or not, we share a bond where I can detect changes within you, and I was aware of your fear. I just expected the worst,' Kassy said as she brushed her hair, staring back at him. 'You risked our plan being discovered. This is not a game!'

'Okay, I was a little reckless. I'm not used to lurking around in the dark. Next time I will be more careful.'

They were silent for a time, the uneasy silence between two people who had nothing in common except the circumstance that had been thrust upon them. It was a silence shared where they were both becoming to know one another, but on which no trust had been built. Maybe it was the only bond they could expect.

'What do we do with this information when neither of us are gamblers?' Kassy said.

'I have an idea that may just work. For it to work, I need to call on someone who owes my father a debt. It is time to call in the favours my family has so gracefully dished out over the last cycles.'

The next day Bertram set out on foot for the Lyre family home, a wealthy family who lived in a manor in the hills on the other side of town. Gerald Lyre had been one of the most trusted officers under the command of Arlo when Scuttle had fought with Cavere. He had personally helped deliver Arlo back to his estates following his crippling injury. The man was of questionable integrity and had a hand in most criminal schemes in the town. Gerald had returned from the war wealthy beyond reason and had quickly become known as a hard man who would fund the locals of Fallon's March in their personal pursuits—for a fee, of course. He often protected the town's folk and mediated disputes—for a cost, of course. Some took this help, seeing it as a simple way to meet their means, but when they failed to hold up their end of the deals, they were quickly made examples of. The Lyre family was both loved and hated in the area and though Arlo had and still loved Gerald, he had warned Bertram not to get involved with the man or his large family.

The first problem was convincing Gerald that he was indeed Bertram Paxton.

The day was cloudless, not hot, making travel a delight. Even the intruder within him revelled in the freedom of the wild again. By setting out early, Bertram would make the Lyre estate before the noontime chime.

The Lyre manor stood upon the highest of the hills near Fallon's March, even higher than Heaven's Reach, which was in sight from the Lyre estate. Stone walls surrounded the manor. They were fitted with long spikes on the top and manned day and night. Gerald was a suspicious man, which had more than once seen him come out on top during dangerous confrontations. Arlo had once let slip that Gerald ran a strong thief guild in Stormwatch, which he controlled from his estate where those in his employ were trained.

Bertram did not bother trying to hide his approach, since the Lyre family would well know of it, anyway. Although Bertram felt the need for urgency so they could rescue Arlo, he counselled himself against hurrying. Still coming to terms with the changes that had come upon him, he needed to clear his head and try to focus on doing things right the first time. There was no room for error. He would go to Gerald and spill out everything that had happened to Arlo, then use gold to get Gerald to use his men to storm his home, and rescue Arlo. The price would be high, and Bertram wasn't sure he was willing to pay the heavy price Gerald would demand on top of the favour he owed. The favour was owed to Arlo, not himself, and Bertram knew he could not assume the Lyre lord would even honour the debt unless it was Arlo himself who presented at his gate.

They approached Bertram before he made it so far as the gate. Riding hard on drakes that were the preferred choice of mount in the hills and grasslands around Fallon's March. There were twelve

Chapter 20

riders in all, wearing clothing free of any family heirloom that approached him. The formidable drakes hissed at Bertram until their riders slapped flanks with heels to stop them. They surrounded him, and one dismounted as Bertram raised his hands to show he was no threat.

'Seems if you are looking for Fallon's March, you are way off track, stranger,' the man said, standing at ease opposite Bertram.

'I'm not lost. I know where I am headed, and it is indeed the Lyre manor,' Bertram responded.

'May I remove my pipe while we talk?' Bertram asked, and when he got the nod, he did so slowly and offered his mixture bag once his pipe was filled.

The man whom Bertram knew was one of the Lyre sons accepted, and the two of them sat facing each other, smoking quietly.

'This is all very pleasant, stranger, but the day passes us by while we sit here. What business do you have with my family?'

'Your father will know me. I am a local, although because of necessity I am disguised to protect my identity.'

'That does not help me in making sure you are not an enemy wishing my father and our house harm,' chuckled the man, drawing a mouthful of smoke and blowing smoke rings that drifted away on the wind.

'Our fathers served together for Scuttle in the fight against Cavere. He would have come himself but sent me in his stead due to unfortunate circumstances that have come upon our family. I cannot divulge my true identity to you, and for that, I apologise. Bind me and gag me if you wish, but I must speak to Gerald. It is a matter of honour over a called-in debt.'

'This is becoming very interesting. My father has no owed debts that I am aware of, and you are obviously unwilling to reveal your identity. What is stopping me from sending you away with your tail between your legs?'

'The Lyre family and your father's honour is well known in these parts. The bond he shares with my father was forged with iron, blood, and loss, which makes my petition more than just an average request. I know Gerald doesn't like to have others in his debt, and he will be happy to clear it from his conscience.'

'Stand, then, mysterious stranger, and place any weapons on the ground, then place your hands out for binding,' the man said, standing back up.

Bertram did as instructed, and another man bound his hands with rope, then gagged him. Finally, they placed a sack over his head, and he felt himself pulled up onto the back of one of the drakes.

The short ride was uncomfortable, and Bertram was afraid. Now he was helpless, but it was too late to reconsider this meeting. He would soon be in the lair of a dangerous man.

They left him in a room with a fire. Bertram could feel its heat as sweat not only from the fire but also from fear dripped down his face, and he struggled to contain his laboured breathing beneath the hood. The strange thing he realised as he sat there, bereft of sight, was that he could hear well—no, better than well — and it brought his thoughts briefly back to the previous night as he spied on Angus with his gambling friends. His hearing was incredibly sharp. He had always had great hearing and the conversation with Kassy about everybody now having an affinity with one of the elements of nature played on his mind. He had loved the wind more so lately, which made him feel at his most free. He had been born in the spring months, the air element, so maybe there was some affinity between the winds

and himself, but what and how to find out, he didn't know. What he knew in that moment as fear threatened to freeze the blood that ran through his veins was that he could hear a lot and distinguish the differences in sounds that came to him from the manor.

Chapter 20

Somewhere someone chopped food on a wooden cutting board. In a room to his right, two people coupled while below them a servant was being corrected for her lax behaviour.

Footsteps approached. Someone in hard boots and one in soft, maybe slippers. The door opened on silent hinges; the slippers stopped before him, and whoever it was, a man by the sounds of it, coughed.

'Remove the sack from his head, Joseph, we are not barbarians,' said a clear, concise voice that hinted at a well-educated man.

They pulled the sack clear of Bertram's head, revealing a man before him with clear, brown eyes and a beard down to his chest. He was frowning as he regarded Bertram. 'Take off the damn gag then get the poor man a towel. He is practically dehydrating before my eyes from the sack you idiot, Joseph.'

'We didn't know if he was a danger to us, Father. You're always preaching caution with strangers.'

'I suppose you are right. Oh, and get him fresh water after you remove his ropes.'

'Is that a good idea, Father?'

'Would you like to discuss this with me later?' the man replied, turning an uncompromising look at his son, who practically ran from the chamber after he removed the ropes binding Bertram's arms.

Behind the man whom Bertram knew was Gerald stood two men similarly bearded and looking unamused.

'Are you okay?' Gerald asked Bertram as he pulled a chair closer to sit on.

'Considering the situation, yes, I am. I asked to come here fully aware of the implications,' Bertram said, wiping his face on his sleeve.

'My sons tell me you come to request I fulfill a debt owed to your father. Is this true?'

'It is and let me introduce myself. I am Bertram Paxton.'

Gerald sat back and almost comically blew air from his mouth in a whoosh. 'Paxton. Now that's a name I haven't heard for some time,' he said thoughtfully. 'Go on.'

'My father, Arlo, was a commanding officer with you in the Cavere campaign.' Bertram let that information sink in, and then fresh water and a towel arrived, which Bertram used before continuing. 'Trouble has beset our house, and we need your aid in a few matters, which is why I am here.'

'How is Arlo these days?'

'Crippled yet strong of heart and mind as much as always,' said Bertram after he drank down the cool water.

Gerald smiled. 'We always joked that he would use magic to restore his legs once the Severing had ended and magic returned.'

'If you know my father at all, you also know how much he mistrusts magic. He refuses to acknowledge it could help with his crippled legs.'

'Well, that at least explains why he isn't here himself,' Gerald said. 'I only ever saw you as a young boy. Now you don't look like him though, so how can you prove he is your father and you are not some impostor bent on causing strife between our families?'

'You pulled Arlo from the wreckage of a collapsed building, then carried him on your back across the battlefield to safety. When he was left to rot in a military makeshift hospital, you came back for him, just like you said you would, and personally delivered him home to his wife and teenage son. He referred to you as the shield and the goddamned luckiest man he ever knew. '

'Anyone could have gotten that information from a conversation with Arlo? You are going to have to do better than that! Risking my scrawny ass to save Arlo that day paid the debt in kind, don't you think?'

'Yes, it paid the first debt for when he paid a small fortune to have you released from the dungeon of Acclaro after a powerful merchant found you in bed with his wife.'

Chapter 20

Gerald eyed him with interest now. 'Go on.'

'He told me the second debt you owed him still was because he lied and vouched for you when you killed a certain general who was intent on seeing the regiment you both commanded killed to the very man just so he could rise up through the ranks and take credit for the outstanding achievements you both commanded on the field. Without his help, you would have been hung right there in Cavere like a mere criminal.'

'And your mother?'

'Ran off not long after Arlo returned a cripple. She could not deal with his affliction and sought a better life.'

'If you are who you say, who and where is your brother?'

'Tal would have been my elder brother. He died in childbirth, which also played a part in my mother leaving us,' said Bertram, knowing full well he was being tested. Few besides his family knew of Tal, and at Bertram's words, Gerald appeared to relax.

'Joseph, have food brought to the balcony. Our friend Bertram is true of word and a trusted man in my eyes.'

They retired to the balcony that afforded a wonderful vista on Fallon's March far below.

'Arlo told me of you, Bertram. He was wonderfully proud of the scholarly talents you showed and constantly feared for your safety while we were on campaign. Tell me of the problems that now beset you and my oldest friend.'

'I have had a part in my father's strife. I brought a group of unsavoury folk to our door, and when they couldn't be forced from my home, I agreed to help in a quest for an item of power. I was stupid and was used as a decoy to bypass a guardian, which nearly killed me.' He pulled his shirt up to show the myriad of scars that now creased his chest and abdomen. 'Now I would have my revenge and see my father, who is kept hostage in his own manor, freed. The manner of revenge, however, is important in that they die knowing at the end that I still live.

'This group goes by the name Lords and Dames. They are currently holed up in our manor where they keep Arlo captive until he signs all his land and assets over to them.'

'The one named Angus Strongblade is truly a fearsome and cunning warrior with a love of gambling. He has already had a hand in parting coin from many of the honest Fallon folk, but grows bored, looking for a better challenge. I understand you have an unmatched gambler in your family whose prowess borders the legendary. I would ask for his help in leaving this enemy of mine with a debt that cannot be repaid.'

As cheese, wine and olives were brought out on a platter, Gerald indicated they would eat before discussing this terrible business further.

With bellies full they sipped wine, and finally the conversation returned to the task at hand.

'You present me with two tasks, Bertram. My debt is repaid in one. What can you offer me that will balance the remaining one?'

'As you know, Arlo is not short of coin, and yet I see that is of little value to you. My services are sadly lacking, unless you require my scholarly talents.'

Silence sat between them as Gerald pondered Bertram over his wine. 'My men tell me you now have a thriving crop of wraith plants on Arlo's land, close to the road to Fallon's March. Wraith is in high demand among the nobility these days and greatly interests me. The profit from that field and being able to splice the established trees to grow my own would save me considerable time and trouble. I would require the handing over not only of that crop near to harvest but also the land it grows on.'

'If I may be so forward with you, Gerald, my father has always made it plain the land the wraith sits on is never to be for sale. He has plans for that land. Could I maybe offer that we will farm the wraith and deliver it to your lands every harvest for the next five cycles?'

Chapter 20

'You bargain when the life of your father hangs in the balance?'

'Because of my father's condition, he has planned for that bountiful crop to fund his retirement and set our house up for the foreseeable future. Should I give the land along with his prize crop away, I fear he will choke the very life from me.' Bertram shrugged apologetically. He sat back, knowing well that everything hinged on Gerald's next reaction.

Gerald burst out laughing, and when his mirth subsided, he regarded Bertram with glittering eyes. 'I could just see him doing such a thing to you, and I fear he would also attempt to do likewise to me as well, even if I am a trusted friend. Make it seven cycles of wraith and you have a deal, young man.'

Bertram could have yelled with joy but restrained himself.

'Joseph, get the knife and brazier. We will bind this deal in the old way.'

Gerald took an engraved blade bearing his family's insignia of an eagle. He cut Bertram's inner forearm with the blade and then passed a bottle of spirits to Bertram, who drank deeply. Then with expert skill, Gerald cauterised the wound with the hot metal and finished by pouring the spirits over it to cleanse the angry, swollen cut before bandaging it.

Bertram then returned the favour, trying to blot out the pain that now flared over his arm, making him feel ill. When the ungodly business was finally finished, they both chewed some sort of root that took the edge from the pain.

As Gerald walked Bertram to the gate of the manor, Bertram asked him for one last favour.

'This warrior has my father's blade; could I ask that it finds its way back into my hands so I may return this most trusted memory of his service?'

'Let it be so, Bertram. That blade is a part of your father himself, and nobody else is worthy in my eyes to wield it. My man will meet you in the town tomorrow evening at the Cauldron. You won't know him until he reveals my family insignia on his arm. Now travel safely. Are you sure I cannot get transport for you?'

'I appreciate the gesture, Gerald, but I find myself relishing the trek ahead to clear my mind. Thank you. It means much to me that you are as honourable as my father said you were.'

Bertram began the long walk back to the mill. He was not sure at which point he began running. He could hear his heartbeat rising, matched by that of the intruder within, its presence behind his eyes. He felt joy at his minor victory, wanting to shout it to the corners of the world. All that came out was a long howl of unbridled power. Then he was loping on four legs across the fields and forest, all his senses alive.

The taste of blood and meat brought Bertram back. It was almost dark, and he was in the forest. It took him a moment to realise he recognised this area as being close to the mill. His clothes were gone, leaving him naked and kneeling beside a deer carcass with gore covering his hands and arms as he chewed rich meat. The intruder had taken him over.

It laughed from within as he realised this.

'Twist this all you want, Bertie, but you didn't even fight me. You wanted to run free just as much as I did. We ran, we feasted, nothing more.'

Bertram, feeling revulsion now, forced the meat down his throat, then stumbled away to the edge of the woods towards the mill, torn between losing control and the memory of that feeling of total release.

Once again, Kassy was waiting for him when he arrived at the mill. Her face showed no emotion as she looked over at him, but she said nothing. Once inside, Kassy fetched water for him to bathe.

When he was clean again, they sat at the table and he explained with unveiled excitement the news that the Lyre family would help them.

Chapter 20

'Aren't you angry with me?' he finally asked, broaching the unspoken topic of his losing control.

'It is your battle, Bertram. I can only try to guide you. The rest is up to you.'

'Wil you come to the Cauldron with me tonight?'

'I long to join you in the hunt, Bertram, but to expose myself so soon would be foolish,' she said, with frustration and fire burning in her eyes.

'You have your magic, though. Isn't there some way you can disguise yourself that way?'

'It's true I could do that, but without my spirit ball, my powers are weakened. If I am exposed, then we lose the opportunity to surprise them.'

They stayed up late plotting Bertram's next move when he met with Gerald's man. Bertram found it difficult to sleep now their plans were underway. He finally found rest when Kassy, whose eyes seemed to be alight with unearthly fire, came and curled up beside him.

Chapter 21

Bertram was waiting at the Cauldron when Sef opened the double doors for business. The big man eyed him and then broke into a big smile, showing a few missing teeth.

'You again? Don't you have somewhere else to sit your lazy ass, Wren?'

'Couldn't resist seeing your winning smile again, my big friend. It makes my spirit soar to realise that there is someone out there who is uglier than myself,' Bertram said, returning the insult.

Bertram strode inside expecting to see Dixie and instead found himself eye to eye with Rae. It startled him more than he thought seeing her would.

'What are you staring at so rudely?' she asked with a touch of defiance. 'Haven't you ever seen a beautiful woman before?'

'My apologies. You just reminded me of someone I once knew. I didn't mean to be so rude.'

'Apology accepted. What's your poison then?' she asked, more relaxed now.

Where once Bertram would have ordered a strong drink, he now found the thought nauseating and wondered whether it may be a side effect of the changes he was undergoing.

'Nothing but hot food, preferably meat, if you have it, and a pitcher of chilled water with lemon,' he replied, still feeling uneasy at talking with Rae.

Chapter 21

Rae raised her eyebrows at his order. 'It's rarely we get a customer who prefers not to choose beverages that would addle his thoughts in here, but everyone to their own, I suppose,' she remarked as he tipped coins in her outstretched hand.

'Business meetings like the one I have tonight require a level head lest I lose any advantage in negotiations if you must know.'

When Rae returned from the kitchen, she had the water. 'The meat is fresh mutton, killed today, but still quite bloody at the moment, I'm afraid,' Rae said regretfully.

'That's fine by me. I like my meat to be quite rare.'

'Fine, I will bring it to your table,' Rae replied, heading once again towards the kitchen.

Bertram chose a table where he could see the bar and the front entrance to the establishment and settled in to wait for his contact.

The food when it came was fresh as promised, slathered in rich onion gravy, and sided with potato and green beans. Bertram had to force himself, with his heightened taste and smell, to eat slowly instead of wolfing the food down.

Bertram had practically licked the plate clean when Rae came to collect it. There were only a handful of other patrons still a chime later. As Bertram was wondering why the patronage was so light this evening, he remembered the upcoming spring festival. He knew from experience that most of the Fallon folk would be hard at work preparing their goods or withholding their coin for the festivities in five days' time.

He finally ordered an ale he had already decided against drinking as he waited, feeling tense as each moment passed. He need not have worried, though; soon after, a man casually strolled in with a calm confidence about him, for all appearances looking like a trader. He was dressed in grey trousers and a blue shirt with a short, black cloak, boots of the finest leather, and a hat to match the cloak. His outfit screamed of wealth as he leaned against the bar, looking around. When his eyes briefly met Bertram's and then looked away, Bertram thought maybe this was not Gerald's man after all.

The man flirted a while with Rae, which actually made Bertram a little jealous, and then with a tankard of ale, he ambled over to Bertram's table.

'Name's Archie, and if I'm correct you must be Wren Sorrenson,' he said, removing his hat and smoothing brown hair tinged with silver at the temples. He slid back the cuff of his shirt to show the emblem of an eagle, the family crest of Gerald.

'I am he and am pleased to make your acquaintance. Ah...'

'Just Archie. Gerald has said you require my considerable talent for breaking a man. Tell me what you know, Bertram, my time is of the essence. I have a family awaiting my return.'

'He goes by the name of Angus Strongblade, but I don't know his family name. A Scuttle native that hails from Stormwatch, Angus is highly trained in the arts of warfare and dedicates himself to it with a quiet fervour, just like his only other love, gambling. He doesn't drink or use any type of drugs and is not swayed by the attention of women. Angus is bored with the lack of talented gamblers in this town and longs for some true competition. He is a part of a group called the Lords and Dames, so be aware of his companions. One named Nix is a flirtatious young lady of eye-catching beauty to distract other gamblers while she gives him the signs so he may know their hands when playing cards, his chosen game,' explained Bertram.

'And your wishes, Wren?'

'I hope to see him lose and, knowing it will bruise his ego, ask for a chance to win back his lost coin, only to have the stakes raised to a level where he cannot pay the debt. When he loses, I would see him given over to the Lyre family to be broken before he knows of my involvement. He has a blade stolen from my father, which I want returned to my care,' finished Bertram.

Chapter 21

For a long moment, Archie just stared at Bertram without flinching or showing any sign of his thoughts at all. 'I must confess I am now interested in knowing what this Angus has done to merit such devilish attention from you, Wren. You don't appear to be the type to hold a grudge.'

'Everybody has their limit, Archie. I have reached mine, and now he must pay for the hurt he brought me and my family. How will you get his attention?' asked Bertram.

'Each evening I will present myself here asking about him and putting out the word that I want a challenger with the heart to come test my skill. If he is, as you say, a man led by his own considerable ego, then he will not turn down the challenge. You will play my acquaintance in the matter, a business partner in certain circles. You will let me take the lead in this matter and act as my second to witness our games, which gives you plenty of reason to be present. Should things go wrong, I won't be held responsible; however, you should know I have not lost a game in four cycles at cards or dice. It is as if the gods blessed me, that's if there still are any gods left. Are we clear, Wren?'

'Crystal clear,' answered Bertram.

'Well, it's settled, then. I will meet you at nightfall at the Iron Horse Inn at the opposite end of town. Do you know of it?'

'I do, Archie.'

'Good, don't tarry. My time is precious to me, and if you waste it, then our deal is over. Goodnight, Wren. I will see you tomorrow evening.'

Archie placed his hat carefully on, emptied his tankard, and left the Cauldron.

Before Bertram could leave, Rae was there with cloth in hand, wiping down the table and collecting the empty tankard, then stopped to regard him.

'I can't shake the feeling I somehow know you, Wren Sorrenson. You remind me of a friend,' Rae said as she worked.

'A mere coincidence then, my lady. I am not from these parts; however, I frequently travel the coast near the Scented Isles for business, so maybe you have seen me there sometime,' he suggested, rising from his seat.

'Not likely. Has anyone ever told you that you have the most curious eyes flecked with gold and mystery?'

'Not recently, no. Good evening to you, Rae,' he said as he walked off and immediately realised his mistake.

'How do you know my name?' she called after him, but Bertram kept on walking.

Chapter 22

Business was slow once again the following night when Bertram met Archie at the Cauldron. The Lords and Dames were also absent, so the two of them mingled and asked the whereabouts of Angus, who liked a game or two, with Archie boldly stating he could beat him easily and how he was disappointed that he had yet to meet this gambler of note.

Two days before the festival of spring, they finally had their chance when they entered the Cauldron to find not just Angus but all five of the Lords and Dames in attendance. Bertram and Archie presented themselves at the bar, both ordering ale.

Rae delivered the drinks to them and casually leant into Bertram.

'A word of caution, Wren Sorrenson. The man you have both been so liberally asking about is here with his friends. They are not to be trusted and have already caused much trouble in this town in the short time they have been here.'

'Duly noted, though I fear my friend here longs to test the mettle of one of them in cards.'

Taking their drinks, the two made their way to a nearby table.

'Shouldn't we approach them?' asked Bertram.

'No, we wait for Angus to come to us. He will seek to gain an advantage and have us show deference by coming to him. We give him nothing,' replied Archie pointedly, ignoring the looks the group had fixed on him.

It was Nix who approached them first, strolling over with that noticeable sway to her hips.

'I'm sorry,' drawled Bertram. 'I still have no need of your company, neither does my friend here.'

'It is not of my concern if you prefer a cock to the delights of a dame,' she shot back. 'My friend has heard you two have been looking for him and wishes me to ask you to join us so he may hear himself the boasts being made in his absence.' Nix ran a hand down the fine material of the embroidered shirt that Archie wore.

Archie brushed her hand away as one would an irritating fly. 'Does your friend Angus always send a woman to do his bidding?'

If looks could kill, then Archie would have certainly met his end. Nix stood a moment staring at the two of them, who blatantly ignored her and then, realising she would get nowhere, stalked away again. The waiting game began, and Bertram and Archie had a few visitors whom they had spoken to at length over the last two nights who came to see the reason Archie had not approached Angus yet.

'If Angus is indeed such a great gambler and is bored looking for a challenge, then it is his place to approach me. I have nothing to prove, you see. You all know me from around town and how I haven't lost a game of cards, dice, daggers, or feast in four cycles, and yet this guest to our town has been heard saying there is no decent challenge here. Well, if he is

true to his word, then he will challenge me since this town is my home, and Angus is the challenger.'

It was over a chime of loud veiled insults from Archie before Angus rose and made his way over to their table, looking every bit the predator.

Archie looked around as if wondering who this was. 'Can we help you? If you want the privy, it's out back through there,' he said, pointing to the back exit.

Chapter 22

'I am sick of sitting there listening to you insult me,' Angus growled through clenched teeth at Archie.

'I don't even know who you are, friend.'

'Stop playing the fool, man. You know I am Angus.'

Archie made a great show of looking Angus up and down. 'Sorry, it's just that I was expecting someone a little more refined,' quipped Archie to Bertram.

Angus had his hand on his sword hilt now and had gone dangerously silent as Archie watched him with amusement. 'So already you will draw steel, eh? I would have thought such a gambler of renown as yourself could hide his emotions better. Mayhap I was wrong. What do you think Wren?'

'I think he is already rattled, Archie, and that your record has shaken him in his boots.'

Angus stared now at Bertram. 'And who is this idiot beside you?'

'He is Wren Sorrenson, my second in this matter. Do you have a second to vouch for you, Angus?'

'I do,' said Angus, looking behind him as Samual stood fluidly and came over to stand beside him.

'Then sit and be welcome. I hear you have a challenge to set me. Is this true?'

'Well, it matters not whether I am challenger of the so-called defending champion of this town,' Angus said. 'Since you are the champion, then it is up to you to tell me the rules of our pending engagement, Archie,' said Angus, looking composed now.

'Okay then, how does this sound? Two rounds, one of each our choice, and if there is no clear winner from two, then a third is to be decided by chance. You are a guest in my town, so I will give you first choice,' said Archie, all business now.

Throughout this exchange, Samual's eyes never left Bertram. Would he recognise him?

'Wren Sorrenson. My friend Nix tells me you were very rude to her. Just so you are aware, I do not take people insulting my friends well.'

'Then maybe you could keep her on a shorter leash since she is fond of attempting to force herself upon strangers who want nothing to do with her,' he replied.

'Don't push me, Wren. I know where you are staying. You are nothing to me.'

'So already you prove your uneasiness with threats, then? Would you cause a fight in public and force a forfeit on behalf of your friend Angus before he even has the chance to be embarrassed?'

Samual grew quiet after that, though he continued to stare at Bertram in an attempt to rattle him.

'I choose cards. Have you heard of a game called Peculiarity?'

'Indeed, I have, Angus. Now, to make things interesting, I would like to suggest that the two games we compete in be chosen randomly. To be fair for both of us, a travelling games caravan is in town for the upcoming festival and is managed by an old games master whose knowledge of games is unmatched. This man, Frederico Azam has experience in maintaining the rules and keeping both sides honest. He would be my choice to judge our contest. How say you, Angus?'

'I accept, and if, when we check this man out, if now or after our matches it is found out you have any type of past relationship with him, then your record is forfeit, and any win of yours overturned with the common punishment being the stronger hand of yours severed from your body. This counts for either of us found cheating as well.'

It was decided that both games would be played at the Cauldron in the room upstairs. Both men would bring a second to witness the game and give advice.

Archie smiled and winked at Bertram. 'Looks like we have a deal,' he said.

'On the morrow then, Archie. Then you shall see the calibre of man I am, as I will see who you are. May luck be with you,' Angus said, rising from his seat.

'Before you go, I would change my choice of second,' Angus said ignoring the surprised look Samual gave him.

Chapter 22

'I choose Nix as a replacement for Samual. The lass that seems to truly get under the skin of yourself and Wren both.'

This was of no surprise to Bertram who had seen how well Nix worked as a distraction to open an advantage in cards when he had spied on them at the smith's house.

Chapter 23

Word soon spread around the town regarding the upcoming games, and when Bertram arrived with Archie, they saw the Lords and Dames had already arrived. As they both entered, Angus and the others who stood at the bar turned to watch. The crowd that had gathered burst into cheers when Archie entered. Bertram had known of Archie but before this business had never met him personally, and he had also been told Archie was popular around town, a known family man who helped others less fortunate with his winnings. The support for Archie actually seemed to rattle all the Lords and Dames except Angus, who sat deadpan, sipping water.

'Great evening for a game or two, Angus,' said Archie jovially.

'Guess we will see. All this support means naught when we begin. Then it's just you and me, Archie.'

'I wouldn't have it any other way, my friend. Let's go up—oh, and order drinks or food now so it does not interfere with the game.'

A man approached dressed in fine, black clothes and a white, frilled shirt, with long, white hair tied back in a ponytail.

'Gentlemen, I am Frederico Azam, and you have petitioned me to judge over this competition. I met Angus only yesterday, and he has approved my appointment, but before we start, I must gain the approval of you, sir,' he said, talking to Archie.

'I know you only through reputation within the towns of Scuttle, Frederico, and yes, I approve of you judging this for us.'

Chapter 23

'Fine, then let us retire to the room set aside so graciously by the establishment,' Federico said as he started off up the stairs.

The room had three chairs around a circular table. Two more by the door for the seconds, Bertram and Nix. Nix was dressed in a white dress that Bertram could see had nothing beneath it. A bone corset barely held her bosom, and her face was made up in soft pink and blue that accentuated her eyes and lips. A small table sat by their two chairs with a jug of wine and two glasses.

'Can I offer you wine, Nix?' Bertram asked, playing the gentleman.

Nix feigned surprise, placing one hand on her ample chest and opening her mouth slightly as she turned to look at Bertram.

'That would be appreciated, Wren,' she said cordially, studying him as he poured for them.

At the table, Federico was placing a box on the table.

Federico stood. The room became quiet.

'This is an unusual competition that you have chosen me to judge. If you look closer you will see that the spinning wheel has sixteen equal sections. Each is labelled with a name and all are a different game except the one labelled blank. If you roll the blank you get to choose the game. None of these games are of the usual ilk to be found in gambling and all have one thing in common, the possibility of death or injury.'

Yes, you have heard me correctly folks. The stakes are high and demand that they are matched in monetary value as per both player's requests. 'Seconds place the two thousand ceta wager for the first game on the table before us.'

Bertram and Nix each placed a bag of gold cetas on the table.

'Since Angus is the challenger, he shall spin for today's game,' Federico said.

Bertram studied the room. There were no mirrors, and the curtains of the only window had been drawn. He suspected Angus and Nix had some sort of deception planned but failed to see how any ruse they had planned could be implemented when the game choice would be random.

The chair legs grated loudly on the wooden boards as Angus stood. He reached forward and spun the wheel.

'Whichever segment finishes with the arrow in it decides the game. Good luck to you both. You are going to need it.'

They all watched on as the wheel slowed to a stop.

'Puzzle boxes of Traest' Frederico declared as he invited Angus and Archie to take a look.

'This game requires time to set up. We shall take a break. Then you are all required to be back at the door, waiting for me after exactly one chime. Any absence of either four of you signals a penalty or a loss of a game if later than a quarter chime. I will see you back here soon, gentlemen.'

Without further word, Frederico scooped up the wheel and strode out of the room.

The Lords and Dames retired downstairs to a table, where they conferred in whispers, and then Elspeth rose. Bertram saw her leave by the front door. Would she be readying herself for some sort of deceptive sorcery, Bertram thought, as he watched her leave? He looked back to where the others sat, and Samual smiled, then gave him the one-finger salute.

Archie turned to Bertram.

'Have you heard of this game Wren?'

'No. Not that I can recall.'

'The clue is in the name. Frederico is known for his imagination in conceiving games that will challenge even the brightest minds. I think that if we can discern who or what Traest is then we will have a valuable clue. You claim to be scholarly my friend. Now is the time to tap into that mind of yours and see if you can dredge up anything at all.'

Bertram wracked his mind for memories relating to the name Traest, attempting to identify the name with any of the

Chapter 23

known cultures of the world. A king or another leader, maybe? A religious leader or cult? Any link of the name in his mind eluded him however so he fished for memories of the name in popular mythology. The start time of the game crept closer, and Bertram's searching became more frantic as he attempted to resolve the question.

Bertram was startled out of his deep thoughts as something bumped against the table he leant on with head in his hands. Looking up, he was greeted by the infuriating smile of Samual.

Samual looked from Bertram to Archie and then back again. Then he began to chuckle.

'You don't know do you?'

'Ignore him, Wren,' Archie said rising to his feet. 'It's not over yet.'

Samual wheeled away to join his friends, leaving a last insult as he went.

'Better get yourself another second, Archie. Oh wait, there is no time for that, is there?'

Frederico summoned them upstairs when time had taken its course.

He produced two rectangular boxes, each appearing identical with a stone case and inlaid pearl upon its top face. The pearl had movable squares and each showed a small part of a picture.

The game will take place with each player and their second in a different room. You must solve the picture puzzle to show the correct image and then the box will open and the second part of the puzzle begins. Only once a player solves the picture will he be able to get the item inside and then be told the next stage of the game. I wish you both luck.'

Frederico placed a sandglass on the table. 'You will have six chimes from when the sandglass is turned. Angus and Nix, you will accompany my man outside the door into the next room. I will supervise Archie and Wren in here.'

It may have seemed simple to an onlooker. After all, it was no different to a child's puzzle of the same nature. Move the tiles until the picture is revealed, but this was no child's game. If the puzzle lay untouched between the movements of the squares for longer than a few moments, the squares randomly changed position. The task of solving it took Archie's undivided attention as Bertram fought his building anger at not being able to provide an answer to who Traest was.

Half a chime had passed when Bertram heard a door open in the hallway outside followed by the high-pitched laughter of Nix.

Had they solved it already?

Archie cursed as the puzzle again reset itself.

'Come on Wren! Give me something.'

Bertram slumped down into his chair, then straightened suddenly. He had an idea.

Bertram pushed his mind out of the room, searching for Kassy. The intruder lay quietly observing but Bertram could feel its anger towards him. He ignored it and focused on Kassy until their minds touched.

While the invasion of his mind from the intruder was heavy, clumsy, and childlike, the feeling of Kassy entering his mind was almost instant and took mere moments to know what he faced. Kassy told Bertram a story that also came to him in images of a dragon named Traest which slumbered deep beneath the ocean. A seaman named Davin who had dived down deep to recover his wife when she had been washed overboard in a storm found his form when he spied the yellow of the gold crown upon the dragon's head. Davin returned with a crew to claim the golden crown, which was the size of a small house, but when they began their work the dragon awoke in a fury at the attempted theft. The crew and their boat were smashed to pieces. Davin, the only survivor felt the dragon's might when it invaded his mind learning everything about him. It took the dragon less than a day to find the city Davin called home.

Chapter 23

The people of Sainthome awoke in burning homes. Any that were lucky enough to escape the hungry flames were greeted by the immense form of the dragon within the eye of a ferocious storm that levelled the ancient city. As the dragon revelled in the deaths and despair of the people below, Davin huddled terrified within its talons as he watched all he held dear destroyed. When it was finally over the dragon put the sailor down at the edge of the ocean and then rose to its full height causing the sailor to fall down prone in supplication. 'Don't kill me, I beg of you almighty one. Allow me to live and I will protect your sleeping domain until my dying breath. I will serve you in all things.'

In a voice of thunder, the dragon accepted the man's pleas.

'I am Traest and until I rise once more, you will hide my existence and watch over me. It is said that the sailor still sails the ocean waiting for his draconian master to awaken once more and take the world for its own and only then will Davin be given the final rest.

'Traest is a dragon,' Bertram yelled excitedly.

'The image has to do with water and a boat, but I cannot see anything resembling parts of a dragon. Are you sure?'

'Yes. A man named Davin discovered Traest while out on the ocean. It is said he still wanders the oceans in his fishing boat awaiting the dragon's return. The picture will be of Davin in his boat.' The puzzle went easier after that as Archie quickly managed to resolve the image.

'Now what?'

'Maybe you need to say the name,' Bertram replied.

'Traest!' Nothing happened.

'Davin!' still nothing.

'See here,' Archie held up the puzzle for Bertram to look.

'The figure of this Davin is pointing at the far-off remains of a city.'

'The answer is Sainthome. It's where Davin was from and the city the dragon burned to the ground.'

'Sainthome!'

There came the roar of a dragon in the room, causing both Archie and Bertram to cower in fright. Archie laughed nervously when the sound faded. A faint click came from the puzzle box.

Archie opened the box. Inside was an iron cylinder about a hand span in length with five segments that radiated the soft glow of different colours. Archie grabbed the cylinder and then let it go with a cry as needles shot out from the cylinder to stab into his hand before retracting back inside the cylinder.

'Shit! I shouldn't have been so hasty,' he said looking at the wounds of his hand.

'There is a note beneath the cylinder,' Bertram said.

On the note were the following words.

The point at which the people of Fallon's March are closest to the gods.

Archie and Bertram looked at one another and both answered at once.

'Heavens Reach!'

Frederico walked over to them, clapping slowly.

Congratulations on solving the first part of the game. Now the stakes are higher because those needles that pierced the skin of your hand, Archie, were poisoned and any moment now you will begin to feel the effects. You have six hours before the poison stops your heart. Retrieve the antidote from my man at the location you believe the note refers to and return here to solve the final stage of the puzzle box. One final thing. Your second must stay here at the Cauldron.

Archie's face paled. 'I better get going then. With any luck, Angus won't know of Heaven's Reach.'

'Hurry back, my friend so we can finish this,' Bertram called after him.

Frederico moved to follow Archie out, then stopped and regarded Bertram.

Chapter 23

'Join me for a drink lad. Both seconds must remain with myself and my man downstairs until the contestants return.'

'I don't see why not. I could use one to steady my nerves.'

Frederico locked the door behind them, and then they both descended into the tavern to join Nix and the other judge.

Nix greeted him with a smirk. 'Took your time, Wren. I would say Angus has nearly a chimes lead on Archie.'

'You seem awfully sure Angus has got this in the bag. Don't get ahead of yourself Nix.'

Bertram saw Museo sitting beside Samual at another table. There was no sign of Elspeth.

Her attendance doesn't mean anything. Bertram tried to reassure himself unsuccessfully.

It was close to three chimes later when excited voices could be heard out front of the Cauldron. Both Nix and Bertram stood in anticipation. The figure that strode into the tavern shouted three words that made Bertram's hope disappear.

'Lords and Dames!' Shouted Angus, striding over to Nix and downing her drink. 'Let's go Nix we have a game to win.'

Bertram was still waiting with Frederico when Angus descended to the tavern room with Nix. The judge came next, handing the puzzle box to Frederico who opened it to reveal the cylinder pulsing with white light.

Frederico nodded.

'I declare Angus the winner of game one. The other contestant has yet to return and when he does, if he does then he will not need to finish the last part of the puzzle box.'

Bertram was growing worried now. Nearly five chimes had passed as he waited, forced to ignore the celebrations of his enemies. The trip to Heavens Reach by horseback would take less than three chimes. On foot maybe four and a half.

Where the hell was Archie?

Many patrons stayed to see if the local man Archie returned. It was their voices outside that alerted Bertram to Archie's return.

The cries of excitement turned to ones of concern. When Archie staggered through the door, Bertram hardly recognised him. Blood caked the left side of his head turning his tunic red where it had soaked through. He hobbled on bare feet that were bruised and bleeding.

Bertram helped the injured man to a seat.

'Dixie, some water please.'

Once Archie had drunk his fill the crowd around him hushed waiting for his story.

Frederico moved to stand before Archie.

'I must inform you that Angus won the first game. I wish you better luck tomorrow. Now excuse me as I take my leave.'

Bertram passed Archie his freshly packed pipe waiting as the man smoked slowly.

'I was making good time to Heaven's Reach expecting to meet Angus on his way down. Close to the base of the hill, I began to feel I was being watched. When I stopped to look behind me I was surprised to see Angus some fifty feet away. Even now I am not sure if he had been waiting for me or had followed because he didn't know the location the note spoke of. 'It's an advantage to be a local after all, Angus greeted me.

I ignored his attempt at conversation and galloped my horse to the top where just as Frederico had promised, one of his men waited with the antidote. On the way back down, Angus was nowhere to be seen. My excitement grew. I was going to win this. I had nudged my mount to a run to be sure of beating Angus back here when we struck something I couldn't see which threw me from my mount to strike my head on the rocks to the side of the path. When I came around my horse and boots were gone. I was dizzy with blood loss but forced myself to rise which was when the pain of both feet made me aware of a deep cut on both of them. Even though I hobbled back to where signs in the soil told me where I fell. There was nothing there that could have caused my fall. I return here badly injured but more aware now

Chapter 23

of the character of the man I compete against. Tomorrow I will be ready.

Once they were outside away from prying ears, Bertram leading his mare and Archie walking beside him, they headed towards the road to Archie's home that he and his wife shared with her brother.

There was no way to prove it, but Bertram suspected that the mage Elspeth was behind the ambush. He shared his theory with Archie once they were alone.

'I saw Elspeth leave at the break, but I'm not sure where she went.'

'It would appear, my friend, that the Lords and Dames are more devious than I previously thought. If she leaves during the game tomorrow, Lyre men will be waiting for her. We have tomorrow to come. I am lucky, so let's hope Aspre shines her holy light upon me. One thing is certain. Angus is going to be overconfident, especially since they got away with cheating and we cannot prove a thing. He will demand a higher prize, and I will up it until it's a fee he cannot pay. Then he is mine. If we can stop Elspeth then we can still win, otherwise I am destitute. I just wish we had some magic of our own to avail,' Archie said, stopping now they had reached the branch of the road towards his home.

'I may be able to help with that, Archie. '

Archie gave Bertram a curious look.

'I know just the person to help make sure Elspeth doesn't interfere again.'

'If that is possible, it will be very well received, my friend. Now I must rest, check in on my wife and children, and forget this night. See you tomorrow, Wren.'

Bertram watched him go, then mounted up and rode as fast as possible back to the mill. He had favours to ask of Kassy this night and knew she wouldn't be happy to help even if it meant one of her enemies would be brought down.

Chapter 24

Back at the mill, Bertram relayed the events of the day to Kassy. 'So, they would cheat with the use of magic like us,' she pondered out loud.

'Yes, and I have something to ask you. Now that they have the advantage, Gerald's men will be ready in case Elspeth tries to leave again. It would be a fine thing if you could aid us with your power, Kassy.'

'That is a risky thing, indeed. I would need to be close to my spirit ball, Bertram.'

'I would bet my life that when Samual leaves the manor, he takes it with him since it is of such value. If you come with me to the Cauldron, you would have access to the ball's power, would you not?'

Kassy began pacing. 'I guess that just might work, Bertram,' she said, smiling. Then she outlined what she would need in order to help Archie the next night. They planned until the early morning, and Bertram once again became aware of the intruder inside him growing restless. The full moon of Aspre was due again in three days, and it was stirring.

The next day when Bertram left the mill to head for the Cauldron, Kassy went with him to the main road near the town. She had taken her most natural form of a red fox with multiple tails and at the road stopped to stare at him.

Chapter 24

'I can feel its power already, Bertram. You were right. I will wait for you out back near the privy as we planned, then let's see how they fare with magic against them.' Then she shot off at a run towards the Cauldron. Archie waited for him by the road as always, and Bertram fell in beside him, leading his mare.

For the first time, he detected a sense of anxiety around the gambler.

'I have put in place some protection from Elspeth's sorcery,' Bertram said, patting Archie's shoulder.

He felt the relief wash over Archie. 'That is fine news indeed, Bertram. I cannot afford to lose this game. Not only will my wife want to kill me, but the sum of coin I have procured for this match from Gerald would leave me in his debt likely for life, and though I respect and work for the man, he has made it clear he will not be accountable for any losses. As it is, I am already in several thousand cetas of debt.'

'Archie, if it happens, then I will pay it for you since this is all done on my behalf. I am not without considerable fortune. It is just not accessible at this moment.'

The Lords and Dames sat at the bar, just like they had the last evening. Bertram noted Elspeth was there and Samual was wearing a rucksack like he had last night. Bertram knew it held the spirit ball. With a smile, he also noted that Angus was drinking from a goblet: ice water as always.

It would be so much easier if the man was a drunk.

At their entry, Samual stood and clapped slowly while the gathered locals cheered for Archie.

'On time, just like lambs to the slaughter,' he said, elbowing Museo in the ribs playfully.

'Don't be too confident, Samual. Your man hasn't completed the victory yet; he has merely won the first battle,' replied Bertram as he pushed himself between Samual and Museo to take a place at the bar.

'Have you no manners?' said Museo, placing a hand on Bertram's shoulder. 'Where I hail from, such an action could get a man killed.'

Bertram could feel Museo's fingers digging painfully into the muscles of his neck where it met his shoulder.

'Samual, have your lackey remove his soiled fingers from my person or it will force me to defend myself,' he stated loudly, and heads turned to look at the looming confrontation.

'Museo, do as Wren says. We cannot allow Archie a way out of this, and if any of us cause a fight, then Angus is forfeit of this opportunity.'

'This is not finished, Wren Sorrenson,' Museo said. 'It has been a long time since I met someone I despise as much as I do you. Pray you don't meet me during the festival.'

Beside them, Angus and Archie both stood exchanging barbed comments, one drinking water and the other frothing ale. Museo still had his hand on Bertram's shoulder, so Bertram stepped back right into Angus, making sure his arm that he used to brush away Museo's knocked over the jug of water and goblet he was drinking from. Cold water poured down over Angus and some onto Archie, and the both of them quickly stood and stared at Bertram.

'You clumsy oaf, look what you have done!' Angus complained.

'My apology, Angus. I was only reacting to the threats of your little friend,' he said, then bent to retrieve the jug and used the moment to grab the goblet, which he hid beneath his tunic.

Museo clenched his fists at the latest insult from Bertram, and Samual stepped between them, then led Museo away before he could react further. Thankfully, that was when Frederico called for them to head upstairs. Bertram hurried out the back of the Cauldron under the excuse of the need to use the privy. He gave Kassy the mug Angus had been drinking from, receiving a wolfish smile in response.

Chapter 24

Archie took his seat opposite Angus, who was smiling broadly following his victory in the first game. Frederico took his seat, then turned to Archie.

Frederico placed the spinning wheel on the table.

'Archie, it is your turn to spin the wheel.'

As the wheel slowed, Bertram silently prayed the game would be one that would give Archie some sort of advantage. They all leaned forward to see what game the wheel stopped on.

Frederico clapped his hands in glee. 'It's the blank space. That means that Archie can choose the game to be played. Archie, take your time and choose.'

Archie made a show of not answering right away. He took a long sip of his ale as he looked over the options, allowing the moment to stretch out painfully before answering.

'All Souls!'

Angus looked shocked, and Bertram was sure his own expression matched the warrior's.

The game All Souls had been used to decide disputes before the Severing. Since the return of magic. It was an ancient game that the King of Scuttle had outlawed in Stormwatch after a death had caused riots and nearly burned the merchant district to the ground. Many priesthoods complained about the gruesome deaths caused by the game.

'What did you say?' Asked Angus.

'Let me repeat it for you, Angus. My choice is All Souls.'

Choose something else. It's too dangerous,' complained Nix.

'I think you are forgetting that the choice is mine,' countered Archie.

Frederico shrugged his shoulders when both Nix and Angus turned their glares on him.

'Archie states the truth of the matter. Angus, you may either refuse the game, which will result in a forfeit. Archie will be the winner without needing a third round.'

Throughout the exchange, Archie sat relaxed, face void of any emotion with his eyes fixed on Angus.

This has now become personal for Archie, Bertram realised.

Now it was Angus, drawing out the long silence.

'It's a fool's game that may well be the death of both of us,' Angus said to Archie.

'You are wrong. It is the ultimate game of chance, nothing more. Gamblers like us are always looking for that next big rush. Is that not true?'

'I prefer calculated risks. All Souls is a reckless high-risk game suited for more important matters than who is the better gambler out of the two of us.'

'You could always step away, Angus. Stakes like these are not for everyone.'

'I'm not a coward!'

Archie raised his hands in supplication.

'Easy now. Nobody but you mentioned coward. I guess it's a case of if the hat fits.'

Angus tossed the rest of his whiskey down his throat.

'I'm in!'

Federico smiled. He threw both arms out to the side. 'My friends, we have the game of all games ahead. Listen carefully I will explain the rules only once. First, a question. Have either of you played this before?'

'Only once, when I was in Stormwatch last cycle,' Archie replied. Angus simply answered with a no.

'Angus. Is this worth it? You don't have to do this.'

'I do, Nix. I want to beat this bastard!'

'That's the spirit. I was worried our warrior was naught but a mouse. Glad to see you found your edge, Angus.'

'Shut that ugly mouth of yours, Archie and let's play, 'Angus growled.'

'One thousand cetas per round or bust,' added Archie.

Chapter 24

'That's too much risk, Angus. Remember your own advice. Never gamble beyond your means,' warned Nix.

'It is too much,' Angus agreed.'

'Do you always let women make decisions for you?' wondered Bertram out loud.

'When this is all over, let's see how brave you are then, Wren Sorrenson! I accept the wager,' Angus said.

Frederico waited for both men to quiet before beginning.

'Now that both parties have agreed that the contest will continue, we can address the setup of the All Souls match. Good luck to you both.'

Chapter 25

Frederico briefly spoke to his man outside the door who returned with an iron box. After opening it, the game master passed three disks to Archie.

'Archie, in your hands you hold the three realm discs. Pure diamond for the Celestial Realm, Clear agate for the Middle Realm, and finally black opal for the Infernal Realm. Archie, charge the realms if you please,' Frederico announced.

Since weapons were forbidden in the room during the contest, Frederico passed a small blade to Archie. With one hand above the Celestial disc, Archie drew the blade across his palm, then squeezed the fingers together, allowing the blood to drip onto the diamond disc. Once Archie removed his hand, the disc levitated up off the table until it sat just higher than the heads of both players. A white semitransparent light coiled out from the celestial disc, forming the top third of a sphere on which an image of a Celestial warrior manifested. Within the white light, a sky castle formed on clouds.

Bertram looked on in awe. Nothing could have prepared him for the building tension in the room amongst the bitter stench of magic that set his body to instant attentiveness.

Archie picked up the Middle Realm disc of clear agate. He pumped his cut palm three times, then smeared one side of the disc through the blood before turning it facing blood upwards and passing the disc carefully to Angus.

Chapter 25

Angus accepted both the disc and knife from Archie. He wiped the tainted blade on the tablecloth, ignoring the snicker from Archie, and then he drew the blade across his own palm. Smearing blood on the clean side of the middle realm disc, Angus removed his hand. They all watched the agate disc rise above the table and stop as green hues flowed from it to form the middle third of the playing sphere in which a forest formed with a temple of stone at its centre.

Angus dripped his blood onto the black opal disc. When he removed his hand, the disc slid into position above the tabletop right beneath the middle realm disc, where a muddy light formed the final third of the sphere around a twisted citadel on a lake of lava. This part of the sphere rested on the shoulders of a demonic figure whose eyes glittered with unnatural light.

Bertram's attention was riveted to the sight before him. If he focused on any one realm, his attention seemed to be dragged inwards towards it, filling all senses with the strange realm. So far, Bertram had been able to pull himself back before being overwhelmed. Beside him, Nix elbowed him softly.

'As witnesses, we can allow ourselves to be pulled into the game at any point or retreat here as a simple viewer. I would advise going all in Bertram. It's quite a ride.' Bertram turned to look at Nix. Her eyes were slightly closed. A smear of white partially covered one nostril.

'You used fae powder again?'

'I always do before Angus plays All Souls,' Nix replied, eyes shining with mischief.

Bertram felt the shiver run through him. Angus was not some newcomer to All Souls. He was a seasoned player. Turning back to the game, Bertram saw that five circles filled with sizzling blue energy had appeared at each player's side. These were the players' mana stores which were used up during game actions. Once these were empty, the player would be defeated.

'I have a coin here. One side was marked with a celestial, the other marked with an infernal. One player tosses the other calls,' Frederico announced.

Angus called Celestial as the coin tossed by Archie flipped over and over, landing in Angus's favour.

'First movement to you, Angus. A six wins you your first guardian, while a one heralds an unfavourable event,' Frederico announced.

Bertram noticed that regardless of the result, a tiny amount of mana drained from each player's mana store with each roll.

Angus pumped a fist in triumph as his roll signified his first guardian.

A figure materialised in the Infernal third of the sphere. A woman in a body-hugging dress of skin beneath a coat of bones raised a black iron staff to the sky, screaming as lightning forked about her body.

A sultry voice rolled through the room.

'I give service to the dark lords with whose might shall I extinguish my enemy.'

Looking smug already, Angus's braying laugh accompanied Nix's joy as Archie failed to get a result on his first two turns.

'That is round two completed, which is where I, the nominated judge, roll to determine if an external event occurs for either player that will affect the game,' explained Frederico.

Bertram allowed himself a sigh of relief as the roll won Archie a positive event.

In the celestial third of the sphere, a comet shot across the night sky above the cloud castle.

A chiming voice whispered through the room.

'A victory is foretold for the forces of light. It is written in the stars.' Beside Archie, another mana reservoir formed.

The luck of the game had appeared to change hands, favouring Archie now. Round three began with a one for Angus, who threw his hands up in protest at his bad luck.

Chapter 25

A prayer rang out in the room by a chorus of voices.

'The gods of good, we trust them to deliver us from the clutches of evil. To banish evil as the light of day banishes the night. With faith and the gods of good at our backs, we are safe.'

'Angus. Your enemy's faith costs you double mana for the next two rounds of play,' announced Frederico.

Archie threw a three, which meant another round of inaction.

Fortunately, Angus fared even worse by rolling another one and getting a second unfavourable event.

Warrior of darkness, your warlock suffers betrayal, leaving her weak and on the brink of death. Miss one turn.

Bertram let the lower third of the sphere draw him down into it where Angus's warlock stood backing away from two dark-clad assassins. Lightning leapt from the warlock's iron staff, leaving one assassin flailing as he caught fire. The second assassin weaved through a dizzying routine of strikes that the warlock somehow evaded before she tossed a cord at the attacker that elongated into an animated rope that soon had the assassin bound tightly on the ground. The warlock caved in the second assassin's skull with his staff, unaware of a third that stalked him silently from behind. After jamming his blade between the warlock's shoulders, the assassin vanished with a smile. The warlock fell to one knee, clawing at the blade in her as a greenish glow flowed out of the blade into the warlock's body.

When the scene ended, Bertram was back in the room. One of the mana reservoirs beside Angus drained to empty, then faded away. Angus grunted as sudden pain bent him over. When he straightened, rivulets of sweat streaked his face.

Bertram knew this was one reason people loved to observe a game of All Souls. It was not uncommon for large fees to be paid to witness such a game. When a player lost a mana reservoir, they would absorb some of the pain from the event into their own bodies. While this was devastating for the players, it was truly a spectacle for the observers.

Archie's first roll came to nothing. He had a second because of Angus missing a turn and rolled a six. In the celestial realm, a winged figure with pure white wings and golden armour appeared and flew about the castle.

'The gods of good are smiling. They send an angelic warrior to lead your armies and reward you for your faith and service.'

'This is bullshit,' roared Angus, making Bertram jump.

'Guess I'm just lucky, Angus,' retorted Archie as he lit a pipe with a big smile on his face.

Now it was time for Frederico to roll for an event. Angus visibly sighed in relief when no event was drawn.

On his next turn, Angus rolled a four. He rubbed his stubbled chin before speaking.

'I wish to spend mana to influence Archie's next roll.'

After voicing this, one of the mana reservoirs drained to half, leaving Angus with two and a half.

Archie took his time rolling, and the die flicked to a three, then at the last moment fell onto a one. The ploy from Angus had been successful and Archie would suffer a negative event.

Bertram was once again drawn into the scene developing in the middle realm as a voice narrated the scene as images played out.

'Plague befalls the land, tearing families apart, decimating the armies of good and destroying supply routes and hope of reinforcements. From these pestilent dead rise an army of the dead who fall upon the survivors in a bloodletting frenzy. Belief in the good gods is waning and whispers to the gods of darkness abound.'

When the scene cleared, Archie was breathing hard, his breaths coming in laboured gasps. Weeping sores had appeared on his skin. Archie was down to four reservoirs now compared to Angus with two and a half.

Two more rounds passed before Angus rolled a six and gained his second guardian.

Chapter 25

'From the burial ground site of an ancient battle, an undead ally arises to the join the warlock of darkness in conquest of the realm.'

The warlock cast a spell that turned day to night and from the grounds about the citadel an undead horde dragged itself from the soiled earth led by a skeletal lich with burning red eyes.

'I will spend half a mana to aid my roll in securing another guardian,' Archie announced. The ploy failed on a roll of two.

'Now I have you! Spend half a mana to move to the middle realm,' Angus said.

With the land unprotected and beset with plague, the Lich king rode forth from shadow, raising the dead under his banner as they marched upon the temple within the forest,' stated a voice thick with hatred.

'Surrender my turn, so on my next, I have two rolls,' Archie said, leaning forward on his elbows among the pipe mixture, smoke billowing about his face.

On his next turn, Angus watched in triumph as his undead army swarmed over the temple with no sign of resistance.

'Absolute darkness extinguishes the light of hope.'

Frederico rolled for an event. A one meant a favourable event for Archie.

'The child of light has been unveiled from the eyes of evil to stand bright against the forces of darkness.'

The scene drew Bertram in. A family home beset by a force of cultists shrieking in the light of fires as they cavorted before the flames to the chanting of a priestess of purest alabaster skin engraved with the sigils of destruction. Through shuttered windows, the terrified family all wailed in fear except for one. A boy of fifteen sat praying. By his side lay a hammer shaped like a bull's head. As the shrieking cultists reached a crescendo, the boy rose to stand before his family, facing the front door naked to the waist with the hammer held in both hands. The door exploded inwards as the boy, now imbued with golden light, smashed through the cultists, shattering bones as the bodies piled up around him. The priestess bathed in the gore of her followers was then upon him, knives diving in to inflict deep wounds as finally, he fell to his knees with a cry of anguish, a prayer to the good gods then throwing his arms around the waist of the approaching priestess. The boy held on as golden fire radiated off him to roll over his enemy helpless in his grasp until she stopped writhing and the divine golden light faded leaving the boy healed of his wounds. He slumped before his stunned family.

'Our child, you are the chosen of the gods. We recognise and follow you. We shall purge the land of evil.'

'Now for my turn, 'Archie said, refilling his pipe with shaking hands. 'Which means I take two rolls as per surrendering my turn last round. My child of light enters the middle realm to face the lich and its undead minions using dispel magic.'

In the middle sphere, an army of civilians, many armed with farm implements, joined the ranks of battling empire soldiers battling the undead. From the civilians stepped the child of light bathed in a golden hue. Ranks of undead threw themselves at this new enemy as the forces of good closed around him protectively to allow him to cast his magic.

'Return now to your home beneath the soil with the carrion. You have no place here in the world of the living. So, mote it be!' His words carried across the battlefield followed by wails of fury as the lich and its army collapsed to dust. The middle realm now belonged to Archie.

'For my second turn, I move my champion into the middle realm,' Archie announced with glee. There was nothing stopping him from attacking the home sphere of Angus on his next turn unless Angus could use his mana, of which he only had two pools left.

Federico rolled for another event.

'Winter falls with vengeance upon the realms, making further advancement in the war for now impossible. Time to reflect and

Chapter 25

plan for the next offensive. Both players gain an extra mana, and we shall take a one chime break before continuing.'

'Cursed lucky for you Angus I had you there,' quipped Archie, standing and stretching.

'Hold your tongue. You have won naught so far,' mumbled Angus, pushing past his opponent.

It surprised Bertram that longer than a chime had passed since the start of the game. Now it was up to Kassy to put her plan into motion.

Chapter 26

'All seems to be going well so far,' Bertram said, leaning in close to Archie.

'Would be better without the breaking event. I had him right where I could win the game. Now the bastard has a second chance. The sooner I finish Angus and be rid of these damn sores, the better,' Archie said, draining his ale.

Bertram watched as Angus sat talking animatedly to Samual, Museo, and Nix. There was no sign of Elspeth so far. Nix moved out the front of the tavern. When she returned, she went straight to Samual and the two shared heated words but Bertram couldn't hear what they said.

'They are worried about the absence of Elspeth. She was meant to be here,' came the intruder's voice.

She would have interfered. Looks like the Lyre men got to her first, Bertram mused and smiled.

Back in the games room, they all took their seats.

'Angus, it is your turn,' Frederico announced.

'I sacrifice one of my three mana to extend the winter in the middle realm.'

The unnatural winter rages on. Travel is impossible, food is scarce and despair rots the minds of the civilian army as they freeze to death. Witnessing this the chosen one questions his faith to his god as hunger takes his mind and he feeds on the dead. When he turns on the champion of light, the warrior is forced to slay the chosen one.

Archie began to shiver, his skin taking on a blueish tinge. He started gagging, only just stopping himself from bringing up the ale he had drunk.

'Never thought I would taste human flesh,' Archie mumbled, looking sick. His mana faded to three now while Angus had two.

'My angelic warrior uses a mana to teleport into the enemy realm,' Archie said, looking as if he was about to fall off his chair.

Angus sat staring at the game before him, mouth ajar as if confused.

'Your move, Angus,' Frederico prompted.

It took a moment for Angus to acknowledge that someone had spoken to him. He shook his head as trying to clear it, and then studied the game. The man's whole demeanour had changed to curling back into himself no longer sitting straight but hunched at the table muttering to himself.

Nix noticed it right away too.

'Angus, are you okay?'

'Activate Soul trap!' Angus said quietly then repeated it louder this time.

'What are you doing Angus, have you lost your mind? Even I can see that is the wrong move.' Archie's realm is undefended.

'Interfere again, Nix and I will be forced to disqualify Angus from the game,' Frederico announced.

The angelic warrior ventures into the realm of darkness. A deadly trap closes about him, trapping his soul.

'Contest the spell with mana,' Archie said after staring at Angus for a long moment of not be able to believe his opponent's choice of action.

'How many pools of mana will you use Archie?'

'I use two pools of mana to match the two remaining that Angus has.'

'Angus, do you contest Archie and meet the challenge or choose another action?' Frederico asked as all eyes turned to Angus.

A range of battling emotions crossed the warrior's face before he answered with a hiss.

'Yes, I meet the challenge with my two mana.'

Nix stood clenching her fists in rage. She made as if she was to say something but a glare from the games master halted her words.

'Sit down, Nix. I wouldn't want you to miss the moment of Angus's defeat,' Bertram said smiling up at her.

'What have you done, Wren? I know you must have done something to Angus. He knows this strategies of this game well. He is not himself.'

'Sit down, my dear. The effects of the game on its players are more devastating than you could ever know. I can attest to that,' Archie said shivering uncontrollably.

'With my turn I use my final pool of mana to banish the sorceress back to her fiery hell,' Archie announced as he stood, arms thrust upwards in victory.

The room erupted into chaos. Angus slumped back into his chair, groaning, and clasping his head in both hands. Nix rounded on Frederico. They have cheated. I don't know how but even you a dim-witted fool could see the change that came over Angus!'

'I saw no display of foul play. As Archie said earlier, the game drains a players mental, emotional, and physical reserves that causes the stoutest minds to crack under the pressure,' Frederico replied.

Bertram rose and met Archie in a bear hug as he congratulated him on the win, as Nix threw her drink against the wall screaming in denial.

'Angus, control your second. She is out of line.'

Angus straightened in his seat, looked up and took in the scene about him. He turned his attention to the game board as the words of an angelic choir rang out through the room.

The forces of light are victorious as evil is banished from the lands.

Chapter 26

'I lost? How could this happen?'

Nix pointed a finger at Archie and Bertram. 'They cheated, that's how!'

Angus slid across the table, then struck Archie to the face with a fist three times. Blood sprayed. Federico reacted by pulling a whistle from his pocket, which he blew frantically. It was the sign for one of the large doormen to attend. Angus kept hitting Archie as Bertram tried to pull him off and was shoved over, knocking Nix down as well.

The form of Sef filled the doorway. He strode over and lifted Angus from the bleeding Archie and turned him around. Angus hit Sef with an uppercut that would have laid out a lesser man. Sef just smiled, then hammered a fist into the warrior's midsection, and he fell with a gasp as the fight went out of him.

'Hold him here, Sef, and get the justicar. Angus has broken the rules and attacked another player. This means he is disqualified and a third game is cancelled. Archie wins by forfeit,' Frederico intoned.

The Justicar, Carson, was a man who had little time for those who broke contracts or committed acts of crime. He had his two deputies, both able men. They chained the hands and feet of Angus. Then the justicar heard the charges against Angus before reading aloud the signed contract that both Angus and Archie had signed before he spoke again.

'Angus, I made you aware of the rules of competition. You have assaulted a civilian in my town, and Archie will be offered recompense. You owe Archie the sum of twelve thousand cetas for the game. I will take you now to a cell to await your fate. What say you?'

'I am innocent and was a victim of foul sorcery,' he pleaded in an unconvincing tone.

'And your proof, Angus?'

We're Golden

When Angus gave no answer, Federico spoke instead.

'Justicar, nobody left this room during the latest round. I saw nothing but the actions of a losing man frustrated by the cold hands of luck.' When they descended to the common room, the crowd looked on in shock and Federico waved for quiet.

'As judge in this competition, I hereby announce that Angus has forfeited the game for attacking Archie after he was defeated. He loses the sum of twelve thousand cetas plus the winnings of game one, to be paid at this moment. As the contract demands, a cheat or player that breaks the rules of the contest shall have his strong hand cut from his body.'

Samual and the other Lords and Dames, minus Elspeth who was still absent, pushed themselves to the front of the crowd.

'Surely a mistake, Justicar. The sum was ten thousand cetas, and I know this man and will vouch for his innocence, as will my friends.'

The justicar turned to Federico. 'Is this true that the sum is ten thousand?'

'Angus himself agreed to increase the amount to a thousand cetas a round, and I have two witnesses who also were present. I watched Archie win fair and squarely as well as witnessing his assault on the person of Archie. You can all see Archie bears the marks of such a crime. Samual, do you have the coin to pay that Angus now owes?'

Samual looked crestfallen. 'I have ten thousand, Justicar, the true sum that was agreed, and that is all.'

'You have heard the judge and know the current debt. Can you pay the fee for him?'

'Sadly, no, but I can get the money in time.'

'Unfortunately, that will not do. Your man is now not only condemned to maiming but is at the mercy of good man Archie.'

At this the crowd broke into excited conversation as they led Angus from the establishment. Ale and mugs struck him to the cries of 'cheat' from the crowd.

Chapter 27

They congregated at the Justicar's building. Federico, as the judge, was present, and so was Nix since she was the second for Angus. Archie, whose face was heavily swollen, arrived and came to stand beside Bertram. The smith would wield the blade and cauterise the wound as an apothecary stood by to treat with herbs and medicine for the pain.

Angus walked from the cell in chains. His sword arm stretched out over a small anvil. 'It now makes me wonder if you were cheating when we played together, Angus, and won my savings,' Bertram heard the smith tell Angus as they tied him in place. Then, wielding an axe, the smith swung the heavy blade down and cut the hand from its body, which fell to the stone. Angus screamed and slumped with the shock of the blow. Nix burst into tears.

After the wound was cauterised in the fire and Angus had passed out, his wound was lathered with herbs and bandaged.

Looking a little sick, the justicar turned to Archie. 'All that remains is the fee still owed and the recompense for the assault on your body,' he said to Archie.

'I will take Angus as my property to pay the debts he owes me. I ask he be charged one thousand cetas for the assault I have suffered at his hands.'

The justicar and judge agreed that was a suitable sum to be added to the debt of Angus, who was still in chains. Angus was loaded on a cart so Archie could take him away.

Nix was distraught as she watched the wagon roll away, and Bertram rode beside Archie up front, driving since Archie had trouble seeing.

'A fitting end, my friend,' he said to Archie.

'And no less than he deserves,' replied Archie. 'Oh, I almost forgot. Here is the blade Angus wielded. I am led to believe it is yours.' Bertram took the sword proffered him and felt a lump in his throat. He had his father's blade back and now just needed Arlo to be freed.

'What will you do with him now, Archie?'

'I owe my own sizable debt to the Lyre family and I will use this man, plus my winnings to repay that then leave this place with my family to start a new life.'

'May I ask a favour of you, Archie?'

'If you must, but I know not how I can grant such a thing.'

'I only request to be present when you turn Angus over to the Lyre family.'

'Well, I can do that. I leave for the Lyre estate at noon tomorrow, so meet me here, Wren.'

After leaving Archie, Bertram headed out across the fields, though only in late afternoon the silhouette of Aspre was visible above him. By tomorrow evening the white moon would be full in time for the start of the festival. Bertram had hoped to attend the festivities as Wren.

Sorrenson, but with the full moon so close he would be safer staying at the mill. In that time Tamul would be at its most powerful as he ruled the night alone, free from the good moon's influence. Bertram tried to concentrate but found it hard to tear his gaze away from Aspre. The intruder's presence was then there inside, even though already there it sometimes faded or became more prominent like now.

'Don't return to the mill, Bertram. Kassy will only chain us, try to control us for her own purposes. We are her prisoners. Mark my words, Bertie. If you are the man I know you can be, then resist her and go far from here. We don't need her, Bertie. The moon calls to us. Let's run beneath it, hunt and be free. You remember how it felt?'

'We are returning to the mill. Without her, you wouldn't even exist.'

'You call this a life, trapped in a weak body where I may never rise and run free? We are prisoners, nothing more!'

It relieved Bertram when the mill came into view with the familiar figure of Kassy on the lookout waiting for him to return.

Bertram entered the mill, then climbed up the repaired stairs to the second level, where Kassy waited, her eyes alight with that unnatural glow.

'We did it, Kassy. I still can't believe it worked.'

'The goblet worked perfectly and being so close to the spirit stone meant my power was strong again. It felt wonderful to feel it again. Tonight we struck a blow against our enemies, as we will tomorrow night.'

'Tomorrow night? What do you mean? The moon will be full, and I cannot leave. Unless you think I have enough self-mastery to resist the lure of the intruder.'

'You still don't have the strength to do that. I can see the intruder behind your eyes here now and would guess it's been quietly goading you to let it free, am I right?'

Bertram only nodded and sat down, tired now, and Kassy came to sit beside him.

'It will get easier, Bertram. You must trust me with this. To let the intruder out too soon before you can call it back could cause many disasters. Last time you were lucky since it only longed to hunt, but it will kill without a second thought. We cannot risk a party of townspeople hunting us.'

'What are you planning to do tomorrow night, then?'

'Not so fast, Bertram. First, we eat what I have prepared, and then I will explain it to you.' They dined on bloody meat charred on the outside and with cornbread and gravy. The meat thankfully sated the other for now, and it slunk away into the recesses of his mind to rest and wait for its next chance.

Then Kassy shared her plan.

The next morning, with the promise to return before mid-afternoon chime fresh on his lips, Bertram arrived at Archie's home, where the gambler was waiting for him. Angus sat chained and gagged in the back of a cart. He eyeballed Bertram with so much hatred and fought against his bonds like an animal, growling curses from under the gag.

They were escorted into the Lyre estate to an awaiting Gerald, who greeted Archie with a kiss on each cheek and a vigorous handshake for Bertram. 'I see you bring him here as per our agreement,' he said to Bertram.

'Yes, and before you take him for whatever use you have for a maimed man, I would ask for time alone with him.'

'Of course, my friend; I am a man of my word, unlike this scum.'

'This is Angus, who I gambled against. As you most likely heard from your sons, I caught him cheating, and you can see his hand removed as the contract we signed demanded.'

'Sit him there and remove the gag. I would talk to this deceitful man.'

They removed the gag, and the first thing Angus did was hock phlegm at Gerald, striking his cheek where he stood before the chained man.

Gerald stepped back to wipe the phlegm away with a kerchief. 'Well, at least he has spirit. I like that.'

'Go fuck yourself,' Angus said, smiling up at him.

'You are in a world of trouble, Angus, and since Archie here has deemed to bring you to my home, I can only guess that he intends

Chapter 27

to give or sell you to me. I, unlike Archie, am not a kind man. Normally I would never take damaged goods like you; however, since one crime you committed was against a man whom I would follow to the gates of death, I find myself in this situation.'

'I did nothing against you. I also don't even know you. If you think threats will make me do your bidding, then you are the fool here, not me.'

Gerald nodded towards Bertram. 'You may have your moment, but don't damage him any further. He will need that other arm to work.' Then he, Archie, and Gerald's two men left the room.

Bertram stood just behind Angus.

'Stand before me, coward. Wren Sorenson, you will regret the day you ever messed with me. My friends will see to that!'

'I must confess that I have deceived you as to myself. I am not Wren Sorrenson. That is just a fictional character, although while being him I have enjoyed the freedom his role has allowed me,' Bertram began.

'I don't care for anything you have to say, Wren. You and I both know I was a victim of sorcery,' Angus spat out.

'I think you forget that you also used the nefarious powers of Elspeth's earth magic during the games, Angus. You showed you couldn't be trusted to play fairly, and so we were forced to act in a like manner,' said Bertram as he took a seat in front of Angus.

'Who are you that you know of Elspeth and her powers?' Angus narrowed his eyes.

'We are golden.'

'What?'

'Those words, do you not remember them?'

'You speak nonsense, man. Your mind is addled.'

Before he even had time to think about what he was doing, Bertram was out of his seat and had Angus by the throat. He jerked the man's chin up so their eyes met. 'Let me remind you then, Angus. While I lay with my guts spread around me and my life's blood cooling. You laughed at those very words uttered by Samual as he mocked me.'

Angus stared back at him, and then his eyes widened. 'Bertram?'

'Yes, Angus, it is I, Bertram, back from the dead.'

'How? I saw you dying with my own eyes.'

'And yet here I am. The one favour you allowed me was to not finish the job, but that speaks volumes about the ego of the Lords and Dames. Unfortunately for you, I am not the weak, timid man you once knew and took advantage of as a decoy so you could steal the spirit ball.'

Angus laughed. 'You are wrong. You are still weak, Bertram. Samual will see you fall short of saving the crippled piece of shit that was your famous father.'

Bertram could feel the intruder there beside him begging to be allowed to show itself, and for the first time he consented with the warning that if it went too far, this would be the last chance it got. The intruder came forth swiftly with a growl that was beyond frightening. Bertram's eyes changed to gold, his chin broadened, ears lengthened to points, and facial hair sprouted, all while slowly his teeth elongated. Then the intruder was in control.

'You made a big mistake in betraying us, little man, and your error gave me life. I can feel your fear, warrior. Should I rip the balls from the very body you inhabit? If I had my way I would, but I do trust in one thing: Gerald Lyre has unimaginable torments prepared for breaking you, and that, for now, is enough. Your precious Lords and Dames, however, will be given no such quarter,' growled the intruder through Bertram, squeezing the throat of Angus until he choked and thrashed about.

'Enough, let him go. You have done what was needed, and if you cannot stop now, you will get no more chance. I will fight you every time,' Bertram screamed from within his own head.

Reluctantly, the intruder released Angus, sliding back into his mind. Relief flowed through Bertram, and he felt shaken at what it

Chapter 27

was like to be forced into to the back of his mind as a spectator. In that moment, he could relate to the intruder better than ever before. When he was fully himself again, Bertram realised that from the pungent smell, Angus had pissed himself. He slapped Angus back to full awareness. 'Angus, worry not, my friend. We are golden.' Then he called for Gerald to enter the chamber.

'Oh, Wren you have literally scared the shit from the man,' Gerald laughed as one of his men gagged Angus again. 'Take him down to the questioning room. I would have his secrets and knowledge of his family. We may bleed a fortune from them with any luck.'

As Angus was dragged away, Gerald turned back to Bertram and Archie. 'Bertram, my debt to Arlo is now repaid. The second part of our plan begins and I will have the information you need once I wring it from Angus. I will find out everything he knows of these fool friends of his that would hold my dearest friend hostage in his own home.'

'Many thanks, Gerald. I can be found in the Cauldron most nights and will await your contact.'

He then turned to Archie. 'My friend, yes, it is I, Bertram, and now you know my motivation and true identity. You honour yourself with prowess for your part in it all. I truly thank you and consider myself in your debt.'

Bertram left the Lyre estate so Archie could discuss his release from the debts of Gerald, and Bertram felt happy in the knowledge the gambler would have enough coin to do that, as well as move on with a new life for his family. For the first time, he could feel the satisfaction of the intruder there beside him. They made a formidable team, he realised, but how long would the intruder be happy to stay in the background, especially with the full moon tonight? This thought gave Bertram extra speed as he returned through the afternoon enjoying the run through the countryside.

Chapter 28

Kassy left Bertram chained up when Aspre was nearing its zenith. She had ignored his complaints about missing the festival. 'You don't have the restraint and willpower yet, Bertram; it's too dangerous, and I won't risk it.'

When he looked up imploringly at her, she suddenly spat straight into his eyes, which stopped him in shock. 'What did you do that for?' Bertram growled as he wiped the spittle from his face. Where the spit had hit his eyes, it now burned. 'What did you spit in my eyes?'

'It will allow you to see through my eyes so you won't feel entirely trapped here.' She left him there with the power of Aspre pouring down upon him, his body on the edge of frenzy.

Fallon's March was alive with the festival. Beautiful lanterns shone their myriad of coloured lights powered by magic. Music drowned out many noises as revellers danced in the streets or flittered between street food vendors, sampling the many delights. With the fae powder rushing through her veins, Nix felt detached, which was what she needed right now. The maiming of Angus, then his disappearance, had shaken her. Nix imagined herself one of the fae, given the lease to return to the human world while the moon lasted. With all thoughts of her friend Angus left behind along with the rejection of the other Lords and Dames, who had

Chapter 28

refused to join her in the town, she threw herself fully into the festival. Nix became one with all the beautiful souls who, like her, threw caution to the winds on this special night. She danced with strangers in the square, liberally sharing fae powder and in return, sampling other substances that found their way to her.

A muscular, masked man in the visage of a bear pulled her into an alleyway, and they rutted urgently. Nix was back out in the square eating sweet treats and drinking cool, minted water in no time, which was when she noticed the woman.

Tall with blood-coloured hair down to her lower back, she danced with her hands raised beneath the moon with abandon and total freedom, uncaring of the stares of other revellers around her. She mesmerised everyone with her simple, flowing, yet graceful moves that highlighted her lithe, muscular body through a thin white dress that fell to just below knee level.

The woman had noticed her too and slowly danced over to Nix, who was still sitting down. Flicking the long red strands out of her eyes, the woman climbed upon the lap of Nix and kissed her. The sweet smell of sweat and the faint odour of musk assailed Nix as she wrapped her arms around the woman.

'Who are you?' she asked the woman as she was dragged from her seat to dance.

'I can be whoever you want me to be. I am everyone and they are me, as one with the Mother. Let's not ruin the moment with names this night of nights. Let's be free of the roles and personas life has thrust upon us. Just be.'

They danced for chimes in the square until fatigue and the lessening of drugs faded from their bodies. They retired to the comfortable seating down by the river, where children played and families sat with picnics.

'I don't think life gets better than this,' said Nix, running her hands through the woman's hair and admiring the dark silken skin of the woman's face.

The woman turned to Nix. 'I think life is too short not to be celebrated with total abandon, and to do any less is a crime against our very nature.'

'I haven't seen you around here. You are blessed with incredible beauty, so I surely would have noticed,' said Nix.

'I am from the coast and spent most my life at Whaleson City, but my heart belongs to the Scented Isles and always will, which is where I was born,' replied Kassy taking Nix by the hand and kissing her from the wrist up to the shoulder. Then she pulled Nix closer by the hair and kissed her again, washing away her questions.

'You are a free spirit, Nix, and yet I feel deep down you are so lost and sad. Such sad eyes that try to hide the pain and regret you have, but they are not fooling me. Spring is about renewal and is a time to leave such things behind. One way to do that is to unburden ourselves. Let me start. I give myself forgiveness for failing my children when they needed my help, and I stood by, frightened, while they were slaughtered in my home. Beneath the forgiving moon of Aspre, I let that go, and it shall burden me no more.' Then she fell quiet and stared at Nix, who reached for the small container clasped in the woman's hands that held the fae powder. Kassy placed a hand firmly on that of Nix. 'No, not now. This is a time for clarity and closure so you can truly be free. What do you feel the need to let go and forgive yourself for?'

Nix couldn't meet the woman's golden eyes as she stared back at her, unflinching and allowing no escape from the intense gaze. Tears began streaming down her cheeks. 'There is so much that haunts me. I am a terrible person, and my deeds and those I have been party to haunt my dreams,' she said between sobs.

'Slowly, child. Start with the most recent. This is something not to be used to handle all our misgivings at once. There will be many moons like this for that,' Kassy replied tenderly and wiped away the girl's tears.

Chapter 28

'I met a man in this town who I truly liked and could have loved. He was kind and welcomed me and my friends with open arms. We betrayed him, used him, and I watched as he died before my eyes and then, even then when I could have uttered words of kindness, I mocked him and left him to die alone. All so that my friends who treat me like a child and a whore would continue to accept me. Daily, I try to rationalise that I had to do that or end up like this man. My friends have no mercy. They would kill me without a second thought and find a replacement just as quickly.'

'I have a secret to tell you,' Kassy said once Nix had finished drying her eyes. 'First, use some of that fae powder. It will make what I am about to tell you that much more enjoyable.'

Nix clapped her hands together eagerly. 'I love secrets,' she said. 'Can you do this, please? My hands are unsteady.'

Kassy unclasped the box, which was made from seashells and pearls. She took the small sniffing spoon and heaped it with the pink fae powder. A part of her wept inside. Nix was mentally little more than a child, and it saddened Kassy to know what must be done. To shove those emotions aside, she focused on the bodies of her two dying sons and how Nix had laughed as they lay dying and had even finished her youngest with her knives as he lay unable to defend himself, calling his mother's name.

Nix snorted the spoon of powder up one nostril, then rubbed her nose and breathed deeply. 'You really packed that one. I can only imagine the effects when you tell me this secret. It will truly heighten the moment and what comes next. At a guess, I would say you are going to take advantage of me. I would like that,' she said, running her fingers through Kassy's hair.

Kassy smiled and packed the spoon again. 'One more, my little sprite,' she said. 'Then we will truly have some fun. Nix paused and looked up at Kassy. Two? That is more than I have ever taken. Are you sure it's safe?'

'Do I look like someone who wishes you harm, darling?' She purred and squeezed the girl's hand reassuringly.

Nix took the second spoonful, and her eyes closed. She smiled and laughed. 'It's so strong,' she said, opening her eyes. 'Everything is so beautiful. Now you take some,' she said, leaning against Kassy.

Kassy took two spoonfuls also so as not to arouse the girl's suspicion. It didn't matter since the powder would have no effect on her.

'Now come with me, my friend, let's go somewhere more private,' Kassy whispered to Nix.

'Hmmm, I like the sound of that,' Nix replied and allowed herself to be pulled to her feet. They found a section of trees by the water thick enough to hide themselves from the view of the families on the riverbank.

Nix jumped up and down. 'What's this secret? I want to know already,' she said, laughing as Kassy beckoned her forward to whisper in her ear.

'Sign this contract now, you old fool, and all this misery will end. Then you can die in peace,' said Samual, slapping the contact down in front of Arlo, who sat tied to a chair in the dining room.

'I will do no such thing until you bring my son before me, and if he is alive, then you will get your damn signature,' retorted Arlo defiantly.

Samual backhanded the old man across the face and stormed from the room.

Downstairs he passed Elspeth, who looked a mess. When she had left the Cauldron during the break for the dice game between Angus and Archie, a group of men in the darkness had jumped her. They had roughed her up nicely and broken the fingers of her hands, which since she had healed using her magic. The healing had cost

Chapter 28

her, and now, while still showing the dark bruises to her face, she looked ten cycles older as she walked gingerly from broken ribs. Samual knew Archie was behind it. The gambler, Archie, and his second, Wren, had somehow found out that Elspeth was leaving to use sorcery during the card games. Archie had disappeared off the map, which left Wren Sorenson, but the fool was as elusive as his counterpart. Samual longed to have an in-depth talk with the man and give him a taste of the violence Elspeth had endured.

Samual knew his Lords and Dames were falling apart with Angus having his hand chopped off and then sold in slavery to a man called Gerald Lyre. Gerald was supposedly a terrible man and not one to cross. Now Angus was lost to them, which left them down one warrior, and not just any warrior either. Angus had been an exceptional fighter.

Museo was downstairs on the front porch and looked up as Samual arrived.

'Have a drink, Samual. All this worry can wait until tomorrow,' he slurred, and Samual smashed the crystal goblet from his hands. It shattered.

'Our group is disintegrating, and all you can do is get drunk. You should be out there watching over Nix, you fool!'

'Always with Nix, is it? Watch Nix, see to Nix. Well, I'm sick of running around after the wanton whore. She is no better than a child, and we all know you only keep her around to warm your damn bed, Samual,' Museo shouted back, standing chest to chest with Samual.

'Don't push me, Museo, I am not in the mood right now. I have enough problems to drive me mad.'

'We all do, Samual, so don't take it out on us. We should never have attacked the Vixen and stolen the spirit ball. All it has given us is ill luck. Now we have lost our strongest warrior, Elspeth was beaten to a pulp, Nix has run off, and the fool Arlo won't sign his estate over to us until we produce Bertram so he can see his son is alive,' his voice dropped to an exaggerated whisper, 'which we know he is not!'

Samual threw his hands in the air. 'To the infernal hells with this. I am going to my room. Inform me if Nix returns; I would have words with her.' Then he stormed off into the manor as Museo shouted after him. 'Yes, my lord, I will do that, my lord,' in a mocking tone.

It was an ungodly chime of early morning when Samual was shaken awake by Museo, who appeared stone sober now.

'Samual, dress and come downstairs. Nix has returned.'

'Just send her up,' Samual replied sleepily. 'I wish to sleep more.'

'I can't do that. Nix is not herself, and you need to see her. You are the only one who can ever get any sense out of her. Now come downstairs.'

Samual thought briefly of throttling the man who annoyed him more and more these days, but it was the tone of Museo that made him rise and get dressed. Museo had genuinely looked worried, even afraid.

When Samual got downstairs, he found Museo and Elspeth standing over Nix in the library, where she lay babbling and drooling on herself. Her bare feet were muddy and bleeding, and thorns pierced the skin of her back and neck, showing grey against the pale pink of her skin.

'Get her up, Elspeth,' Samual snapped.

'No way am I touching her. Those thorns are from the wraith field, Samual, and I have no wish to be affected by their poison.'

'What the hell was she doing in the wraith field?' Samual asked.

'Your guess is as good as ours. We can't get any sense out of her at all.'

Samual looked around and spied his long, leather gloves and donned them, then he knelt beside Nix and sat her up.

'Nix, what has happened to you?' He noticed her eyes were large and the pupils dilated. 'She is messed up on that damn fae powder,' he said, thinking out loud.

Chapter 28

'The red-haired woman, she did this to me. She is a monster, not a human. She told me things Sammy, bad things, and then she took me and impaled me on one of the wraith trees. I can feel the wraith in my blood; it's eating me from the inside. I'm scared, Samual. Please hold me,' Nix said between sobs.

'You are making no sense, Nix, what lady?'

'The one with the long, red hair. She got into my head with some sort of magic and showed me what we did to her, and how it made her feel. She gave me the pain we caused her, and it's too much. I cannot take it anymore.' Nix covered her ears and rocked back and forth, crying hysterically.

'What is she babbling about?' Samual turned and asked Museo.

'We don't know Samual; all she keeps saying is the red-haired woman gave her all the pain we caused and then impaled her in the wraith field.'

Elspeth was kneeling beside Nix and was looking at the black striations on her back. 'Already it spreads, and soon she will become lost to us to wander the astral world more and more,' she said.

'Can't you help her? Dammit, Elspeth. Use your magic to pull her free.'

'Samual, my magic is too dangerous for me to use right now. I am weak and would become very ill from the cost required. I cannot cast until I am fully rested from all my injuries.'

Samual cursed and swept everything off the table. 'We need to know who this red-haired bitch is. Museo, you should have gone with her to the town this night. Now she could be lost to us.'

'Don't point the finger of blame at me, Samual. You could have gone, but you don't trust us to stay here and watch over Arlo and the precious spirit ball.'

'Can you blame me? You are a follower, Museo, not a leader, and it's as if I need to wipe your ass for you.'

'I won't listen to this anymore Samual. You insult me too much and always look down on the rest of us. If it wasn't for the debt I owe you towards my sister, I would already be gone.' Museo left the room.

'Leave him alone, Samual. We are all hurting from the loss of Angus and now this. Just give him tonight to calm down. We will all benefit from rest, and tomorrow we can begin the hunt for this red-haired woman who has dared to hurt one of our own.' Elspeth put a swollen hand on his arm. 'Please, just leave it and have a drink with me. Soon my power will be accessible again, but until then we need to be united.'

'You speak wise words, El. I am sorry for my outburst; I just hate seeing us fall apart. We have become weak, and I am used to being the predator, not the hunted.'

Elspeth passed him a glass of brandy. 'Here, drink this. It will settle both our nerves. All is not lost. We just don't know who our enemies are at the moment,' she said, drinking down her own brandy.

When Samual returned to the dining room, he unchained Arlo from the chair and carried the man up to his chamber.

'Things aren't going to plan are they, Samual? I heard you all arguing. It's nice to see you having problems.'

'Shut up, you old fool, you know nothing of what is happening.' Arlo chuckled.

'Don't laugh at me, Arlo,' warned Samual.

This only made Arlo laugh more until he held his stomach from all the mirth. 'Not so cocky now, are you, Samual?'

Samual grabbed Arlo by the hair and pulled his head back.

'Let me tell you something then, Arlo. Bertram will never be coming back to rescue you. He is dead. We used him for bait, and he was attacked. Once we acquired what we needed, we left Bertram alone to die a sad death!'

'You jest and try to hurt me.'

Chapter 28

'No, this time I tell you the truth. Bertram is dead, and you will be soon as well. I would prefer you sign the contract and your fortune over to us, but if you don't, then Elspeth will

use her magic to counterfeit your signature. In the end, I always get what I want. This time will be no different.'

Samual left Arlo there to feel the full weight of his words. It felt good to hurt someone and focus all his anger on the old man. Let's see how strong he was now that he knew his precious Bertram was dead.

Chapter 29

Bertram was awake. He saw the tear tracks down Kassy's cheeks. She had been weeping.

As he had watched through Kassy's eyes, Bertram had felt sickened by Kassy's easy manipulation of Nix. When Kassy had impaled the woman in the wraith field, he had wished Kassy had never given him her sight and prayed it would soon end. Nix had screamed for too long, screams that would echo through his mind for his entire life. He turned his eyes from Kassy, reminding himself that this was no woman. She was a creature of myth, a monster. Which meant he was a monster too.

When Kassy had done weeping, he finally turned to look at her.

'What is it, Kassy? Are you hurt?'

'No, I just weep for my lost sons and what my enemies made me do tonight. Nix was an enemy of ours and needed to pay for her part in killing my children and stealing the spirit ball. The problem is that it gave me great pleasure to break her.'

'Is she dead?'

'No, she still lives. I gave her all my pain and sent her mad. If the insanity doesn't kill her, then what I did later will.'

Bertram just waited for her to continue as she dried her eyes. 'The wraith will trap her in the astral or she will become a victim of possession from entities that prowl that realm.'

Bertram shuddered. He had heard about what happened to the poor souls infected with the thorns from the wraith trees. Nix was

Chapter 29

easily swayed and just a tool for Samual like the others in their party, but Nix was not evil. With good friends, her life could have been so different.

Bertram awoke fully refreshed, feeling more energised than he could ever remember feeling in his life—a side effect of Aspre in her zenith, Kassy had explained. From the window in the mill, he looked out upon the fields clothed in white tendrils of mist, which hardly ever came this early. Iktar was almost a month and a half away, but since the return of magic, the seasons have fluctuated, maybe because of the Elemental Tower of Goetz. If they were to stay in the mill much longer, he would need to take measures to ensure they stayed warm during the winter. Fires were a danger to their continuing need to stay hidden. To see smoke arising from the mill could bring suspicion that he had no wish to invite upon himself and Kassy.

Kassy was still abed, her red hair flowing out around her head like a pool of blood highlighting her pale, beautiful face. Bertram pulled on his boots, collected his coat, and descended from the mill. From here he could see lights on in the landowner's manor, which tempted him momentarily to visit the supposedly crazed man to see what he was doing at this early chime of the day. However, that manor was not his destination; his father's was.

'I see the witch has finally unleashed us from the chains. Pity we missed the glory of the moon,' rumbled the intruder from within. The other's discontentment and anger were soon replaced with joy as Bertram loped across the fields towards the only home he had ever known. The mist was thicker now; Bertram was among its grasping fingers, which would aid him in his task.

As he neared the barracks, he could smell the taint of the dead bodies in the nearby trench. They had deserved a better death than this, and to Bertram, it seemed a crime that they had yet to have their corpses buried with the honour they deserved as his father's men. Bertram made his way to the manor, noting the lights to the kitchens and his father's chamber were aglow. Arlo had always been an early riser, and it heartened Bertram to know that even his father's imprisonment couldn't stop him from practising his precepts of life. At the kitchen outside the door, he shrank back out of sight as one maid returned with two buckets of water she had drawn from the well.

'Hurry, Nellie, we can't afford to have breakfast for the masters late again, Samual will flay us for it,' scolded Tess from inside.

'They can all burn in the infernal lands for all I care. I still think we should just run away while they sleep. We would be well away when they even realised,' replied Nellie.

'Hush, you foolish girl, if one of them should hear us, we are good as dead. Anyway, would you so willingly abandon Arlo when he has given us everything?'

'They will kill him. You know that as well as I do, Tess. It's just a matter of time. We know we will be next,' whined Nellie.

'Enough, Nellie, we will find a way. Soon someone will notice the absence of Arlo and his men and come to find out what's amiss; then we can get a message out, but until then we stay for Arlo!'

Bertram smiled grimly as he made his way around to the side of the manor, where one of the thick Eldruth fruit trees grew high alongside the upper hallway between the four bedrooms on the second floor. The window latch there was faulty and was how Bertram used to sneak in and out of his home over the cycles during his youth. He clambered up through the thick branches easily then took the branch that would allow him to see inside the hallway.

Peering inside the dusty window, Bertram could see a figure slumped in a chair outside Arlo's chamber. It was Museo, whom Bertram had remembered saying he was a lover of the night and far from a morning person. They had Arlo guarded, so Bertram shimmied along the branch farther to look in upon his father's chamber. Arlo was in his chair at his table. Papers lay strewn on the floor as he wrote frantically in a book. His appearance was dishevelled, and for the first time in his memory, Bertram could see his father was unshaven. Bertram was tempted to knock on the glass and allow Arlo to see him, but he refused to entertain the notion further since there was no way he could carry Arlo down the tree to safety. His father was alive and well, so that was good, but his rescue would need

to wait until Bertram could learn the patterns of his enemies well enough to get Arlo away from the Lords and Dames.

Making his way back along the branch, Bertram took the other branch that would lead him up to the only room on the third story of the manor, which Arlo had used as his private study, and had the faulty window latch. The branch buckled alarmingly beneath his weight for a moment, making Bertram pause and pray silently for it to hold. He made it to the window and saw with relief the room was empty. Using his dagger, Bertram pried the frame open and then lowered himself down onto the rug. Before he did anything else, he crept to the door and placed the wooden pole across to bar the door from being opened from the other side, hoping nobody would try the door while he was inside. He had little time and wasn't sure what he hoped to find, but he remembered Samual's admiration for the study, which allowed a splendid view from two different windows out over the fields around the manor.

'A place where I can see myself penning my next significant works,' Samual had told Bertram.

Looking around, Bertram spied dirty plates and goblets on the fine oak desk. Ink had spilled in one place, which if left uncleaned would forever tarnish the fine desktop. And then Bertram spotted it. A book bound with a fine cord made from dark leather with no title. It wasn't one from the manor library, or Bertram would have known of it since he had read every volume more than once. A quick search of the room proved uneventful, and when the sound of muffled voices arguing carried up from below, Bertram knew it was time to go. He grabbed the book and then quickly climbed out the window, making sure he pushed the frame back in and dropped the broken latch to look like he had never been there. Bertram was already racing across the field when the intruder brought to his attention his mistake.

'You forgot to unbar the door, you fool,' the intruder accused, and with a sick feeling in his gut, Bertram knew he had.

'You could have told me earlier, you know?'

'You were inside, Bertie, and had the chance for revenge. We should have murdered them all in their sleep. I am not the one to be blamed for your weakness. Now they might find out someone has been there. You told me you don't need my help many times, so unless you ask and I am willing to help you, then I will remain silent.'

Closer to the mill, the intruder spoke again.

'There is a doe up ahead; can you smell it? Fresh meat, Bertie, is just what we need,' and Bertram had to agree. 'Not now, we can eat later,' but the intruder seemed to explode into Bertram, who, unprepared, raised no resistance. He was crouched, making sure he was upwind of the beast. The intruder crept forward to within a short distance before the doe's ears flicked up in alarm, its head rising to gaze around, which was when the intruder burst up and charged forward with a howl that reverberated through the morning. Even Bertram thrilled to the hunt. The doe almost escaped them but was brought down as the intruder lunged, catching one of its back legs, and then they were upon it, mouth descending to tear at the soft flesh of its throat, ripping the life from it.

The intruder gorged itself before Bertram regained control. They lay panting upon the blood-drenched grass beside the still-warm doe. Bertram gathered himself and slung the doe over his shoulder, then recovered the book from the ground in the undergrowth before making his way back to the mill.

Chapter 29

A dishevelled Kassy came downstairs while Bertram was skinning the doe. She said nothing, but her eyes told him she disapproved of his loss of control again. Burying the innards behind the mill, Bertram took Kassy a haunch of meat. She watched him as they ate in silence.

'You have been busy while I slept,' she finally said, wiping blood from her mouth.

'I went to the manor. When I was a child, I used to sneak in by a damaged window. My father is alive but kept under guard. I found this book; it's Samual's. Maybe it can help give us an advantage against him.'

'What you did was stupid, Bertram. I know you wish for nothing more than to save your father but to risk our plans without me knowing. Anything could have happened without me there to back you up.'

'I know, Kassy, but I am tired of doing nothing. How long before they kill Arlo or use your spirit ball to force you to serve them? What are we waiting for?' Bertram fired back.

'We must make them turn against one another, tear their trust apart. With Angus gone and Nix terrified, they will bicker amongst themselves, wondering what is happening. This brings us to a point of much danger now, Bertram.'

'What can we do now without revealing ourselves until we are ready?'

'We sow the seeds of suspicion within them even more and with the people you know so well in the town, drawing attention to your father. You may have more allies than you know.'

Chapter 30

With the end of the festival, the town of Fallon's March returned to its quieter state. Few of the caravans, theatre troupes, or other travelling groups that roamed the festival trail remained as the town recovered from three nights of celebrating the simple joys of life. Bertram returned the waves and nods in his direction from townsfolk who had come to accept, at least partially, his being here since the events at the Cauldron.

Bertram ached to be finished with this entire business so he could get back to the mill where Samual's book awaited him. There must be something inside he could use to his advantage so Arlo could be rescued. He thought of Nix as Kassy plied her with stimulants, then tore the woman's sanity away to replace it with madness, and he shivered. Then again, what should he have expected Kassy to do? The Lords and Dames had broken into her home, killed her two sons, and stolen her spirit ball, the seat of her power. Now Kassy was vulnerable. It confused Bertram as to why Samual had not forced Kassy to go to him. Was it that he didn't yet know how to use the powerful item?

Though Bertram had fought it, his mind kept returning to Nix and what she had been through. The simple way she went with any decision made for her and the way she threw herself into anything joyous while shutting out all that threatened to interfere with her life of fantasy had been her downfall. He pitied her, and yet there had been times she had been calculating, cold, and filled with

Chapter 30

eagerness to see others hurt. Bertram knew he couldn't waste his time pitying any of the Lords and Dames. Nix had forged her own path long before their lives had crossed, but to impale her in the wraith trees...did she deserve that?

Two carts heavily laden with stock for the Cauldron sat with their horses stamping their hoofs impatiently as they waited outside the establishment. Sef towered over the two drivers, who each accepted a mug of ale from the big man before wandering away beneath a tree where they squatted and lit their pipes.

Sef spotted Bertram and called out. 'Wren, good morning to you. I had thought you may have left town with the festival since we haven't seen you in what, three days?'

'I prefer to avoid the temptation of drinking every day, Sef; otherwise, I would achieve nothing at all,' Bertram replied, feeling genuinely happy to see his friend.

'Well, since you're here, maybe you can help us since all my oaf of a brother seems to do is talk with everybody who passes when he should be helping me work,' came a deep voice from behind Bertram and Sef.

Bertram turned to see Munn ambling towards the carts. The man was not tall like his brother Sef but thickly slabbed with muscled shoulders as broad as a door. Bertram recalled Dixie once saying if she could birth a baby as big as Munn, she could do anything.

'Quit your griping, baby brother. It's only fitting you do the share of the hard work; after all, you are the youngest and ugliest of the two of us,' Sef replied, faking a punch at Munn, who simply stared at his brother while shaking his head slowly.

Bertram grabbed a crate from one cart along with the brothers, then carried it inside the inn, which looked alien to him during the day. He could hear Dixie's voice in the kitchen scolding someone, even at this early chime, which made him smile.

'What's funny then, Wren?' asked Munn as they returned for more crates.

'Just wondering if Dixie ever stops yelling at someone,' Bertram replied.

'Never, and she is worse during the day since she hardly sleeps,' Munn said.

'Or lets us sleep,' added Sef with a sigh.

'So, are you here for any reason, Wren, or just out of the goodness of your heart to help two tired, worn-out brothers?' Sef asked as they worked.

'Both. I came to ask something of you, and then when I saw you here so overworked decided to help,' he said, laughing at the glares of the two brothers.

'Well, ask then,' Munn shrugged. 'We're all ears.'

'Part of the reason I came to Fallon's March was because I am a scholar who had read many of one of a certain man's writings. A man called Bertram Paxton, whom I hoped to approach regarding his work as well as a possible position in our guild at Stormwatch,' Bertram explained.

Sef paused, then nodded as if agreeing.

'Bertram would have liked that,' Sef said.

'You speak in past tense, Sef. Has something happened to Bertram Paxton, or has he left Fallon's March?'

'We knew Bertram and his father, Arlo, well. Bertram was a regular at the Cauldron when he wasn't busy helping run his father's manor. Nearly two months ago he went missing, and we haven't seen him since,' Munn explained as the three of them got their breath.

'Hasn't anybody looked into Bertram's disappearance?' Bertram asked.

'Arlo's man, Martin, who protects the manor and is in Arlo's employ, brought Old Man Paxton to town to enquire if we knew anything. He told us of his worry since Bertram left with a group of troublemakers who call themselves the Lords and Dames. We had them here when they came to town the first night, and they spent

Chapter 30

the night with Bertram, using fae powder and drinking heavily. Then, according to Arlo, they had convinced Bertram of their need to stay somewhere, to which Bertram offered them the hospitality of house Paxton. Bertram left the next day with these new friends and hasn't been seen around Fallon's March since, even though these friends returned. This was ten days before you arrived here, Wren.'

'It's strange then that a few days ago I went to the Paxton manor to present my invitation to Bertram and stopped before doing so when I saw two of the Lords and Dames who had been in the company of Angus when he was at the Cauldron for the gambling with Archie. I think their names were Samual and Nix,' Bertram said. 'They stood out in front of the manor, literally screaming at one another. The topic they were clearly disagreeing about was Arlo signing his lands over to Samual. I watched for a while, which I am loath to admit since I am not the prying type, but I never did see any guards or servants, which is why I decided to leave. Do you know if Arlo has talked with Justiciar Carson?'

'It may well be that he has indeed done that, but you would need to ask Carson himself,' answered Sef.

'I find it hard to believe that Arlo, who is a godly man who refuses to accommodate foolishness, would allow such people as these Lords and Dames to reside in his home. There is no way he would willingly sign his land over to anyone,' said Munn, raising his eyebrows in surprise.

'I will finish helping you both, then maybe seek out Carson,' Bertram replied. Now he had planted the seeds within the minds of the two brothers, Bertram allowed himself to settle into the strangely calming task of unloading the carts. Sef and Munn thanked him once they had unloaded everything.

'Next delivery is tomorrow afternoon, Wren. With strength like that we have a job for you, should you be looking?'

'I'm afraid I'm not cut out for this work. I most likely won't be able to walk come tomorrow,' Bertram called back as he wandered back into town. The many shops lining the main road through town were opening their doors. Bertram stopped at one selling hot tea with fresh pastries, and he settled down to await their arrival. The work had caused him quite a sweat; he loosened his top shirt buttons, closed his eyes, and deeply breathed in the fresh morning air.

'A little early to be sitting about doing nothing, Mr. Sorenson,' someone said, startling Bertram enough that he nearly fell off the bench. He looked up to see Rae standing before him with a large basket in hand containing a bundle of cloth.

'You underestimate me, dear Rae. I have just come from the Cauldron, where I helped Sef and Munn unload the carts of stock. Now I'm merely trying to recover. This brief respite I have earned with sweat you see now beading my forehead,' he added, looking up at Rae, who was now giggling.

'Those two would find any excuse to get someone to do their work, you know.'

'Here, sit with me for a moment. I won't keep you long,' Bertram said, scrambling to make room on the bench and calling for another pastry to be added to his order.

Rae sat, then readjusted her skirts as she stared at him.

'What?'

'Sorry, it's just I still feel I know you, though I am sure it's not possible. It's just you remind me so much of a friend of mine,' Rae apologised.

'Bertram Paxton? '

'Excuse me?' Rae asked.

'I bet I remind you of a Bertram Paxton. You are one of many who have said that to me. I need to contact that man, but according to Munn and Sef, Bertram has disappeared.'

'Are you related?' Rae asked Bertram.

Chapter 30

'No, we are not. I would know if I had a brother, and my mother kindly reminded me often that after having me, she and my father had decided that having more children just wasn't worth it,' Bertram said with a wry smile.

They shared the tea, and then ate the pastries in silence.

'Well, I wouldn't say you're that bad, Wren. Strange, for sure, and a little secretive. But at least you have your good looks going for you,' Rae responded, refusing to look at him as she fumbled with the basket she held. 'How is your uncle these days, Wren?'

'Mad as usual. His paranoia keeps him locked away most of the time.'

'Is it true what people say about him then, you know, that he murdered his family?' Rae asked.

'Not true at all. His family died of the withering disease. It's a family weakness on his wife's family side, which is why he never suffered from it,' Bertram replied and was relieved that at least he didn't have to lie about one thing to Rae.

'Well, anyway, Wren, you have interrupted me for long enough. Good morning to you.' And then Rae walked away quickly.

'Rae, wait a moment, please,' Bertram called after her.

Rae stopped walking. She glanced back over her shoulder at him.

'Can we meet tonight after your shift? There is something important about Bertram I need to talk to you about,' Bertram said.

Rae paused for so long that Bertram thought she might not have heard him correctly, and he was about to ask again when she answered.

'If you think I will ride out to Old Man Dufell's manor in the dead of night, Wren Sorenson, then you are mistaken. However, if you meet me at the Cauldron, we can speak awhile.' Rae then hurried away, leaving Bertram staring after her.

Bertram angled his way down towards the small lake, delighting in the reflecting sun on the clear water. He could smell the sweet flowers from this distance easily, which made him remember happier times with his parents here a lifetime ago.

Museo rested his back against the tree trunk and pondered on the conversation Wren Sorenson had shared with the serving wench Rae. It was true that the man was similar to

Bertram. How had he not noticed that before? The same casual gait as he walked, the interest in the littlest things around him or the crooked grin he gave often. Can't be Bertram, though; this man is not casual. He is confident, at ease with his surroundings, jovial, not harbouring an inner anger that rendered him powerless. The Dufell estate, though, that was interesting information. Samual had been tearing his hair out trying to locate Wren, and now they knew he was the old man's nephew. Museo kept his distance as he followed Wren down towards the lake.

Chapter 31

Once Bertram had skirted the lake, he continued back into the town where he would cut across to the fields that bordered that side, then cut across to the track that led to the mill and Dufell's lands. His path took him close to the glass blower's business, where an amazing display of clever creations sat arranged on shelves that could be viewed easily from the few glass windows in the town. The owner was a widely travelled man who had recently returned to Fallon's March after learning how to create glass windows, but the small furnaces he had added at the back of the shop had yet to prove successful in creating glass panes for windows. Instead, he had used a clear, obsidian, volcanic rock that had to be shipped to Stormwatch from west of the Bay of Storms. Bertram only knew of this because his father had been approached by the shopkeeper to fund collateral in order to complete the shipment.

It was while looking in the window that Bertram caught the reflection of a figure passing by behind him, who turned to look at him before continuing on. In the glass, Bertram had glimpsed a long moustache beneath the figure's wide-brimmed hat, and he turned to look as the man hurried on, his identity hidden from the hat and the long, deep-blue cloak he wore.

Could that have been Museo? Bertram wondered. Deciding against heading for the mill, he headed the opposite way into the town towards the market area, keeping a calm demeanour about him in case he was being followed.

'Of course, we are being followed,' the intruder drawled. 'Head to the fields now, Bertie. We can ambush and kill him, or do you want to give away your cover?'

'I will lose him in the town. I was born here, and he wasn't. It will be easy to give him the slip.'

Though it was only mid-morning most of the morning haggling was now complete since store owners and farmers in the town preferred to conduct their business as early as possible. Bertram moved through the stalls, feigning interest as he went while trying to glimpse the darkly dressed figure whom he had thought was Museo. Bertram avoided buying any of the meat, vegetables, or fruit on view. If he needed to flee, he would be better served without having to lug any purchases with him. Slowly he meandered his way past all the perishables towards the trade wares and timber yard before ducking into a small alleyway, where he stood examining his nails as if waiting. Bertram could easily see if anyone made their way past his position and he could still use the alleyway to escape into the narrow roads that wound through the many homes nearby.

'We are being stalked,' came the voice of the intruder.

'Maybe we are, or maybe not. I'm not sure yet,' Bertram sent back.

'Lure him here, then kill him. We cannot afford to have anybody follow us, Bertie.'

'Don't you think I know that? Anyway, we don't know if we are being followed yet,' Bertram replied.

'There he is. By the logging saws. Can you see him?'

And Bertram could. The dark-clothed man walked quickly, throwing furtive glances as he went. He moved easily without drawing attention to himself, and Bertram could see from beneath his cloak that he carried a rapier. Museo carried a rapier, too. Coincidence? Bertram tracked the figure's movements until in apparent disgust the man kicked up a plume of dust and then turned back towards the food market.

Chapter 31

Bertram stayed where he was for another quarter of a chime, then turned to leave down the alleyway towards the houses. As he neared the opening of the alleyway, the figure he had watched stepped out to block his way.

Bertram turned, then sprinted back down the alleyway, ignoring the call of the man behind him, whom he now was certain was Museo of the Lords and Dames.

'Wren Sorenson, stop! I just want to talk to you!'

Bertram didn't stop, though, and instead burst out into the timber yards, narrowly avoiding two workers carrying a long pole of timber. He ignored their shouts of dismay as he ran down through stacked piles of timber and out onto the cobblestone roadway. The sound of boots striking the stones behind him was enough to know that Museo was in pursuit.

'Find somewhere quiet and kill him,' shouted the intruder within him, but Bertram was too caught up in losing his pursuer. He ducked past a woman scrubbing clothes on the narrow road then dashed down a side road where children played at kicking a ball to each other.

'Watch out,' he called. They looked up in surprise as he ducked between them, running as fast as he could.

'Wren, stop and talk to me,' came the call from behind again.

Bertram almost lost his footing as his boots slipped on the wet cobbles. He turned again to another street, passing more people who stared at him dumbly.

Though Bertram had grown up in Fallon's March, it had been many cycles since he had been in these streets. Now he wasn't sure of his exact whereabouts. His desperation spurred Bertram onward.

Down more alleyways, even doubling back around trying to lose Museo, whose heavy footfalls alerted him that the chase continued.

Pushing himself harder, Bertram turned into another street. He saw he had entered a dead-end alley with a ten-foot wall lined with wicked spikes atop it, blocking his way. He had reached the outer wall that ringed the town.

Bertram was trapped.

Slowing to a walk, Bertram turned with one hand on the sabre at his belt.

He tried to slow his laboured breathing without success.

Bertram watched as Museo turned the corner, slowing now to a walk. He had lost his hat in the chase.

Museo pushed the long, dark hair from his eyes.

'Why are you running from me?' Museo gasped as he stopped twenty feet away with hands on hips.

'You were following me, hoping I didn't see you. I wasn't sure who it could be,' Bertram replied, panting, all focus now on the slim man before him.

'I merely wished to ask you some questions, Wren,' Museo said as he used a piece of leather to tie his hair back.

'I have no wish to answer anything you wish to ask me. In fact, I want nothing to do with you or your damn friends! Don't come any closer,' Bertram warned.

'Or what, Wren? You have nobody to help you now. No Archie, who has left this cursed town, or the two brothers from the Cauldron who you obviously are friends with,' Museo said, with his hand now resting lightly on the long blade at his hip.

'Museo, if you only wanted to talk, you would have approached me plainly, not skulking around following me. Did Samual put you up to this?'

'This has nothing to do with Samual. It is because of my own suspicious nature that I am here confronting you. It wasn't until you arrived out of nowhere that we became beset with problems, Wren.'

'What happened with Angus had nothing to do with me. He was not obliged to take the challenges against Archie,' Bertram replied.

'Let me outline something for you, Wren. First Angus loses his challenge and is proven to be a cheat, resulting in him having his

Chapter 31

hand cut from his body, then he disappears with rumours stating he was given over to the Lyre family, who after some investigation I have found out hold quite a sway over this town.'

Bertram attempted to speak, but Museo talked over him.

'Elspeth was wrongly accused of using sorcery during the challenge with Angus. She was assaulted by a group of thugs and had her hands broken. Then Nix wanders off to the festival only to return with a tale that she was accosted by a red-haired woman who ended up impaling her in the wraith field. Nix later revealed to me that while under the effects of the fae powder when the red-haired woman showed her the pain that had been caused, she had seen something, someone attached to the woman. Hiding behind the eyes were her exact words, and do you know who she saw?'

Bertram watched Museo carefully as the man ambled forward some more with his hand still on his sword as he spoke. When Bertram remained silent, he continued.

'You, Wren. Nix told me she saw you behind the red-haired woman's eyes. Doesn't that seem strange to you?'

'Nix isn't exactly sane, Museo. She uses so much fae powder that to believe anything Nix says would be foolish,' Bertram said.

'Normally I would agree with you, Wren, but I have never seen Nix like this. She was rattled to the bone, and for once there was no sign of the fae effects. Her terrible ordeal had shaken her free of them.'

'You chased me here to tell me of all the troubles your friends are experiencing in the hope I will take the blame for their mishaps?' Bertram asked.

'I know something with you is not as it seems, Wren Sorenson, and I want to know what you and this mysterious woman did to my friend.' Museo drew his sword, to which Bertram drew his own weapon. His mouth was dry, but his palms sweated as if all his fear attempted to escape from them at once.

Bertram knew he was in trouble facing Museo, a celebrated swordsman from Cavere who dedicated much of his life to the arts of swordplay, and yet beneath that fear his anger bubbled. This was one of those who had left him to die and now attempted to blackmail his father.

The intruder was screaming from inside his head, which was highly distracting and disorientating.

'Remember what they did to you, Bertie, they left you to die! This is what you wanted, isn't it? To kill them, rend their flesh, and take revenge? Well, there is no better time than now that you have one of them alone with us. Let me out and I will make sure he bothers you no more.'

Bertram pushed the intruder away from him, focusing on Museo, who stood now just out of sword reach.

'Tell me what's going on, Wren, or I will carve the secrets from you,' Museo said coldly.

Bertram angled his blade at the man's throat.

In response, Museo leaned forward, his thin blade snapping straight out at Bertram's face. The strike got past Bertram's guard easily to slide into the flesh of his shoulder, then out again, making Bertram gasp at the pain.

The sight of blood on Museo's blade sent the intruder into a shrieking frenzy. Bertram slashed diagonally down at Museo's throat, but the man simply batted the attack aside and then slashed across Bertram's left thigh, making him stumble. He was outmatched against a superior fighter, and he knew it.

The next few moments were a blur as Museo attacked from every possible angle in a flurry of strikes that Bertram somehow met with his own blade as his reflexes took over, and the long lessons overseen by Arlo and the guard, Martin came into play. Museo ducked a brutal swipe of Bertram's blade then danced back out of reach, hardly breathing hard, while Bertram was breathing heavily through his mouth.

Chapter 31

'You have some training in the blade then? But how long do you think you can last against me?'

The commotion had attracted attention from the adjoining street, as behind Museo, a group of people had gathered. Bertram knew he couldn't risk staying here to be maimed by Museo or be caught up in a public duel, which was against the law in Fallon's March. Even now shrill whistles could be heard in the town, alerting him to the fact that the garrison soldiers had been notified that something was happening.

Bertram feigned a low strike, then angled the blade up at Museo's grinning face. Steel met steel with Museo's counter, slamming his arm to the side, leaving him unprotected. Then Museo darted forward, crashing his sword hilt into Bertram's face and slamming his head into the wall behind him.

The strike allowed the intruder to break free of Bertram's control with a surge of strength. It grabbed the blade and used it to pull Museo closer, ignoring the damage the razor-sharp steel did to Bertram's hand. It smashed a fist into Museo's face.

Museo attempted to tear his blade free. The intruder grabbed Museo by the shirt and then slammed him into the wall. Bertram faintly registered pain in his side as Museo released his sword and danced out of striking distance. He now held a short dagger in his opposite hand, stained with Bertram's blood. The man's calm demeanour had disappeared to be replaced with fear now as he stared, wide-mouthed, at Bertram. He flicked his free hand to his belt, and then there was another blade in hand as the intruder attacked again. They slammed together, one dagger falling to the cobblestones, the other connecting with Bertram's side.

Museo fell under the power of the attack as the intruder rained blows down upon the man's chest and forearms, where they protected his face. Revelling in the release it had craved, the intruder screamed its pleasure to the sky as shouts of alarm reached down to Bertram. The garrison men were closing in. Bertram surged up with all his willpower, seizing control of his body again.

'Leave me alone,' he snarled at Museo, who was staring up at him in part wonder, part fear. Looking up at the tall wall behind him, Bertram leapt, easily clearing the spikes to land on the other side. He ran in the mill's direction and, once he had realised there was no pursuit, slowed to a walk. The pain of his wounds was all coming back now that the adrenaline was leaving his body. He felt raw and on fire. It was uncomfortable when he twisted to the side, and he realised with horror something was stuck into his flesh behind his left shoulder. Reaching around, his hand found the hilt of a dagger, which he pulled free with a curse. It was Museo's other blade.

The dagger wound didn't hamper his movement at all, but blood flowed freely down his side, soaking his shirt. The wound to his shoulder was painful when he raised his arm, deep but clean, and his face ached where Museo had caught him with the hilt of his blade. In an exhausted shuffle, he wound his way back to the mill. He could feel the intruder's anger at being denied a kill, but he tried to ignore it while berating himself for losing control so easily. He couldn't deny it anymore. When he became too emotional or his life was

threatened, the intruder could simply walk in and take control of him. Sure, it was damn useful, as he had just found out, but it could easily be his downfall too, and now he had been forced to reveal Wren was more than he seemed. Museo was now a problem that would not be so easily turned away next time.

Chapter 32

Kassy saw him coming. She met Bertram on the ground floor and then helped him upstairs. As he rested, she grabbed clean water, bandages, and herbs, then silently dressed his wounds. The wounds to his shoulder and back needed stitches, which she threaded with ease, listening as he told her what had happened to him.

'They know Wren is not who they think he is, and it's only a matter of time, Kassy before they work out who the red-haired lady was who attacked Nix,' Bertram said. 'Our plan is falling apart.'

'All it means, Bertram, is that we must speed things up, that's all. They don't know your true identity yet, though it seems your persona as Wren has come to an end. We must not act too hastily without aid from the Lyre family until you are feeling better. Soon we will be ready to assault the manor to save your father and reclaim my spirit ball. The thing that worries me is that you were witnessed leaping over a ten-foot wall with spikes, which no ordinary man could do. The intruder cannot be allowed to take you over even in matters of life and death. You need to be in total control, but you are still split in two. The intruder within you is a constant drain of your energy as it claims your strength and power.'

'Kassy, It's different with the intruder now. We have come to an understanding of sorts. I can control him if needed.'

Kassy threw her hands in the air, then pushed back her hair. The sun's rays through the window made her hair look like rivulets of blood. Kassy seemed to grow in stature as he watched her. Bertram saw something wild, untamed shift behind Kassy's eyes, making the hairs on his arms and neck spring up as if registering danger.

'Fool! Never think you can control the intruder within you. That is a constant battle, a constant threat. If you believe you can control it, you are close to losing. You must destroy it and then its power will merge with you,' Kassy said, then she shook like a hound and was once again as she had always been.

'When the full moon comes, what then? You are still new to being animal kin. You lack the control needed during the full moon to stop the intruder from taking over. You need to act now. What happened with Museo is a clear indicator of that. Heed my warning Bertram, then leave your old life before you destroy it all. This is the only way.'

'I have a life here, Kassy. I cannot, will not walk away from those I love who depend on me.'

'What they think of you will change when they find out what you are now. Rae is a strong young woman with many opportunities ahead of her. From what you tell me of your father, he is wise and he will come to understand that this is for the best. Save them and then leave them. You and I can leave together.'

'To do what, Kassy?'

'Truth be told, I don't know what you and I will do.'

'Kassy, I won't be going with you. I will have my life back, maybe marry Rae and have children.'

'A life I fear will leave you sorely unfulfilled. 'You have been through a lot, Bertram, and still have the rescue to achieve. After, if there is an after for any of us, it will be time for you to walk away. Your life has changed beyond what you had and you can never go back. You must know this?'

'I can make this work. I know I can. So will you…'

'Leave? Yes. Our kind doesn't fare well around communities even though they honour us and love the protection we provide.

Chapter 32

Eventually that turns to distrust, even fear at the abhorrent nature of what we are. Our kind are stronger together and with you beside me, we would be quite a team.'

'If we are victorious you will have the spirit ball. I will have my father, and yet though I feel great sadness at us going our own way, I am decided on this matter,' Bertram said, cringing at the sound of his unsure voice.

Her voice softened. 'Come with me Bertram, it is for the best. No matter what you choose, your path will always lead back to me.'

'I can't. I am needed here with Arlo and my Rae.'

Kassy nodded. 'Get some rest. I can sense the intruder in you. It will await you in your dreams, so be wary Bertram. It is time to claim your power.'

Bertram slept little as the pain from his fight with Museo kept him from the accelerated healing Kassy assured him his body could now make use of. Kassy only awoke him for food but soon he drifted into sleep again since he found it difficult to even just keep his eyes open. His unwanted companion, the intruder, was thankfully quiet too, which left Bertram only at the mercy of dreams, which were a confusing mash of memories that always led back to his father, who was still a prisoner in his own home. When he finally clambered up out of his unconscious mind, his night vision easily picked Kassy at her favourite place at the window as she stared out across the fields below.

A thought had followed him from his dreams, the witch Elspeth.

'Kassy, while working on scholarly writing regarding the changes that the return of magic caused regarding nature and man, I found information scarce. Guarded by jealous philosophers, this knowledge was kept from me as I sought answers. Recently you mentioned it was an advantage to know what element of magic Elspeth favoured. Can you explain more about that?'

Kassy's golden eyes found him in the darkness.

'The return of magic by the Coterie of the Heart was directly manipulated by the Mother to make sure the abuse of power our world had seen before the Severing never happens again. Now you are aware already of the hostility nature has towards man and the other races, but something less clear is that if you can know the birth date of any one person, then you can know the time in each cycle of their life when they are strongest and weakest. This is important when dealing with one who draws magic from the Mother. The two priesthoods of Tamul and Aspre are different. They draw directly from the moons, who are the only remaining godlike beings besides the god of time. Do you follow this reasoning, Bertram?' Kassy said, coming to sit beside Bertram.

'Yes, I do. If Elspeth draws from the earth, that is the season she was born to?'

'For one who takes the path of power, they would be foolish not to use their birth element as their key element since to choose another would dilute their potential when they are at their most potent. This, however, doesn't mean they can't access the other elements when using magic; it simply means by choosing their season's element they are vastly more dangerous. The cost they must pay from their own body, mind, and soul is much less than if they draw from the other elements, especially its opposite,' Kassy said.

'Okay, that makes sense, and so in this situation with Elspeth, whom we know draws from the earth element, the best time to strike at her would be in the air element?'

'Yes, that is correct; her power will wane while the cost of magic for her will be higher. Now unfortunately we are not among the air months of the cycle, but are close to Iktar, the first month of the water element, which is one of Elspeth's neutral elements. Elspeth will be weaker, which will be of much use to us when we move against our enemy.'

Chapter 32

'While I was in Stormwatch visiting the Auspex University, I had reason to notice that it was rare to see newborn babes in public, if at all. I mentioned this to one of the master scholars who was helping me at the time, who brushed it away by labelling it as common superstition,' Bertram mused.

'These things take time to become known to the masses, Bertram. Such powerful knowledge cannot stay hidden forever. I have learned directly that any who wish to take the path of power have to commune directly with the Mother,' Kassy said.

'And the magic that runs through us. What cost does that have, Kassy?'

'That is different, Bertram. Most call it a curse linked to nature itself and therefore the Mother. I don't see it that way. I see it as a calling. We are in both worlds, able to know the calls of the Mother like no other while being also among the races whom we can help understand the changes to our world.'

'How do you explain the moon's effect on us?'

'The two moons are a part of the reason we are changed. If I were of a different, let's say evil, temperament, then we would be influenced by Tamul's call and not Aspre. It is our animal side that connects us to the Mother, allowing us to learn her secrets if we truly open ourselves and the moons only awaken that side each time they are full, but unlike priests of the moons, we cannot gain power directly from them.'

'Is there a way to reverse what we have become, Kassy?' he asked.

'Not that I know of. Sometimes recently I am saddened by what I did to you out of rage when my sons were murdered. I was filled with hate, and you were the outlet I poured that into. Now I know you were a victim as much as I was. Rest now. We have long days ahead of us. I need to find herbs in the forest and will return by nightfall,' Kassy said, pulling the blankets up around Bertram and then leaving the room.

It was then that Bertram remembered he had meant to meet Rae after her shift. Had she waited for him? He had planned to tell her he was Bertram and Wren was just a creation to hide his identity. It was too dangerous for him to go out now. Samual's diary caught Bertram's attention, and he opened it to a random page.

Chapter 33

5th of Zephyr cycle of nature.

My life is in tatters. It turns out the death of my father has seen me receive absolutely nothing, not the house or property, nor even one of our outer-lying residences throughout the world. Alyissa had seen to that. It was I who had waited by his bedside day after day, mopping the sweat from his forehead, changing his sheets and clothes, and even bathing or emptying his chamber pot like a common servant. And she would dare deny me my worth? My own father, bless his festering black heart, had promised me, his only son, his wealth. The city guard came for me soon after that. Many of the seven they sent were or had been drinking or gambling companions more than once. Louis was there, and the coward did nothing as I pleaded my case, my right, my inheritance. As I write this, I can still hear the words the bitch Alyissa uttered, as if they had been burned into my mind. Let me quote: *Your father hated you even more than your damn mother. All you ever brought him was debt or misery, which is why as per his death scroll you will receive nothing for the dishonour you have thrust upon this, one of the five founding families of Stormwatch.* Then she spat in my face and for that, she will pay.

6th of Zephyr cycle of nature.

They released me from the cells today after one night. My only possessions are the bruises from the guard's batons and this journal. My other possessions were stolen from my person while

I lay unconscious in a cell with eleven commoners. That is hardly the way to treat a noble-born first son. Escorted to the gates, I was forced to wait in the dust until trusty old Angus came to collect me, loyal to the end. We meet the others at nightfall.

7th of Zephyr cycle of nature.

The Lords and Dames are whole again, albeit two members less, since Grinjo fell into the hands of the king's spies. Esmelda lacks the steel to truly be one of ours, preferring the gossip of noble parties and getting hit on by old men as she hopes to find a rich husband. This was not even the best news of the day. As I sat drinking with Nix, Elspeth, and Museo while Angus looked on with disdain at the poisoning of our bodies, Elspeth produced a scroll and passed it to me. I was delighted to see it was the map I had failed to procure from its owner containing directions to the lair of the Vixen. Museo asked about his precious sister, Cari, once again smiling and hugging me when told about her employment for my aunt as a housemaid. He is still unaware that she is really being kept for a higher purpose to serve the feathered one and being kept pure for me. If only he knew what I had done to his family.

Bertram lowered the diary, letting the words set in, and made a mental note to go back earlier to see if any other references to Museo's family were written.

The following day Bertram was up and about even though his wounds still pained him. He obediently let Kassy give him some tonic for the pain before ignoring her protests as he let himself out of the mill to feed the two horses they had picketed behind the structure. It was good to do something normal, to forget everything that bothered him, at least for a while.

A moment came where he paused, then looked around as the feeling he was being watched came over him. Scanning the trees behind the mill that led to the forest there, he spotted nothing. He raised his head, inhaling deeply, but no strange scent carried to

Chapter 33

him. Across the fields, he could see the manor of Old Man Dufell. The manor stood slowly, decaying, and if it hadn't been for the solitary light that would shine at night from the upstairs of the house, Bertram would have wondered if the old man was even alive.

Throughout the day, Bertram still couldn't shake the feeling he was being watched. As he cut food for a stew he was making, he heard the door to the mill open. Kassy was back. When there came none of the familiar soft singing that usually accompanied Kassy's return, Bertram placed the knife down and retrieved his sword from nearby, then moved to the stairs leading down where he paused, listening intently but finding only silence.

'Kassy?' Bertram called out as he began descending the stairs. A clatter came from below, followed by footsteps and the sound of the door crashing shut.

Bertram hesitated, then rushed down the stairs, where he threw the door to the mill open. Complaining came from the two horses behind the mill, and Bertram rushed around the mill to see a figure disappearing into the trees and out of sight.

Bertram returned to the mill and began a search of the lower level, where bunches of herbs hung drying alongside their food supplies. Nothing was missing, so did that mean the intruder was not a thief, and if so, what had they been looking for?

Bertram bolted the door and kept his sword close by as he finished preparing the food. The day wore on into mid-afternoon as Bertram waited for Kassy to return; he busied himself by picking up Samual's journal and began to read where he had left off the night before.

He found an early entry regarding Museo and leant back as the words took him away.

13th of Blaze cycle of New Birth

Now this is what I call living. The war is at its end; the Infernals have abandoned Acclaro and slunk back to the Infernal lands, and magic has apparently returned to the world. Our king is dead and the manoeuvring for his place has seen many deaths in the plays for power throughout Stormwatch. My days of lying low to avoid conscription into the army for the war are over. As I left my somewhat comfortable prison deep within my father's estate I emerged like a butterfly from a cocoon into a time of revelry where strangers embrace you in the streets and women, who now vastly outnumber the men, are hungry to throw themselves almost eagerly into anything that promotes life and happiness. I soon found Nix prowling the streets for her next sexual conquest, and before I knew it, we were copulating like wild animals in the street before heading to the famous inn called The Failing Light to imbibe as much ale and fae powder as we could. In the Failing Light, I pushed myself to the front of an audience, enthralled with the performance of a man who I can only describe as beautiful. Well-formed muscles lathered with sweat and long, dark hair flying about him he threw himself into an impossible dance, both graceful and solemn as he wove the story of the gods returning to the Mother with dance and then with a voice that could make celestials weep. I was at once smitten and jealous of this fine man who impeccably held all who watched in his thrall. It should be criminal to have so much talent, and I knew I must meet this man hoping but not realising then that I wished some of what he had in abundance would rub off on me. Fighting off the attentions of many others, I and dear Nix gained his attention long enough to ply him with fae powder and a seat at our table. His name is Museo Valente, and I must confess that he is clearly the most talented, mysterious person I have ever met. I fear I am infatuated.

Chapter 33

The next entry had no date, and Bertram soon realised it was from the same night, yet later. The ink was smudged and stained rusty brown in colour, so thick in places that some words remained unreadable.

I am covered in blood! As I drifted from the haze of the fae powder and by the gods who know what other stimulants, I recalled in horror what had happened after I left The Failing Light Inn.

When Museo weaselled his way out of my grasp, claiming exhaustion, I felt betrayed and feared the spell he had so effortlessly weaved upon me with his charm and performance would leave me empty, bereft of life, and so I followed him to his home.

Step by step my amazement turned to dismay as he left the noble district to drunkenly weave his way down into low town where the poor dwell like rats. His home, if you could call it that, was a hovel not fit for a beggar and belied the fine clothes Museo dressed himself in. Through a soot-stained window, I watched as he passed out bread and wine to two older people to whom life had not been kind. They must be his parents. Museo upended a pile of coins gathered from his audience from earlier in the night, and the three held each other crying, lost in their closeness as I watched on through the green of envy. Who was he that he should have everything I hadn't? Then I smiled knowing his life was not perfect. He was nothing more than a lowborn minstrel.

A fourth person entered the room dressed in a white nightgown, doll-like and radiant, who I learned as I watched was Museo's sister, Cari. The fighting of two nearby hounds tore me from my voyeurism, and I hurried away to a quiet area where with trembling hands I snorted a large mound of fae powder, then slumped down in the debris against a wall, uncaring of the smell of urine. How long I sat there I cannot determine, but I was no longer alone. Gone was the bright aura of the fae powder that turned every scene into a fairy-like world, replaced by a haze of swirling shadows through which something crept sinuously to my side, lacing me with whispers of dismay that urged me to take something from this impostor Museo Valente. I succumbed.

Creeping back to Museo's home, I watched him bid his family goodnight and retreat farther into another room as his family, including the larger-than-life Cari, spoke in excitement about what they would do with all the coin Museo had brought home and how their days of being poor were over. It was then that I slipped on a stone, which made quite a racket, and the old man rose, moving to the window to peer out as I leaned against the wall of his home, my heart hammering.

'I think someone is out there.' His voice carried to me, and I was stuck with the decision to run or stay hidden. I hesitated for too long, and the door swung open beside me, a figure stepping outside. Without thinking, I turned around the door and struck out with my fist, striking the old man in the face, and knocking him down; then I stomped down on his head before quickly slipping past him into the room where the two women looked on in shock. Grabbing an empty candle holder, I swung it onto Museo's mother's head with a sickening thud. I stood facing Cari, who was standing stiffly while caught in the thrall of fear. Two steps and I had her with one arm under her chin, choking her into unconsciousness. I retrieved the candleholder and knelt above Cari, ready to stave her skull in, but I couldn't do it. Whether it was her complete beauty or the last remnants of my morals that stopped me, I don't know. I put down my weapon, then filled my pockets with Museo's hard-earned coin.

I couldn't leave Cari here since she was a witness. I wrapped her in a shawl, found some soft-soled shoes that fit her, and took her with me out into the night.

With the revelry going on, nobody would assume more than a drunk couple staggering through the streets. And even my father's household guard only chuckled and winked at me as I carried the unconscious girl to my room.

Chapter 33

When I awoke, Cari was naked, gagged, and tied up, sobbing in fear, and this journal was beside me, stained with blood. What have I done?

14th of Blaze cycle of new birth

I moved Cari when night fell again after plying her with sedatives. I had no wish to have her found in my company. The guard found her in an alleyway, or so I heard later that night from the gossip at the Failing Light when Museo failed to show up for his act. Even after all I had done to his family, I still found the need burning within me to be around Museo, and against all common sense I made my way down into low town to the scene of my crime where his house sat ablaze with lanterns.

I knocked twice on the door, which shortly was opened by a dishevelled Museo, his hair a mess of snarls above red, raw eyes.

'Samual, what are you doing here?' he asked in surprise.

'When you didn't show tonight, I asked why, which is how I learned of the terrible thing that has befallen you and your family. I know we are merely new acquaintances, but I was so taken with your performance, as you know, and, well, I just wanted to see if there was anything I could do for you,' I lied.

Museo broke down then, sliding down to the floor, his back against the wall and his head in his hands as he sobbed. I delighted in his grief as I comforted him. I stayed with him all that night listening to his story in the guise of a loyal friend. As the remnants of the dawn light chased away the night, I gave him an offer he couldn't refuse.

'Museo, it's no longer safe here for you. What if the attackers come back for you and Cari now they know where you live and you have gold?'

'Had gold,' Museo corrected me.

'We have spare rooms at my father's townhouse, which my father rarely visits since he prefers the estate. You both could stay there with me.'

'No, Samual, you have already done much for me. I don't want Cari in this cursed city any longer. I won't be able to continue unless she is far from this place,' Museo said.

'I will get her a position at my uncle's manor, then. They are always in need of good workers, and that way Cari will be safe from further harm away from the city.'

Museo stared at me for a long while then.

'Why are you doing all this for me, Samual?'

'Museo, I feel a connection with you I cannot explain. Your act uncovered a part of me that previously was hidden beneath the bane of depression. You brought some semblance of life back to me, and I want to return the favour to you. At this terrible time, you could do with a friend.'

I needn't worry about Cari recognising me. She had retreated deep into her mind and couldn't recall anything about that night besides a man beating her parents to death.

Chapter 34

Bertram lowered the journal in horror. Samual had murdered Museo's parents and then kidnapped his sister, and obviously, Museo didn't even know. Bertram put the journal down, wishing to read no more about Samual for now. Bertram prepared a stew as he waited for Kassy with regular glances for any sign of her return, but none came. The afternoon faded to a dark, moonless night.

The tension building from within Bertram was eased when he finally picked up movement from the trees just before Kassy came into view with a sack over one shoulder. He ran outside, taking the heavy sack from her, then followed her inside. Kassy looked dishevelled and tired after spending the better part of the day harvesting herbs from the surrounding forest. But even this should not have caused her almost comical appearance.

'Before you ask, I was caught in fox form after being chased by several hunting dogs on the far side of town, and it took me most of the afternoon to lose them to then circle back for my findings,' she said before smiling at the cooking food and tasting it. 'I am famished, Bertram. Next time I will send you to do my scrounging.'

They sat down to dip coarse, almost stale bread in the stew, content with the silence between them.

Later, Kassy drifted off to sleep on the cot while Bertram sat in candlelight, reading from Samual's diary.

Kassy sat up on the cot, sniffing the air. 'Bertram, can you smell smoke?'

Bertram had to lever off one board covering the window that faced the Dufell manor. He could see figures out the front of the manor as thick smoke rose from the bottom-story roof. Someone was gesticulating towards the manor. Four more figures surrounded them in a semi-circle. As Bertram watched, one stepped forward and struck the solitary figure, who collapsed.

'Dufell's manor is on fire!' Bertram said.

Kassy rushed towards the stairs with Bertram close behind, scooping up his sword as he went.

They both began racing across the field, the long grass whipping against their arms and chest, when Kassy suddenly stopped.

'Kassy, what's wrong?' Bertram asked, stopping beside her.

'I can't go any further, Bertram. Samuel is using the spirit ball against me. Just be careful.'

Bertram hesitated, then took off at a sprint. He couldn't let Dufell die while he waited. The old man needed help. Flames were now visible from the manor up ahead, hungrily spreading to the upper level. As Bertram neared the end of the field, he strained to see if the assailants were still at the manor, but his sight was inhibited by the thick smoke of the

fire. In a crouch he edged forward from the safety of the field, scanning for possible enemies. He only found the fallen form of old Man Dufell.

Bertram lay his sword on the ground, then knelt beside the old man who was still conscious. Blood covered his shirt from a deep cut to his brow. He fixed pain-filled eyes on Bertram.

'Mr Dufell, can you hear me?' asked Bertram, wiping the blood away with the man's shirt to reveal another seeping wound between his ribs.

'Of course, I can hear you. Looks like you arrived too late though, stranger.'

Chapter 34

That took Bertram back a moment before he remembered he no longer looked like the man Dufell knew.

'What happened? I saw four figures when I spotted the fire. Where are they now?' Bertram asked as he pushed down to staunch the bleeding from the ribs.

'They left already after I refused to answer their questions about a man named Wren. They claimed he was my nephew, but I have none. Are Polly and young Joseph all right? I couldn't get to them,' Dufell pleaded, grabbing Bertram's arm.

Polly had been the man's wife, and Joseph had been their only son. They had died from the weeping sickness cycles ago.

'They are both safely away from here near the mill. You just focus on breathing; you will be fine.'

'Don't lie to me, fool!' Dufell spat out. 'I'm dying. I am not so crazed that I don't know that.' Then he began to chuckle. 'Damn house. I never liked it, anyway. Passed down by my father and brought me naught but grief,' Dufell said as Bertram removed his own shirt, then bunched it under the man's head.

'Keep the pressure on the wound while I get some water, then I will send for help,' Bertram began before realising the old man's head had lolled to the side. He was already dead.

It had seemed a good idea at the time to say he was the nephew of Dufell, but at no time did Bertram care of the danger he had put the man in. Now his blood was on Bertram's hands.

Bertram stayed to bury the old man, which was the least he could do. Then, retrieving his shirt, he plodded back to the mill. It must have been the bloody Lords and Dames. He had escaped Museo, but the man must have found out about his story of being Dufell's nephew, which meant his and Kassy's plan had been compromised, and they both were in danger.

Bertram made it back to the mill feeling weighed down, knowing that his careless decision had killed an innocent man. He submerged his head in the water trough for the horses, then turned to enter the mill only to find he wasn't alone.

Museo stood silently across the clearing in front of the door to the mill. Bertram glanced up at the faint light from the window where Kassy would usually sit. It was empty, and he realised he did not know whether she was inside or if Museo had captured her.

Museo walked slowly towards Bertram, who drew his sabre and prepared to fight.

'You bastards killed old man, Dufell!' Bertram accused, which was met with a chuckle.

'The crazed old fool's blood is on your hands, Wren Sorrenson. If you had not lied about living in his manor, then maybe Samual wouldn't have had the opportunity to kill him.'

'So how did you know to come to the mill?' asked Bertram, carefully watching Museo's sinuous movement.

'I did a little scouting of my own and saw signs of someone living here. After we fired the house and Samual had his way with Dufell, I stayed hidden in the field while the others returned to the Paxton manor. I wasn't sure why I did that, to be honest. Let's call it an inkling of intuition, shall we?'

'Call it what you want, but you are a murderer, Museo.'

'Since we are now discussing what I am, then how about you? Tell me what you are, Wren. No man could have leapt that wall when we fought, and for a time you were not what you are now. Your eyes changed right in front of me; you suddenly came alive with inhuman strength, and your voice changed to one low and deadly. If I am not mistaken, you, my friend, are one of the animal kin.'

When Bertram remained silent, Museo chuckled again.

'Samual has a theory. When we came to this town, it was to seek a treasure held by a creature known as the Vixen, some sort of fox spirit. We travelled for days and entered her lair, where we slew her children and left with what we had sought. It seemed almost too easy. Samual has often wondered if the witch, as we heard her called, had more kin that we had missed, which brings me to you. Samual suspects you are one of her children and she has sent you to have vengeance upon us.'

Chapter 34

'Are you finished yet, or will you talk nonsense all night instead of fighting me?' Bertram growled as he felt the intruder waiting silently but eagerly behind his eyes.

'No, I am not finished, but have just one thing to add. I disagree with Samual's theory. I know who you really are. After the meeting in the alleyway and your dalliance with that lass from the Cauldron, the similarity between you and a man I had thought dead struck me as strange. But then everything that had been happening began to make sense. You are Bertram Paxton, the fop who we lured to the red woman's lair as bait, and since you stand before me then it can only be the truth that before you could die the witch changed you and has been using you since to attempt in getting back her power. This means you know about the spirit ball that is the source of the cursed Vixen's power, which Samual now has.

'Unfortunately for you both, he has learnt how to use it. You now have a choice, Bertie. You can fight us or convince this monster mother of yours to do our bidding. To be truthful,

Bertie, I never felt good about what happened in that cave to you, but it was your choice to come with us. We had to leave and to take you with us would have slowed us down too much, maybe caused all of our deaths.'

'You left me to die while your friends laughed at me. I only came with you so you would leave my father alone. Since then, you have taken over my father's estate while keeping him captive, which is why I have sworn to destroy the Lords and Dames,' Bertram shouted.

'So, you have been to the manor?'

'Yes, of course, I have, Museo. Why can't you just take what you like and leave me and my father alone?'

'It's too late for that now. Samual has his mind set on owning your father's land. He likes it here, you see, and is sick of running. Now that we have unearthed who you really are, but not what you are, then it would be best you come with me to convince this father of yours to sign his lands over to Samual.'

'I will never stand about to see all that my father worked for stolen by mere thugs like you,' said Bertram, and then he charged at Museo, the growl of the other spitting from his lips.

At the last moment, Museo simply leaned to the side, slashing out with his rapier, which forced Bertram into a forward roll to avoid the blade. He lost the grip of his sabre as he came back to his feet just in time to duck a horizontal strike that would have killed him.

Bertram lunged forward, attempting to grasp Museo's waist with his hands, which surprised the swordsman momentarily as he tried to smash his pommel down on Bertram's head. The strike lacked the power to cause any actual damage, and Bertram surged upward, busting Museo's arms outward.

Aware he was still easily outmatched, Bertram surrendered and let the intruder take over. It was his only chance to defeat the swordsman. The intruder rammed one fist into Museo's middle, which bent him over, then Bertram's follow-up knee knocked Museo to the ground. Museo rolled onto his back, letting go of his rapier to grab his coat front, which he ripped open, popping the buttons off.

Light exploded, and Bertram screamed alongside the intruder as they were blinded by the silver breastplate wreathed in sigils that exploded with silver flames that caught Bertram in their writhing fingers causing Bertram to stagger away. He felt as if the skin had been torn away from his body. When he straightened up again, the intruder was gone. Bertram shook his head, trying to clear his sight, which was slowly returning. Opposite him, Museo stood, swirling his blade before him in a defensive pattern. His breastplate still glimmered in the faint illumination from the mill window.

'Bertie, now it's just you and me: a fair fight.'

Chapter 34

'A duel against a master swordsman while having no blade is not fair at all,' Bertram replied, shaking his head to refocus himself from the strange emptiness in his mind.

'You are, of course, right, so let me even things up for you.' Museo kicked Bertram's sabre over to him, then took up a battle stance.

Bertram picked up his blade. If he could defeat Museo, then his plans would still be of use. Bertram was sure Museo hadn't told Samual of their meeting, otherwise, the rest of their vile group would be here as well.

They came together with a flash of blades as Bertram matched every strike from Museo, then Bertram pressed him, grunting with the effort as he smashed his blade in sweeping attacks, grinning as Museo's smile disappeared. When they broke away from one another, he could see he wasn't the only one breathing hard. They circled one another. Then Bertram skipped forward again, driving his blade diagonally down at Museo's throat. Museo deflected the blade, then somehow twisted his rapier to strike at Bertram's sword hand. The guard deflected the blow, but pain ran up through Bertram's arm with the shock shaking his blade once again from his grasp.

Museo was upon him like an enraged beast, no longer exhausted—if he ever was. All Bertram could do was retreat, which made him collide with the water trough of the two horses, who whinnied and shied away in terror. Bertram felt Museo's hilt clip him on the side of his head as he fell, then he was roughly turned over, then punches cracked into his face, making the fight go out of him.

When he came to his senses, Museo had found some rope and was binding his hands. Bertram spat out blood as he tried to fight off the man. He was caught, and he knew it, but there was one more chance to get out of this.

'I know who murdered your parents,' Bertram gasped.

Chapter 35

Museo stopped tying the rope and clambered up on top of Bertram's chest, pinning his arms to his side.

'What did you just say?' he screamed down at Bertram, spit flying from his mouth.

'I know who killed your parents,' Bertram slowly repeated.

Museo slumped down upon Bertram so their faces almost touched.

'That is nothing to jest about, Bertram,' Museo said through bared teeth.

'The Fading Light Inn is where you met Samual and the others. It was the same night your parents were murdered, and your sister, Cari was taken. The crime was a cover up to make it seem a robbery,' said Bertram urgently.

'Anybody could know this,' Museo said, but he didn't sound convinced.

'I have proof in the mill. Just take me up there and I can show you. If you kill me, then you lose. Your sister, Cari, who you think is living grandly at some manor, is instead being prepared for something or someone known as the feathered one.'

Museo lifted a clenched fist as if to smash in Bertram's face, then he lowered it and pulled Bertram up by the shirt.

'If you are lying, I will tear the heart from you, Bertram. I will take you into the mill, but first I will bind you.'

'Yes, okay, Museo, just let me show you.'

Chapter 35

Once Bertram was bound, Museo pushed him into the mill. If Kassy was upstairs, not even Museo could stand against her, Bertram silently hoped.

Much to Bertram's disappointment, there was no sign of Kassy upstairs. He told Museo where the journal was and watched as the man cautiously picked it up as if could cause him harm.

'A book?' Museo said, looking enquiringly at Bertram where he now sat on the pallet.

'Not just any book, Museo, it is Samual's journal. I have earmarked the pages regarding you and your sister. Just read them.'

Museo sat down on the only chair to read, his visage growing stormier by the moment as he read all the marked page entries. Once finished, he approached Bertram, kneeling down beside the pallet.

'Can you be sure it is Samual's journal?' he asked in an emotionless voice.

'I stole it from my father's house while you all slept. It was locked away, but I gained entry through a window that I used to sneak away from my father without him knowing it.'

Museo stood, picked up a chair, which he smashed down against the floor until it broke apart.

'It cannot be true. Samual is mad, but he is my friend. He would never do this to me. Samual was the only one who showed me kindness after what happened to my family, and now you expect me to believe he is the instrument of that horror-filled night?'

'I don't expect you to believe anything. If anybody would recognise Samual's writing, it must be you, Museo.'

'Samual talks a lot about being a writer and spends many chimes at his work, although he has shared none of his work with me or his other friends, so I wouldn't know if this damn journal is his or not. I guess there is nothing to do but confront him so I know for sure,' Museo said with his head with both hands.

'You can't do that, Museo. If Samual is guilty of killing your family, then how do you think he will react to such a confrontation?'

'Yes, I see that…what am I supposed to do then? I cannot just forget this predicament you have put me in, Bertram. If I do nothing, it goes against everything I vowed to do if I ever found out those responsible. I could accuse Samual face to face, which is the best way to gauge whether it was him, but as you mentioned, the most dangerous.'

'Read the rest of the journal, Museo. That will give you the clarity you need in this matter. You know Samual better than most. The only other way is to get Samual alone, and then we both confront him. You get your family's killer, and I get back my father.'

Museo turned to glare at Bertram, his wide, moist eyes revealing the turmoil the man felt.

'I can't do this right now. I need to think.' Museo snatched up the journal. He then headed downstairs.

'At least untie my hands,' Bertram called after him, barely catching Museo's reply.

'When the vixen returns, you will be free from the bonds. Stay out of my way, Bertram!'

Bertram struggled against his bonds before finally succumbing to exhaustion. The intruder crept its way to the front of his mind, nestling once again in his consciousness.

'I see we survived,' it drawled.

'You didn't tell me about what silver does to you! Is there any way to avoid its effects?'

'As long as you don't touch it or be struck by weapons made of silver, we should be fine, Bertie. The breastplate was bespelled,' the intruder snapped.

'Whether you like it or not, we are stuck in this together, so if you plan on hiding any other important facts about you, then maybe you would be so kind as to notify me!'

'The problem, Bertie, is that when we became tied together, you just assumed that I also had lived for as many cycles as you

Chapter 35

have when really it was the birth of me. I have no guide in this, and before tonight I did not know what silver would do to me.'

'Great, so I am being shared with a pup,' Bertram said after a too-high-pitched laugh.

'There is a reason that Kassy didn't tell you about this, Bertram. You think the both of you have bonded, but her children are dead. We were born of hate, a tool to further her own ends.'

'Stop it! Just leave me be. Help me remove this rope,' Bertram replied, feeling overwhelmed. His only answer was the mocking laughter in his mind. Too exhausted to care Bertram slid into a state of wakeful sleep, acutely aware of his mind and the intruder lurking there.

His body felt heavy and lifeless, a useless slab of meat. The landscape of his mind changed into a cavern from which the opening looked down over a deep, evergreen forest. It took Bertram a moment to realise he was panting, and with surprise, he looked down at his body, now that of a fox with white forelegs splayed out before him, tail stiff and ears perking at the sound of movement coming to the cavern mouth. Bertram attempted to ask who was there, but all that came out was a low whine. He sniffed the air and was rewarded with a pungent musk that burned his nostrils. Whatever was coming smelt bad, and Bertram lay there, paralysed with fear of whatever was coming his way.

Another fox trotted into the middle of the opening to the cave, stopping as red eyes located him. Its head dipped, and the muzzle peeled back from sharp fangs as a challenging growl rolled over Bertram. Foxes don't behave this way, Bertram thought.

The fox slowly crept towards Bertram. Its fur was mottled as if with blood and its red eyes were crusted with yellow ichor as if the animal was rabid. The larger-than-normal fox caught Bertram's gaze as he feebly swished his tail and ducked his head at its approach.

In a moment of understanding, Bertram knew what was happening to him. His body might be resting through sheer exhaustion, but here he was amid a battle for control of his mind with the intruder. He would need to fight. Kassy had tried to warn him.

As the fox inched closer, Bertram surged towards it, ears back, jaw snapping, making the intruder dance away. He would not give in to the intruder. Kassy had said the day would come when he would have to battle for his life against the intruder within him, and that moment was upon him.

'Lay back down; I will hold you by the throat but not harm you, Bertram. The time spent together has made me fond of you, but now we need to decide once and for all who is the dominant out of us. Usually, this happens while we are cubs, but in this case, that wasn't possible. Now recognise me as your better, and let's finish this.'

'This is my body and mind. I could have rid myself of your invasion into my mind, but I didn't. I gave you the life you have, however small, and this is what you do to repay me? We could have found a better solution, but it's too late for that now. Kassy warned me about you, and I didn't take it seriously. If you want my life, then you better be prepared to fight to the death because I will not roll over in deference to you, ever!'

In answer, the intruder launched itself forward. The two of them collided in a rush of snapping jaws. The intruder was bigger, stronger, and younger. It nudged Bertram off balance, and he ducked away.

As the other turned to attack, its claws scrabbled on loose stones, making it slip. Bertram attacked, his muzzle snapping forward to close on the other's front paw, teeth sinking deep. He shook his head to do more damage, thinking this would cause the intruder to retreat.

Bertram was wrong. The intruder snapped its jaws down onto his shoulder, puncturing flesh, then bit down at his neck, its teeth slashing open an ear and flesh above one eye. They clashed again, with the intruder pinning Bertram beneath it.

Chapter 35

Rae came into Bertram's mind. He could not let her down again. She needed him more than ever. Instinctively, Bertram scrabbled with his hind legs, ripping up at the gut of the larger opponent with his sharp claws, and fought it away.

Bertram scrambled upright, turning to track the slow circling of the intruder as it limped around him, leaving a trail of blood behind it.

'Still have some fight in you, after all,' the intruder mused.

'We can just leave this be. This is not the usual you; it is the effects of the moons that are full above us.'

'This is how it should be, Bertram. I need to be free to do as I choose, and the only way for me to do that is to destroy you or die trying.'

As they talked, Bertram attempted to escape the situation, to wake himself up, but then he would need to do this again the next time the intruder challenged him. This had to end now, but not in this form. If the other could force him to take this fox's body, then there must be a way for Bertram to change their form to human. It was only a matter of time before the intruder outwitted him within its world.

He noticed the entry to the cave gave off sparks accompanied by a crackling noise-like energy, which was the one thing in the environment that didn't fit in. He charged the intruder momentarily, catching it off guard and surprising it with Bertram's aggressiveness. The intruder lunged at him too late as he weaved around its attack to leap through the cave entrance into the crackling light.

Bertram landed hard on bare feet, jarring his legs as he rolled, then came to a kneeling posture, looking about him. It was a familiar location to him, the Cauldron.

To his left lay the hearth, where a fire sent shadows scampering along the walls. The flames burnt unnaturally brighter than any Bertram had ever seen, and he knew if the other was to change this scene, it would need to go through those flames. He stood there naked, chest heaving with the strain and injuries from the battle and looked across the room where another figure lay in a heap beside the bar top.

The intruder, now in human form, pulled itself up off the floor. It was a teenage boy with one of his feet torn open, missing toes, and leaking a steady flow of blood. Looking confused, the intruder spoke.

'How can we be here? You shouldn't have been able to escape the cave.' It spotted the strange fire behind Bertram and snarled with realisation.

'Bertram, get out of my way,' the intruder warned.

Bertram screamed his defiance. He revelled in the feeling as adrenaline surged through him, and in response, his fear disappeared.

The intruder made a run to reach the fire behind Bertram, weaving one way, then spinning to the other side. Bertram read it easily and smashed his forearm across the intruder's chest, knocking it to the stones. He straddled its chest. Blow after blow fell on the other before Bertram's vision cleared of the fury upon him, and he sat panting, looking down upon the intruder and the damage he had done to it.

'Kill me,' it said, with blood bubbling from between its ruined teeth. Bertram wrapped his hands around the intruder's throat, then watched as he choked the life from its body.

Chapter 36

Bertram easily broke his bonds. When he searched the mill, he found no evidence of a struggle to confirm whether Kassy had been attacked. Bertram doused the candles so the mill and its surroundings were in darkness. The Dufell manor still burned, which would attract the townsfolk, who would send someone to investigate. By then it would be best if he was long gone. He quickly scribbled a note to Kassy and left the mill.

Bertram searched the forest and field closest to the mill, his night vision easily picking out scurrying animals or birds above. He caught the scent of Kassy mixed with that of two other people and followed it, allowing his form to change into that of a fox. The air was alive with delights, the crickets unusually loud, and the ground damp beneath their paws. Nothing existed then for Bertram but the teeming life around him and Kassy's scent. Bertram feared the worst as the scent came closer and closer to his home. He stopped without getting too close, panting softly as the realisation settled upon him. Now Samual had Kassy and his father. To go to his home now would be foolish now that Samual obviously knew how to use the spirit ball and had Kassy under his control. Samual would be waiting for him.

The keenest of hearing picked up voices towards the Dufell manor. With one final, regretful glance at his home, Bertram loped through the night towards them. He recognised the justicar among a small gathering of townsfolk watching the smouldering building, which had collapsed in on itself.

'What do we do now, Telos?'

'Someone must have seen something. From here the Paxton manor is easily in sight, so I will go there to see if Arlo knows anything. Trell, take Lietis and Raif to search the surrounding area including the old mill; I will take the rest of the men with me.'

Bertram backed away, heading for the forest now that the mill was no longer safe. Exhausted muscles shook from injuries and the strain he had put his body under. Beneath a twisted whispering tree, Bertram dug a hole close to the trunk in which to lie low until morning. As he closed his eyes he was aware of a strange loneliness now that the intruder was defeated.

Bertram awoke naked and shaking. His teeth chattered from the cold, forcing him to clench his jaw to stop them. He rubbed his arms, noticing for the first time that they were stained with blood, which was also caked beneath his nails. While stamping his feet to try to get the blood flowing, Bertram focused on his surroundings. The sound of flowing water told him he must be close to the river. Behind him through the greying darkness, he could see the twisted forms of the wraith trees.

Confused, Bertram called to the intruder and then remembered it was gone. It was too dangerous to return to the mill now. He had planned to go to the Lyre family but could not like this.

Rae came into his mind. Her shift would be finished at the Cauldron, and she would be home. He would go to her.

Bertram knocked on the stout door to Rae's cottage. It took another four knocks before the door eased slightly open and a weary-looking Rae peered out.

'Wren Sorrenson? You're naked.'

Chapter 36

'Long story, Rae, and as you can most likely see for yourself, freezing. Can I come in?'

'First, you stand me up, then next turn up at dawn, naked at my door. I am not in the habit of letting naked men into my home, Wren!'

'Rae. Either let me in and hear me out, or I will start yelling,' Bertram said, taking a deep breath.

'Okay, fine, come in then. I will get you something warm and stoke the fire.'

A little later, Bertram sat wrapped in thick blankets. He sipped from his tea, scalding his lip.

'I heard your uncle is dead, his home burned to the ground. It was feared you were also dead. Where have you been?'

Bertram stood and began pacing.

Rae stared at him with curiosity. 'You are so similar to—' Rae began.

'Bertram Paxton. That was one of the things I needed to talk to you about.'

'I told you that Bertram is missing.'

'I know you did.' Bertram wanted nothing more than to tell Rae the truth, explain that he was Bertram, and then take Rae in his arms and console her, but to do that would put her in danger. With the death of Old Dufell on his hands, he could not allow anything to happen to Rae.

'I believe Bertram's father is in danger. The Lords and Dames, as they call themselves, are staying at his manor, trying to force Arlo into selling his land to them. They killed my uncle, and they would have killed me if I hadn't escaped.'

'Arlo is in danger? Something must be done to save him. If he is being held prisoner, you have to tell the justicar. That is your only option,' Rae implored.

'There is one other option, the Lyre family. They have already agreed to help.'

'You can't trust them, Wren. You will forever be in their debt.'

'Then how am I to handle this? Gerald has the men to help rescue Arlo and help bring the Lords and Dames to justice for my uncle's murder. I can't do this alone.'

'Then do as I say and go to the justicar today.'

It was well after noon when Bertram awoke again. Rae had gotten new clothes for him, which she had left at the foot of the bed. Rae wasn't home, so Bertram helped himself to food from the table then set off to see the justicar.

Bertram arrived at the Justicar's office to find a small crowd milling about out front.

'Where is the justicar?' Bertram asked the woman by the door.

'Aren't you that Wren Sorrenson?' she replied, and when he nodded his affirmation, she grabbed him by the shoulders.

'Your uncle's house has burnt down. I thought you may have been inside when it happened, and it gladdens my heart that you are safe. I'm sorry your uncle died.'

'Thank you. It means a lot, but I have information to talk to the justicar about,' Bertram replied.

'Telos isn't here. According to his wife over there,' she nodded to two women talking, 'the justicar went to the Dufell manor last night with five local men. Only the two men who had stayed to search the Dufell lands have returned. They found signs of someone hiding out in the Dufell mill and confirmed that the missing men had planned to check the Paxton manor. Do you know anything or where the men could be?'

Bertram fought the desire to tell the truth, which he couldn't without endangering them, too, but he had to tell them something.

'I have just come from the Paxton place, where Arlo told me he noticed nothing until this morning. Sleeps like a log,' he said. 'The house guard said that the justicar and his men asked questions then left when it was obvious nobody had seen anything. I have to tell the justicar when he returns. I will call on him tomorrow.'

Bertram had the distinct feeling he wouldn't be seeing the justicar or the three men who had been with him ever again.

Chapter 37

With the urgency of rescuing Arlo foremost in Bertram's mind, he forced himself to a cautious approach on the long walk to the Lyre manor, choosing to stay in his human form so as not to attract the wrong attention from the Lyre family. The coming days would require clear focus if he was to save his father and Kassy without causing any more deaths. As he strolled through the lightly forested woodlands, he realised he had expected some form of contact from Kassy, but the more he thought about it he realised she was not her own master anymore, Samual was. Bertram arrived on Lyre land feeling refreshed rather than tired. Since his change, it seemed that nature restored him more deeply than food or rest.

Bertram heard the approach of horses long before he saw them. He knew guards regularly patrolled the Lyre lands, which made any unhampered approach difficult. How long had they been monitoring him?

Three riders ahead approached at a trot. Gerald's iron-grey hair and chiselled features gave away his presence immediately. A younger version of himself flanked him, whose horse skittered sideways as he sat at ease with an arrow knocked to a bow. Three rabbits hung from his saddle. The third rider was extraordinarily tall, with dirty, straw-coloured hair that curled about a pale, pocked face.

'Bertram, my good man, I was merely discussing with my sons yesterday about when you would return,' Gerald said, skilfully sliding from the saddle to grasp Bertram's hand in his.

'My youngest, Julian, became sick of me bothering their preparations, resorting to dragging me out for a spot of hunting,' Gerald added as he loosened his trousers, then moved away to urinate.

'My other acquaintance is someone you should be happy to see, Bertram. His name is Spiris, and it is he that will take care of the witch for you.'

Spiris climbed slowly down from his mount and ambled over to Bertram. He removed a leather glove, then shook Bertram's hand.

'Well met, Bertram Paxton; it is a pleasure to put a face to your name,' he said, smiling, and Bertram found himself drawn in by the man's strange, smoky eyes that flowed from blue to opaque and back again.

'I welcome anyone who can aid me in saving my father,' Bertram said, feeling immediately at ease with Spiris, wondering if it was magic the man used to do this.

'Did you find out something about Elspeth, Gerald?'

'What?' Gerald replied, holding a hand over his heart and grimacing. 'Did you think I would just sit about doing nothing while I waited for you to finally return for our help? Bertram, you injure me. Now slide up behind one of us and let's return to my home. I have much to share with you about your enemies.'

The Lyre household was a frantic hive of activity as they moved through it to a room that Gerald referred to as his war room. A detailed map of the Paxton manor had been painted upon the surface of a large table, complete with pinned notes and scrolls, allowing them to be easily read.

The collection of information displayed before Bertram astounded him. His father had often spoken of Gerald being one of the best tacticians he had ever served beside during their campaigns together. Seeing the amount of organisation that Gerald had already put into his father's rescue, Bertram couldn't believe it.

Gerald fell into a large chair at the head of the table with one leg stretched out in front of him.

Chapter 37

'You have acquired quite a group of dangerous enemies, Bertram. With the help of our late friend Angus, I managed to at least glean some important information regarding them.'

'Late friend, Angus?' Bertram queried.

'The poor fellow never fully recovered from the overzealous ministrations of my boys,' Gerald replied, shrugging.

'Let's begin with Nix Borello, seemingly the least dangerous of the four Lords and Dames, or so she would prefer you to think. Wanted for murder in Stormwatch, Nix ran away from her family with Samual Hayter. It was reported that they returned later that night, and Nix stabbed her parents to death while they slept. The reported deaths were explained as a ritual of some dark magic, a sacrifice to the feathered one.

'When Samual's daddy worked out his son had been involved in the murders, he arranged for Samual to be cast out of the city, never to return. Beautiful young Nix was imprisoned to await her death. She seduced her guards, then murdered Samual's father as Samual watched. Nix is totally smitten by Samual, and she will defend him with her life. She has no interest in his money since she has more wealth than he does, which is carefully hidden away. The girl is infatuated with Samual and is by far the most predictable. Recently she caught the wraith disease. You wouldn't know anything about that Bertram?' Gerard asked.

Bertram accepted mulled wine from one of Gerard's sons.

'Your reluctance to answer just shows my feeling was correct then,' Gerard said with iron in his voice.

Bertram paced with his cup to his mouth for a moment before speaking.

'There wasn't much to it. Another friend has interests in seeing justice served upon the Lords and Dames, and that friend impaled Nix in the wraith trees.'

Gerald let out a low whistle. 'Now that's a terrible, slow death. Another friend? If you want my continued help, Bertram, you and I need to be clear about all things. Who is this other friend?'

'You wouldn't believe me if I told you the truth.'

'I shall be the one to decide that. Now tell me or we are done!'

'The Red Vixen is the subject of many tales between here and the coast, where the Perfumed Isles lay. A sly creature so terrible a foe that for centuries has protected the common folk in return for tributes. The Lords and Dames sought the Red Vixen for her power source, a spirit ball that, if lost to her would render her totally within the holder's control. They found her lair, which was where I was injured, and now Samual has the spirit ball. The Red Vixen, whom I have been hiding out on the Dufell lands with, is now captured, along with Arlo.'

Gerald chuckled, then stopped himself. 'You are serious, aren't you?'

'You have lived in these parts for many cycles, Gerald. You must have heard of the Red Vixen.'

'Only when I was a child. I never actually believed the stories, and I'm not sure I do now.'

'I can vouch that Bertram is telling the truth,' came a voice behind Bertram.

Spiris lounged in a chair as all eyes tracked to him. 'The Red Vixen is very real. I have seen her. This I swear on my magic. The question we should ask is, will her powers be used against us?'

This was met with many mutters of agreement.

Gerald motioned for quiet. 'All right, quiet down. Let's continue with what we know, then we can return to the topic of the Red Vixen if need be.'

'Let's continue with Samual,' said Gerald, motioning for another wine.

'Now that daddy was dead, Samual became Lord Hayter and immediately began plotting to become king of Scuttle. The former king, rest his soul, was murdered in the betrayal by the infernal lords outside Acclaro.'

Samual failed an assassination attempt against two other candidates. When they searched his estate, the king's guard

Chapter 37

unearthed evidence that he was fraternising with Infernals. Meanwhile, Samual was busy escaping Stormwatch in the company of the other Lords and Dames.

Next, we have Elspeth Quince: a bitter loner whose vanity holds her back from her true, terrible potential. This Machiavellian woman suffered terrible abuse throughout her childhood, leaving her a bitter, twisted creature. Her interest in the stars and death was mocked until strange occurrences began to plague her siblings, who hated her. While her parents were away doing business, Elspeth burnt her remaining siblings alive. Her father, a prominent military man, drew her close to him. Since then, he lavished her with his wealth and rushed to please her every whim while many believe he was a thrall to her power. There was little we could learn about her study of magic which began on its return to the world other than Elspeth threw herself into her studies with abandon, sacrificing much to the Mother in return for her power. Not satisfied with the power the Mother offered, Elspeth turned to another darker power: the infernal lord, Quail, Devourer of Souls.'

Bertram nearly coughed up his wine as he fought the feeling of despair that threatened to overcome him. Their enemies were bad enough without infernal lords.

'That leaves Museo Valente, a truly talented dancer, musician, singer—and, of most interest to us, sword master. His parents were murdered, and our friend, Samual, a newly found acquaintance of Museo, helped catch the two killers. With the city no longer holding any interest, Museo agreed to travel with Samual and his friends. On a more immediate note, Museo has been absent from his friends since last night, when it is suspected they were to blame for the murder of Lord Dufell. You have something to add, Bertram?'

'Museo followed me into the town two days ago. I escaped him, but he found out about the mill on Dufell's land where I had hidden with Kassy, who is the Red Vixen. Museo confronted me there after I buried the old man. He had worked out that I am Bertram Paxton back from the dead and would have killed me….' Bertram trailed off.

'What stopped him?' Spiris asked.

'I told him the truth about his family.'

'And what truth was that?'

Bertram grinned. 'Samual was the one who murdered Museo's parents. He then arranged for the sister to be passed about like a whore at his uncle's manor. I think we might have an ally in Museo, or at worst a very reluctant enemy. Museo is struggling with this news; whether he believes it is unknown, and that makes him unpredictable.'

'How did you find out this information?' Gerald asked, leaning forward, elbows on the table.

'I broke into my home and found Samual's journal locked in a room. Thankfully, I read enough to save Museo from killing me. With just the three of them, we should have the advantage.'

Gerald shook his head, putting down his goblet. 'They were three, but if you include the mercenaries the Lords and Dames have just hired, then it's more like two score.'

That news did nothing to improve the despair Bertram was feeling. 'So, what do we do now?'

Gerald leapt to his feet. 'I thought you would never ask. Now grab some more wine; you are going to need it for the new negotiations of our partnership. With these new considerations to account for and the danger to my beloved kin being greater, I must protect our interests, then I will explain our plan.'

Chapter 38

Aspre strained to break through the thick cloud cover. Its brightness turned into a pale shroud as a small force hurried out of the woods towards the Paxton manor. They stopped just out of the woods to the west of the manor as Gerald motioned them to gather close.

Spiris rose to tower over them where they crouched. He began moving his arms in an intricate pattern, his mouth moving rapidly as he uttered words that Bertram found he couldn't remember once they were spoken. A mist coalesced around the kneeling men, which alarmed Bertram until he saw he was the only one who seemed to hold any concern about it. As the mist thickened around them, making sight difficult, Spiris then touched each man on the head, and to Bertram's amazement, his vision cleared completely.

'Stay where you are. I will now veil the manor to confuse our enemies.'

They waited for the mist to descend upon the manor, which seemed for Bertram to take an eternity as he squatted swathed in fear, his senses in overdrive. He could feel the rage at what the Lords and Dames had done to his father and to him like a heat within him. Now that the intruder was gone would he be able to call on that anger and hatred? The knowledge of the intruder taking over if things became too dangerous when he was backed into a corner had been comforting. Now it was gone.

Gerald crept over to Bertram's side. 'You will enter by the window with the faulty lock with me, Spiris, and three of my men. Spiris will use his power to ensure we make no sound.'

Gerald signalled to the waiting men with hand gestures, and they crept off toward the manor, leaving just the group who would enter by the window.

They were about to set off to the rear of the manor when a voice carried through the night from their left toward the front of the manor.

'Samual, you diseased whoreson! It is I, Museo Valente, one who once called you friend and is now here to confront you on a matter of family honour. Come out and face me, you gutless cur.' The cracking sound of breaking glass followed Museo's words.

'Bertram, come now while we still have this distraction,' Gerald whispered, taking his arm.

The group hurried through the night. Bertram's magically aided sight made it almost daylight. The others parted for Bertram, who scampered up the familiar hands and footholds to the window ledge. He moved along for the next man until they all crouched just below the window. Gerald nodded at one of his men to open the latch and go in. This is it. Bertram felt the rush of excitement, or was it fear? A low growl rolled up from deep down in his throat, earning him a strange look from Gerald.

The Lyre man grasped the latch and turned.

There came a flash of blinding light. The man fell back, hands and face burnt and blackened, crying out in pain. Gerald slapped a hand down over his mouth, the man writhing beneath him, then raised his dagger before striking down with its handle, knocking the man unconscious.

The window lay open now, a temptation that beckoned along with the possibility of further traps. Someone had magically trapped the window, which meant Samual knew his diary was missing, and the Lords and Dames may already be aware of them

Chapter 38

if they had heard the cry of the wounded man. Bertram climbed through carefully, expecting the worst. He crouched by the door, waiting until the other four had followed him. Bertram tried the door but it was locked by key.

'Let me through, I can disarm the lock,' came Spiris's voice. Then he was beside Bertram. A haze of blue light built in the man's open palm, then he gently blew it at the lock and the light floated down into the keyhole. Moments later, they heard a click. Loud shouting came from the front of the manor.

Gerald put a finger to his lips, motioning them to wait.

'What is this nonsense, Museo? Come inside.'

'I think the mist is a little too theatrical, Elspeth, don't you?'

'What? It has nothing to do with me. It's natural, you idiot!'

'Natural? Ha! It's a clear night until you get close to the manor, then this.'

Bertram's enhanced hearing picked up the twang of a bow, then a grunt of pain.

'Back in the house, now! We are under attack,' came Samual's scream.

'Thorns of the Mother protect us, escirclez, aspete, clalexus, tiedis,' came the words of Elspeth. The smashing glass from various areas of the manor was a sign that the assault had begun.

'Bertram, go, now!'

Bertram turned the door handle, revealing the empty landing beyond with the narrow stairs leading down to the second level into Arlo's room, then down further to the kitchens, allowing easy meal access for the serving staff. The five of them hurried down the stairs to the landing. One of the Lyre men pushed past Bertram into his father's room with Bertram close behind, his eyes flicking around the chamber at the dishevelled bed sheets and blankets askew across the floor amidst half-eaten platters of food, spilled wine, and clothes. The total disarray of the chamber was the exact opposite of how Arlo liked to live.

The man before him had taken up guard at the only other entrance to the chamber that led out into the second-level hall.

'Hall's clear,' he called back, and they spilled out behind him, moving with intent since each of the Lyre men knew the layout of the manor from chimes of memorisation. Four other bedrooms branched off the hall and the manor's only bathing chamber.

'Leave the rooms and head to the stair hall up the front. Jelse, you wait by the back stairs so we don't get surprised from behind, and Luis stay here at the top of the stairs in case the rooms have anyone in them.'

That left Bertram, Gerald, and Spiris. The clashing of blades and screaming reached them from below.

'Ready?' asked Gerald, drawing his sword, and Bertram nodded.

Spiris chanted, and a gaseous form was writhing about in his hands. Bertram took the middle position as Gerald led them into the battle below.

Three men fought a frantic battle in the vestibule below. One was a Lyre man, the other two Samual's mercenary hirelings wearing chain mail coats over leather armour with falchion swords that would be perfect for indoor fighting.

Gerald roared, then shoulder-barged one mercenary into the wall. His follow-up strike almost took the man's leg off below the hip. Their sudden appearance also startled their own man, who paused and paid dearly for the moment of indecision as his opponent slashed him across the chest, sending him to the side with a howl and leaving Bertram facing the mercenary.

'What's wrong, boy? You going to shit yourself?' laughed the mercenary through his blond, jutting beard.

Bertram's sword felt suddenly heavy in his hands. His legs seemed to quaver, and he felt ill. 'He leapt forward with an overhead slash that the mercenary blocked. They exchanged three quick strikes, then came together with both blades held vertically between them.

Chapter 38

Bertram hooked a foot behind the mercenary's ankle, then pushed hard, and the mercenary fell back against the wall. He managed to keep his feet, but his blade dropped, and Gerald's long sword took the man in the face.

Bertram was breathing hard.

Beside them, Spiris raised his voice in a command that sent the throbbing gaseous form shooting out from his hands.

It enveloped a group of three mercenaries closest to them in the hall where they had one of Gerald's sons cornered. The gas rolled over the four of them, having an instant and devastating effect as they all dropped their weapons and vomited.

'Don't fear the spell. It won't affect us three,' called Gerald, pulling Bertram after him into the hall. Gerald made easy work of two sick mercenaries while Bertram dispatched the third. Down the hall, Bertram could see Museo dancing about two Lyre men, easily making them look like unskilled boys. Behind him, Samual had a Lyre man against the wall, slamming his head into the stone repeatedly, leaving a dark smear of blood until the man slipped lifeless to the ground. Gerald's oldest son, Thomas, led four men out to join Bertram and Gerald from the parlour. Mercenaries gathered about Samual at the door to the dining room.

Samual locked eyes with Bertram. Blood had speckled his face, and he smiled.

'Wren Sorrenson—or should I say Bertram? Don't look surprised, Museo had told me of his feeling that you had risen from the grave. I'm happy you are here now. You can convince Arlo to sign the deeds to his lands before we kill you.'

Bertram pointed a wavering finger at Samual.

'If you have harmed either Arlo or Kassy, I will send you to the infernal lands where you belong.'

The mercenaries around Samual opened the dining room doors. They ushered Samual out of sight. Museo followed.

'Museo,' called Bertram, which made the sword master stop.

'He murdered your parents, and yet you still trust him?'

Museo hesitated, caught between decisions. He then pulled the doors shut behind him.

'Damn it, I was counting on his help,' Bertram said. Gerald rushed over to his son. 'Get some water, somebody. The rest of you stand back from that door. It is the only entrance, and now we are forced to fight a prepared defence. Louis, take three men outside. Cover the dining-room windows in case they decide to flee.'

'There has been no sign of the witch or Nix. Best to send some men up to search the bedrooms, Gerald,' Spiris said.

'They must have my father and Kassy in the dining room,' Bertram said as Gerald's son, Thomas moved with three men up the stairs.

One of the Lyre men turned to Bertram. 'They also have Rae. I saw her through the window when we attacked.'

'I feared Samual would drag Rae into this.'

'The good news is that they are all still alive. You may be able to bargain for their safety yet, Bertram,' Gerald said.

'I will not sign the papers for our land to go to those murderers!'

'If all goes well, it won't come to that. If we can gain entrance, then Spiris will reduce the numbers with his magic. I counted seven of theirs dead to two of my men.'

'I will prepare my offensive spells,' Spiris told Gerald, moving over opposite the door to the dining room.

Bertram and Gerald were looking at the mage when the wall came alive behind Spiris, revealing Elspeth, who snaked an arm around the neck of Spiris. A knife plunged into his side three times. Then Elspeth pushed the stricken Spiris at Gerald, who was charging at her. The two men collided, going down with a flail of arms and legs. Elspeth was moving her hands quickly now as three Lyre men moved in on her. She slashed her arm down; the wooden floor rippled, buckling up and twisting itself within moments to a wall of thorns blocking the way forward for Gerald's men.

Chapter 38

Bertram raised his sword, then shuffled forward as Elspeth turned her attention to him. Thrusting her hands out, she screamed, 'Iceendre.'

Four bolts of white shot out, striking Bertram in quick succession. Bertram gasped at the chilling cold that enveloped him, stealing his breath and energy, and making him slump to the ground.

Elspeth stepped forward to smile down at him, then she stepped down with the heel of her boot on Bertram's hand, grinding it with her weight as he howled. Bertram attempted to rise and grab her leg, but she stepped over them. Then her form dissolved through the dining room doors.

'The air mage won't be bothering us any longer,' Bertram heard her say to Samual's high-pitched laughter.

Chapter 39

Bertram lay curled up in a ball, his teeth chattering, wounds burning with ice fire. He watched as Gerald rolled Spiris over to inspect the mage's wounds. Bertram examined the wound to his hand which was already beginning to heal as broken bones straightened and popped back into place.

'How bad is it, Gerald?' Spiris asked between gasps.

'Bad enough. Fortunately, you won't die for a few chimes at least, but by then, you will be unconscious from blood loss. Don't die yet my friend, we need you to do one more thing.' The Lyre men who had been cut off by the thorn wall had given up attempting to cut through it and instead headed for the stairs from the kitchen that would lead up to the main bedroom.

A series of loud thumps came from upstairs, followed by screams. Bertram climbed unsteadily to his feet, trying not to think of what was happening up there. Between his worry for Arlo and Kassy as well as the pain that was flooding through him, it was too much to worry about at that moment.

Then Gerald was at his side.

'Bertram, you need to pull yourself together. You don't have the luxury of panicking now. Lives depend on you.'

Bertram nodded, then forced himself to move his arms to force some warmth into his body. The cold was worse than the deep winter months. There wasn't one area of his body that wasn't feeling the effects of Elspeth's magic.

Chapter 39

One of Gerald's men appeared at the foot of the stairs in the adjacent stair hall doorway. He shambled towards them, then pitched forward on the stones. Gore covered his back through shredded leather armour. Gerald went to him and rolled him onto his side, shaking him. He dragged the man into the hall and realised it was futile; he was dead.

Gerald cursed. This wasn't going to plan.

Bertram stood up, which was when he saw another figure in the doorway to the hall, moving fast.

Nix ran into the hall, blood staining her white shirt, trousers, and her bare feet. She lashed out with a leg, catching Gerald full in the face before he could rise from beside Spiris then spun towards Bertram with a knife in each hand.

Bertram was totally unprepared.

There came a cracking noise. Lightning flashed, striking Nix and tossing her against the wall.

Spiris had saved his life. The mage groaned in pain, then fell onto his side after the spell took its toll on him.

There was no sign of the other three men who had gone upstairs. Silence descended upon them.

Nix wiped her mouth with the back of one hand and looked over at Bertram.

'You were there, weren't you, Bertram? Like a parasite latched onto that bitch, watching as she impaled me in the wraith. I could sense you, feel you, and you did nothing.'

'Remember how I felt when you left me for dead? You knew the danger you were taking me into, and now you expect me to show sympathy to you? Things didn't have to be like this, Nix.'

They stared at each other as the life faded from her eyes.

Thomas arrived with two Lyre men arrived from the kitchen. 'There she is. We had her cornered upstairs, but she escaped us. Marcus, Snotts, and Les are all dead.'

That left nine of the Lyre men, not including Gerald and Spiris. The mercenaries had so far proved to be fierce fighters.

Gerald wiped his bloodied nose. A trail of blood ran from one ear, and for the first time, the man looked old as he accepted Bertram's outstretched hand.

'Gather yourselves. We attack now. Spiris, I need you to blow that door off its hinges. Can you do that one final thing, my friend?'

Spiris pushed himself up against the wall. He began chanting in a soft voice. The air around Bertram crackled with power as a wind sprang up, gaining slowly in force and intensity. Bertram scurried away from the dining room doors as men nervously gathered themselves, slapping backs or sharing intense looks and nods.

Spiris was shouting now, though Bertram couldn't hear the words. They were torn away by the wind that spiralled around the mage. He punched out his arms at the doors, and they exploded inward, sending figures scurrying within.

Spiris dropped his arms, falling unconscious against the wall. Gerald and his men rushed into the breach with Bertram close behind. The long table had been upended on its side, which forced them to split towards each side of it. A volley of crossbow bolts met their entry, taking down two Lyre men. One of them was Thomas, Gerald's son. The mercenaries intercepted them at each end of the table, attempting to narrow how many attackers could engage them at once.

The Lyre men pulled at the table together, tipping it over so they could take the centre of the room. Museo stood with his sword point down on the ground; Elspeth leaned heavily against the wall, clearly exhausted as she swayed unsteadily.

Samual stood behind Arlo and Rae, who had been tied to chairs. He held the spirit ball, which swirled with silver energy. Kassy stood beside Samual, her arms stiff and a grimace twisting her features, seemingly battling Samual's control.

Chapter 39

The mercenaries fell back as the Lyre men swarmed over them in a well-coordinated attack, felling three more of the hired warriors.

Gerald stepped forward, ushering his men just behind him.

'I know not what mercenary company you are, but you need to ask yourself this one question. Is today the day you wish to die?'

'Kill them! I paid good gold for your services. Now kill them!' shouted Samual.

The three remaining mercenaries traded glances, then sheathed their swords, hands raised. The Lyre men parted to allow them to pass.

'Jonas, watch our backs so these turncoats don't attack us from behind,' Gerald told his third son, who took up a position just within the doorway to the room.

'Samual, this is foolishness. We can solve this without further bloodshed,' Museo said, looking sideways at Samual.

Samual laughed. 'Is the famous sword master getting cold feet?'

'Now I know my son is alive. We can work something out, Samual. Your friend is right,' began Arlo, but Samual's fist cut his words off. Arlo's head snapped to the side.

Bertram growled, stepping forward, the anger raging in him. 'While I live, you will get nothing from my father. So come kill me, Samual. Leave the other innocents out of this.'

'Kassy, kill them all.' Samual raised the spirit ball, which was pulsing with what looked like lightning.

Kassy took a step forward and then paused. The exertion of just doing that sent rivulets of sweat down her forehead. Samual looked at the spirit ball and it flashed red. Kassy gave a gut-wrenching scream.

'Samual,' shouted Museo. 'Stop this, now!'

'Kassy, we have discussed this already. If you continue to disobey me, then I have no option but to destroy you.'

'Samual, enough already; we can still get out of this. We can leave with our lives,' Museo pleaded, stepping in front of Samual.

Kassy gave a quiet cry. A tear ran down from one eye as she moved swiftly forward, the Lyre men moving to intercept her. With startling speed, Kassy grabbed the first man and threw him back into the other three, taking them all down in a heap. Then she ducked a sword swing, backhanded the warrior, and spun between two others, chopping one's legs down with a roll forward then smashed a palm into the next. It seemed to Bertram that she chose strikes to only disable not kill the men against her.

Gerald timed his moment perfectly as he struck Kassy with a silver pendant he was holding, which had the immediate effect of making her thrash about on the ground. Gerald moved a step closer, and Kassy scrabbled away until she hit the wall, then covered her face.

'By the infernal hells, do I have to do everything myself?' Samual said. He spoke three low, guttural words and the ground beneath Gerald and the remaining Lyre men turned to liquid that enclosed around their ankles.

Bertram summoned all his pent-up anger and pain that this man Samual had brought into his life. Claws tore from his fingernails and he felt his jaw extend, jagged teeth cutting through gums, bringing an almost sweet pain with it that fed his fury even more. He leapt at Samual. The spirit ball flared. Kassy leapt to intercept Bertram, catching him in mid-air and slamming him down. Bertram fought Kassy, their forms part man, part fox, as they snapped at each other's throats. Kassy's jaws tightened around Bertram's throat. Bertram whined. He had lost, but the jaws didn't tighten, and above him, Bertram could see the exertion in Kassy's eyes as she fought against Samual's wishes. In his mind, Kassy spoke.

'It will take time for me to forgive you for your part in my children's death, Bertram, but you are one of us now, family and all I have left. We're golden!'

Chapter 39

The bolt of power from the spirit ball lifted Kassy into the air above Bertram. Her hands moved to her throat as she began gasping.

Bertram stood up on unsteady feet as Kassy writhed beside him, choking. Gerald and his men were still stuck. Samual raised an outstretched arm at Elspeth. He whispered words and Elspeth curled over in pain as motes of dark energy like ashes floated from her form to envelop him.

Bertram felt a flicker of doubt in his mind. The realisation that Samual was also a mage was a dangerous revelation to only find out about now.

Museo turned to Samual, his knuckles going white around the sword hilt as he pointed his blade.

'Is it true, Samual?'

'What? Do you really want to do this now, Museo? Let's deal with these scum first, then we can talk. Now kill them, you weak fool!'

'I am not a fool, Samual, and I want to know now if you killed my parents then sent my sister to be some rich man's whore!'

Samual hesitated a long moment, then glanced at the Lyre men and Bertram before turning to Elspeth, who was shaking against the wall. Her dark hair had white tinges to it, and she had bitten her lips, leaving a snaking trail of crimson down her chin.

Samual slapped her across the face.

Elspeth opened her eyes with a cough.

'Get it together, I need you, now,' he yelled at her.

From behind him, Museo was weeping. 'You did it, didn't you, Samual? You bastard, you can't even admit it to me!'

From where she choked in the air, Kassy still fought weakly. Her arms fell limp. Arlo was thrashing against his bonds as Samual thrust the spirit ball into Elspeth's hands.

'Just hold this. I am sure you can handle this simple task.'

Then Samual turned back to Museo.

'Stop snivelling, Museo. Have you lost all respect for yourself?'

'The journal is yours, I know it, Samual. Your writing cannot be mistaken as much as I would like to believe it to be.'

With a rasp, Samual drew his blade.

'It's simple, Museo. I fell for you and your mysterious ways: the exquisite singing, dancing, and swordplay. You had everything, even the perfect family. I chose you to join me as one of the Lords and Dames. With your skills, we could go anywhere, but it turns out you were weak and needed a push, or you would never have left Stormwatch.'

'That night I had made enough gold for my family to move somewhere for a better life away from danger. Then you come along and decide you want me to join you, but with no loose ends, so you murdered my parents. You then lied to me about sending my sister to your sick uncle as a plaything?'

'At least she is alive. It wasn't your destiny to stay in that soul-dredging life you had. I gave you an identity, a path to power alongside me. You should feel honoured.'

Museo stared back, stunned.

'You are truly mad, Samual. Blinded with this power you continuously search for, willing to sacrifice everything and those around you for it. It ends here, so prepare yourself. Our alliance is at an end.'

Museo snapped his sword out as he leant into a deep lunge. The moment he moved, Samual flicked his free hand at Museo, who slipped turning his front ankle. Museo corrected well, falling into a roll, and then coming up onto one knee in a defensive position. Samual sprung forward, slashing down strikes in a furious combination that forced Museo's blade wide before Samual caught Museo with a kick to the chest, making him gasp as it connected. Museo staggered backward, but Samual surged after him, only denied the killing stroke when Bertram swept out a leg from where he lay almost tripping Samual. Samual flicked his blade in an arc that cut a crimson line across Bertram's chest.

Chapter 39

'Stay back Bertram, or I will carve your unborn child from your lover myself!'

Bertram reeled back in shock. A child, Rae was pregnant with his baby? Bertram looked at Rae, who was weeping.

Samual turned back to Museo, who now had to put all his weight on his back leg.

'You can't even give me the respect of a fair fight.'

'Poor Museo. Life isn't fair; I would have thought you realised that,' Samual said, stepping forward slowly and then feinting an attack.

Gerald and his men were still struggling to get free of the ground, which had begun to slowly loosen up around their feet. Bertram forced himself up onto his knees. He needed to help Museo.

Museo batted aside three hard strikes, then Samual stabbed low, the blade sliding into Museo's thigh just above the knee. He fell with an anguished cry. Samual punched him in the face with his hilt and stood over him with his blade resting on Museo's throat.

'I'm truly sorry it comes to this, Museo. You could have been so much more.' Then he leaned forward as if to drive the blade down into Museo's throat.

Bertram barrelled into him. The blade slipped, still driving deep into Museo's shoulder, making him cry out but stopping Samual's killing blow.

Samual smashed the sword hilt into Bertram's face then jumped back, blade raised before him. Even so, Bertram's claws hit Samual, whose form shimmered leaving him with no sign of injury.

Behind them, Elspeth was chanting in a soft voice. Bertram cringed as he prepared for death by some nefarious magic, but then Elspeth simply winked out of sight.

Samual cursed, then hurried over to where the spirit ball sat on the ground. Arlo had got a hand free and was reaching for it when he got there.

'No, you don't, old man,' Samual said, taking the spirit ball in one hand.

Bertram knew this was maybe his last chance. He leapt at Samual, barrelling into him as he turned. Samual staggered backwards, somehow keeping hold of the spirit ball which he grasped in his hand.

Kassy streaked past Bertram, pushing him aside to get to Samual, who shouted one word: 'Stop!'

Kassy froze.

'I will crush it, and you know it will kill you,' Samual said, stepping away from Kassy.

Gerald's right foot came free. One of the other Lyre men was totally out with his sword ready as he pushed in on Samual.

'Kill them all, Kassy!' Samual screamed, and she turned towards Bertram, Gerald, and his remaining men, a puppet for Samual.

Kassy smashed a fist into Bertram's face, knocking him to the ground. She swept the first Lyre man aside with an arm and continued forward towards Gerald, who was fumbling in his jacket for the pendant he had used to ward her away earlier. She got to him first, smashing a fist into his chest with such force his trapped ankle broke with an audible snap.

Kassy turned to Bertram and he could feel her regarding him. If she refused to kill them, she died, and if she killed them, then this was all over. He raised his hands.

'Kassy, it's me, Bertram; remember, we are family,' he pleaded.

Gerald's son attacked with a roar and Kassy grabbed his arm, breaking it, and then took his sword. She turned again towards Bertram, and they both looked at Samual when he cried out in pain. Arlo was biting his arm.

Kassy took the chance offered as the spell over her broke. She made for Samual, who got his sword free, and then stabbed down and Arlo let go with a cry. Kassy struck like a wild beast, nails

Chapter 39

scratching down at Samual's throat and chest. She drew thick rivulets of blood in her attempt to tear the spirit ball from its chain.

Samual broke free from her grasp.

'Give me the ball, Samual,' Kassy said, standing ready to pounce at him again.

'I would rather crush it. If I'm going to die, you will too!'

Bertram pushed himself forward to where a crossbow lay on the ground. He grabbed it and spun without aiming. Any other time the bolt would have flown past its target harmlessly; this time, however, whether by true luck or the grace of the Mother, it flew true, striking Samual in the chest just below the right shoulder.

Samual dropped the spirit ball, and Kassy lunged to break its fall.

'Vocase servose domin vestarus!' Samual shouted.

The air beside Samual seemed to thicken as a form coalesced. Bertram saw Arlo and Rae begin bleeding from the nose as he felt the blood flow from his own.

'Beware, he has summoned an Infernal. Don't look at it,' Kassy yelled, leaping backwards.

With a loud, ripping noise, the air tore open. Intense, red light filtered through around the edges of it; then a bird-like head broke through the opening, its long beak open. Jet-black eyes flicked around, then it pulled its body through. It was large, at least half again of Bertram's size, with mottled fur and feathers covering its body.

Gerald began screaming and wet himself. His son and other men ran. Bertram wanted to run too, but the fear for Arlo held him back as he averted his gaze. In his peripheral vision, he saw Rae struggle free of the remaining bonds to rise behind Samual, who was laughing now.

The Infernal was entirely through the opening; it shook itself, and some type of vermin flew from its unholy body in a swarm descended on all in the room except Samual. Bertram tried to slap them away as they bit him.

Rae struck a knife held in both hands into Samual's back. Samual howled and careened away, with Rae following. She struck Samual again, opening a gash along Samual's chest.

Samuel fell back against the wall with a crash. Above Samual, the heavy framed painting of Bertram's mother dropped, striking Samual from above and knocking him down.

With a beat of its wings, the Infernal reached Rae, screeched, and then tossed her across the room.

There was nothing Bertram could do but try to fend off the vermin attacking him. They were thick; trying to get in his mouth, nose, and ears. Blood flowed from bites to his face and neck.

The Infernal reached down and picked up Samual, then with a long screech it stepped through the rip with the sorcerer and was gone. The hole closed behind them.

The vermin fell to the ground, writhing about as they died, their link to the Infernal realms gone.

Bertram felt his body returning to its normal form.

Chapter 40

Bertram felt his body return to normal now the danger was gone. He crawled over to his father, touching him on his shoulder, and Arlo screamed, trying to move away.

'Father, it's me, Bertram, your son. It's me,' he said, holding Arlo in his arms.

Arlo opened his eyes, focusing on Bertram, then wept.

'Bertram, is it gone, the Infernal?'

'Yes, Father, it's gone now. You are safe.'

'I never thought to see you again. They said you had died.'

'It takes more than that to kill a Paxton,' Bertram said, smiling.

Behind them, Kassy gave a loud cry. Bertram expected to see something terrible but was relieved to see she was holding up her spirit ball by its chain. She flashed him a smile, the relief clear for all to see.

Gerald lay breathing hard, the broken bones jutting from his leg. Now the danger was gone. His son had returned and was splinting Gerald's leg.

'Gerald! You owe me for the damages,' Arlo called across to his old friend.

Gerald winced, then craned his head to look at Bertram and Arlo.

'Bertram, the fee just doubled because I had forgotten your father's terrible sense of humour. I have had enough of the Paxton's for a lifetime.'

Bertram smiled at Gerald, but his sense of humour failed him as his eyes found Rae, and he hurried over to her.

'Rae, are you okay? Tell me you and the baby are fine, please.'

Rae scrabbled backwards. 'Get away from me. You are no longer the Bertram I loved. Now you are a…'

Rae struggled to find the word.

'A monster!'

'I can explain. I am still the man you knew.'

'No! I saw what you are now. You are dangerous, no more than an animal. Stay away from us.'

'It's still me dammit,' Bertram yelled, losing his patience which made Rae cringe further away from him. He could feel the eyes of the others in the room on him now, feel the flush of embarrassment climb his cheeks.

'I'm sorry,' he began, but knew it was useless and instead slowly backed away.

'I have always loved you and maybe I should have listened when everyone said to take you for my wife. We all think we have time,' Bertram laughed. 'But time is a fleeting mistress. I never dreamed something like this would happen to me, Rae. I know we can make things work if you still love and trust me after the deception I was forced to make in becoming Wren Sorenson. Can you forgive me so we can start over as a family?'

'I do love you, Bertram, but not what you have become.'

Bertram blinked away tears. Forced himself not to beg. Kassy had warned him but as usual, he thought he knew better. The right thing was to leave this place and leave Rae and their baby so they had a decent life ahead of them. He said nothing, just nodded in acceptance and turned away.

Bertram went to Arlo. He helped him into one of the remaining chairs.

'I'm sorry for everything. Hopefully, in time you can see that what I have to do now is the best for everyone.'

Chapter 40

'I know Bertram, I know. To me, you will always be... You must drive out whatever you have within you now.'

'I will father. I am your son and I love you,' Bertram replied staring at Arlo who only looked away from Bertram.

Bertram felt himself choking up as his father refused to acknowledge him further and say he loved him back. He looked at the others around him.

Gerald held a hand on his sword hilt warily. 'Gerald, I thank you for all you have done for me. I know Arlo will honour our agreement and can only hope that will somehow compensate for the losses you suffered here.'

Finally, Bertram turned to Museo, who was now under guard from the lyre men.

'Museo, I think that under different circumstances we could have been friends. You are partly to blame for what has happened to me and my loved ones, but I forgive you that and hope you can free your sister. '

With a final glance at Rae and Arlo, Bertram turned and walked to Kassy's side. She placed a hand on his shoulder and squeezed.

'It gets easier with time. Come now let's leave while we still can.'

Together, they walked from the Paxton manor and the life Bertram had always known. Away from the manor and safe once again in the woods Kassy changed into a red fox and began to run. The urge to run became all-encompassing. Bertram gave in to it and allowed the change to overcome him. He lost himself in the heightened sensations of his new form forcing away the fear of the unknown, the many regrets and the rejection of his loved ones and ran into a new future.

The End.

Printed in the USA
CPSIA information can be obtained
at www.ICGtesting.com
CBHW051748300724
12430CB00040B/535